BRIDGET CRACK

BRIDGET CRACK

RACHEL LEARY

First published in 2017

Allen & Unwin
83 Alexander Street
Crows Nest NSW 2065
Australia
Phone: (61 2) 8425 0100
Email: info@allenandunwin.com
Web: www.allenandunwin.com

Cataloguing-in-Publication details are available
from the National Library of Australia
www.trove.nla.gov.au

ISBN 978 1 76029 547 9

Set in 13/17.5 pt Adobe Garamond by Post Pre-press Group, Australia
Printed and bound in Australia by Griffin Press
10 9 8 7 6 5 4 3 2

The paper in this book is FSC® certified.
FSC® promotes environmentally responsible,
socially beneficial and economically viable
management of the world's forests.

The river rises to the flood. The river will not tell.
What is here for the telling? And who is here to tell?

Pete Hay, 'By the Living Harry'

1

A GOOD PLACE

Bridget stood on the boggy patch of ground looking up at the road. She yanked the spade out of the ground, shoved it in again and with a grunt brought up another chunk of waterlogged soil. The blister on her middle finger burst and she swore, put it up to her mouth. The sun had reached the field above and just below the road, evaporated the fog and melted the frost. The patch of dirt where she worked was still cold, the hill on the other side of the creek shading it. Below her, fog clung to the creek and the low land around it, rays of morning sunlight filtering into it, the grass under the fog coated in frost. Despite the digging her hands and cheeks were pink with cold. She looked behind her at the saddle between the two hills where Pigot and Chambers had gone that morning. Nothing. No sound but the rush of the creek and the distant bleating of sheep.

She shoved the spade into the ground, strode up the slope to the cottage, yanked open the door to the lean-to and then pushed the next door that jammed into the cottage's dirt floor. Inside she felt on top of the cabinet for the pipe, then for the smooth leather of the tobacco purse. She leaned over the fireplace, held a stick in the embers.

Outside she sat on an upturned log, exhaled smoke into the brisk morning air, looked across the field where the trees had all been cleared, the rocky slope dotted with black stumps. Quiet. There was no one out here. The cottage sat at the end of a road that went nowhere. No one came to the place. There was nothing out here but sheep and crows and Charles Pigot and Grant bloody Chambers.

She sucked again, the smoke rough in her throat. When she had come out here a month ago, Pigot had said the missus was away, was sick and with relatives in Hobart Town, would be back soon. There'd been no sign of any missus. None was coming. There wasn't even a missus. She knew that now. Pigot was a man who lied easily, no trace of deceit in his black eyes, so sure was he of his right to lie. A man who did not answer to anyone, or to any God. She knew—there was no missus, never had been one in this cottage, not a sign of a woman anywhere, no leftover mark.

Chambers, a convict servant like her, repulsed her. Lizard eyes, flesh rotten with some unnamed shame. He'd grabbed her once down by the creek, 'Come on, what's wrong with ya?' He'd slipped on a rock and she'd got away from him and since then the wanting in his gaze had been lacquered with anger.

For the last two days he and Pigot had been away over the hill felling trees, her there on her own all day. Pigot said he wanted the ground dug and ready to plant. She said why didn't Chambers dig it, she wasn't digging, it wasn't her job to dig. Pigot had paused where he was, about to put a log on the fire. Then he placed the log slowly, deliberately. He straightened, turned around to face her, fixed her with shiny coal-coloured eyes. 'Your job, is what I tell you your job is.'

Bridget sat smoking while the fog thinned over the creek. She hacked a piece of fabric off the bottom of her dress, wrapped it around her hand and walked slowly back down the field.

A little while later she saw a figure coming down the hill. One of them coming back. Which one? Chambers. He was limping. She had noticed it as they left this morning. He went into Pigot's place, came out with something in his fist, walked down towards the hut that sat close to the damp of the creek, didn't look over at her as he passed by about twenty yards away. What was he doing back? It wasn't lunchtime yet. She heard the hut door open and close and soon a stream of smoke came from the chimney.

In the cottage she put damper, butter and smoked meat on the table for Pigot, took hers outside the lean-to and ate there. When she heard the dog bark signalling Pigot's arrival, she walked off back down to the mud patch.

After he had gone again, he and the dog disappearing up the track and over the rise on the top side of the road, she went up to the cottage, got the bucket and took it down to the creek, drawing water from further down rather than her usual spot so that she didn't have to go too close to Chambers' hut while he was there.

...

Pigot came in again at dusk, hung his coat on the back of the door and sat down at the table. She put a bowl of hot soup and a spoon down in front of him, the butter and damper already there. He slurped a spoonful. 'Take one to Chambers.'

'What?' She had long ago dispensed with calling him sir. Chambers never did and Pigot didn't seem to want it. He was no gentleman, of that she was pretty sure.

Pigot slurped again, his face close over the bowl, didn't answer.

She was confused. Chambers had his own rations, was given them every week and cooked for himself in his hut. She never went there.

She turned away from Pigot, spooned soup into a bowl, went to the door and out, down the track towards the creek.

Chambers was lying on a straw mattress in the corner, the fire casting a blanket of light over him. His right trouser leg was rolled up to the knee exposing a yellow boil on the shin, the skin around it red and tight. Bridget stood in the doorway holding the soup bowl. Chambers didn't move. She went quickly over to him and put the soup down on the ground where she was still out of reach. She shut the door behind her and hurried back up to Pigot's cottage and into her lean-to.

...

In the morning Pigot sent her down to the hut again, this time with oats. Inside the fire was nearly out. It was cold but Chambers' face was shiny with sweat. The boil had broken overnight, pus and blood oozing from the middle of it. The leg was more swollen, the whole of it from the knee down fat and red. She put the oats down and he pointed at a bowl of water next to him. 'Can you get more salt?' She realised then that it must have been salt he'd had in his fist yesterday when he left Pigot's cottage. She had to move closer to him to pick up the bowl. She grabbed it quickly.

Pigot was still sitting at the table eating.

'He wants salt.'

He spooned oats into his mouth, kept his gaze on the table in front of him. 'Then get it.'

She went to the sack in the corner, took a handful. She had just reached the door and pulled it open when Pigot spoke. 'Touch my pipe again, I'll drown you in that creek.'

She paused, wondering whether to deny it, then went out and down to the hut.

Pigot went up the slope and over the road by himself that morning, just him and the dog. After a while she heard the steady stroke of the axe begin. As she dug she looked over at Chambers' hut.

By lunch, when Pigot told her again to take soup down there, the fever was on Chambers hard. As she went to leave he reached out, clamped his damp hand around her wrist. 'Tell him I need a doctor.'

She pulled her arm off him. 'He's getting one,' she lied, didn't know why she'd said it.

Back up at the cottage she stood in the doorway. 'He needs a doctor.'

Nothing from Pigot. He put a spoonful of soup in his mouth.

'He's going to die down there.'

Pigot raised his head. 'And you care, do you?'

'Can't just let him die down there.'

Pigot looked back down at his bowl. 'If he's not better in the morning, I'll get one.'

In the morning, he'll be dead, she thought.

...

In the morning Chambers was alive but the leg was swollen and hot, the fever even worse. He was delirious, talking about a storm brewing, yelling at her to shut the door, shut the door. Then he was crying, blubbering that it wasn't his fault, something—she didn't know what, couldn't understand what he was saying—wasn't his fault. She sat on the stool next to his mattress. Pigot had not harnessed the bullock. He had gone over the hill with the dog just as he had the morning before. He was not going for the doctor.

She sat with Chambers most of the morning. She didn't care what Pigot said or did. She couldn't be over there digging while twenty yards away Chambers lay here like this. He hadn't eaten last night and wouldn't eat this morning. She managed to get some water into his mouth. He was restless, his eyes protruding and glassy. He thrashed around on the mattress for a long time and then fell into a deep sleep. She went out and up to Pigot's cottage, stood outside it looking up the slope and over the road, could hear the faint stroke of the axe.

Down in the field she dug for a while and then went to check on Chambers. She stopped outside his door then opened it slowly. He was still, his eyes open. He was lying on his side, staring at the wall. She had known before she opened the door. Somehow had known.

Outside the cottage she stood looking up at the road, the rush of the creek behind her.

When Pigot came down for lunch she put the soup in front of him, waited to see if he was going to ask anything, enquire after Chambers, but he only spread butter on the damper and stuffed chunks of it into his mouth. He left again and in the afternoon she planted potatoes in the dug dirt.

When Pigot returned in the late afternoon he went down to the hut, came back up, went into the lean-to and came out with the spade, took it down towards the creek. Bridget could hear the rough sound of the spade going into the dirt. In the twilight she saw him drag the body out of the hut, saw him roll it, pushing it for the last part with his boot, into the hole. He picked up the spade, shovelled dirt into the grave.

...

Later, she lay awake feeling the presence of Pigot on the other side of the wall. She had not spoken to him that night and he had not said a word—ate his dinner as though nothing at all had happened. Eventually she got up, lifted the lean-to door so it would be quiet and not drag, and went outside. The moon, almost full, cast blue light across the field. The bullock was moving around in the yard beyond the end of the hut, the faint sound of the creek running—those the only sounds rippling the silence. The brightest of the stars spun dusky fingers of light at her. Can't stay here, it said.

Have to get away from this place.

In the morning Pigot didn't go over the hill, but stayed in the field next to the hut among the stumps and picked up the rocks that lay scattered all over the place, added them to the pile that he and Chambers had made. Bridget walked down towards the creek, saw Pigot's tall form bend, pick up a stone, walk over to the pile and drop it, pick up another one, the dog sitting by the pile sniffing the air and watching his master. At the creek she dumped Pigot's bedsheets in the scrub on the bank, picked her way down to the water with the shirt, squatted there and dunked it, rubbed the collar against a rock. Her movements were fast and scattered this morning; she couldn't concentrate. As she came back up from the creek with the wet washing she glanced across the field again. He was standing next to the rock pile, one foot up on it, looking towards the woods. While she was hanging the washing she heard him walk past the bullock yard and into the cottage. Maybe he was going to harness the bullock after all, go into town. But as she hung the shirt over the line she heard him whistle for the dog. The dog ran after him as he walked down the track towards the creek, a gun by his side. Roo hunting. They were almost out of meat. He was going roo hunting. Would probably be gone for a couple of hours then.

In the lean-to she grabbed her shawl from the mattress and from inside the hut took a wad of damper, the last of the smoked meat, wrapped them in the shawl. She pulled the door of the lean-to shut, her breath fast, heart hammering. She looked down to the creek. No sign of him; he had disappeared into the trees already. She looked up at the road and then had a thought, went back inside. She grabbed the pipe and tobacco, hurried back out and walked quickly across the rocky field to the road. She ran until the road went into trees and was out of view from the creek below then slowed to a quick walk.

...

The road wasn't really a road—more a rocky, scrubby cart track that disappeared completely at times only to reappear for a few yards in a gully as two muddy wheel ruts. She kept up a fast walk. Maybe he would get back to the hut to find her gone and would just sit there, put his feet up on the table, smoke his pipe. He would look for his pipe . . . Should have left it, shouldn't have taken the pipe. Well, it was too late now; it was part of the bundle she held against her stomach.

The day she had come along here had been overcast, the cloud low around the hills. It had been early in the morning when they'd turned off the main road, the crisp air as shocking as a slap. For the rest of the day she'd sat on the back of the cart while it jogged over rocks and holes, her arse raw from the rubbing of the hard wood. There had been one house, a big place off in the distance nestled into the crook of a hill, a cart track turning off the one they were on and leading over the tree-studded plain towards it. After that there was nothing: the cry of yellow-eyed crows and the occasional kangaroo darting across in front of them, bounding off into the scraggy mess of wattle and gum that flanked the track. Pigot sat up the front hunkered down into his coat, the bullock dragging her on the cart through mud and over sheets of rock towards a far-off and criminally silent horizon.

She didn't know how long it had taken to get from that turn-off to the stone hut that sat in a dip near a creek, the land around the creek damp and sprung with sedge. It had seemed like a long time. She had not been along the track in this direction, hadn't left Pigot's place the whole time she had been there. After the first two weeks had gone by and there had been no sign that Pigot was going to take her to town for church, she had told him she needed to go. She knew masters were supposed to make sure the convicts in their service went to church on Sunday. But Pigot had said that if she wanted to go to church, she could go, had motioned towards the track. 'Road's up there.' She'd thought about doing it, about walking off then and there, had gone and stood outside; a bitterly cold day, the rain having stopped for a while but not long before it had been coming in almost sideways. She had turned and gone back into the cottage where the fire crackled in the hearth.

She hadn't even wanted to go to church, just to get away from that place for a while with that hill looking over her all the time and Chambers skulking, and Pigot casting his long shadow over everything. Just to see some other people, see who was in the town, get a look at the other convicts, see if she knew anyone there, maybe someone she could even get a word with, tell them how rotten the new place was, how she wished she could go back to Hobart Town. Well, now she was going to. She was going to walk to Jericho and tell the constable that

Pigot had let Chambers die and that he'd let her die out there too if anything happened to her, if she got sick; he'd just let her die and she wasn't going back there, there was no missus there and she wasn't staying and she was going back to Hobart Town.

...

She sat on a rock and pulled a chunk off the damper. The day was cool, the thin cloud cover breaking now and then, the sun glowing weakly behind it high in the sky. Around the middle of the day, she thought. Up ahead the faint track made its way up a grassy slope. She hadn't thought to bring water and her mouth was dry now. The wood below the track was solid and dark with trees and she wondered if the creek was down in there. She walked into it, didn't get far before the scrub became thick and tangled. She stood there, the tall gums rising up, each of them trying to see out over the other ones. She had a creeping feeling of being watched. She turned around. Nothing there. Stupid. There was no one out here. She pushed her way further down the slope, listened. No sound of water. She turned around, couldn't see the grass clearing above. She ran back up, cutting grass wrapping around her ankles as she went. When she was back in the light she stood there breathing fast, for the first time wondering if she should turn back. Then she tied the shawl with the remaining damper, the meat, pipe and tobacco around her waist and kept walking.

...

The track crossed a small creek. She squatted, cupped her hands and guzzled. She had just filled her hands again when she heard the new sound. She stood up, listened. Yes. Faint, but unmistakable. She looked ahead at the muddy slope and then picked up her bundle and ran. Halfway up the slope she stumbled, her foot rolling off a rock. At the bottom of the next rise she left the track, ran limping down the hill into the thick of the trees. Behind a fallen tree she lay on the damp ground and listened to it—the rattle of cartwheels. Then it stopped. She waited, listened. She thought she heard it again but wasn't sure. She stayed there a long time with the cold from the ground seeping into her body then she stood stiffly, made her way back up the slope.

It had been this way, she was sure. She had not come far off it. Not that far. So where was it? She turned around. Trees and bushes, no break in them. How could a track just go? Just disappear? Panic wrapped its hand around her guts and squeezed. Behind her there was a noise—a branch cracking. She spun around. Her heart jumped like a frog in a bottle. Kangaroo. Just a kangaroo. That's all—just a kangaroo. She walked a few yards, stopped. The track was close. Close by here somewhere. It had to be. She had been on it not long ago.

She walked one way then another. Branches snagged her dress and scratched her arms. Her foot went down into a hole. She fell forward hard, got up again, walked a few paces and stopped. Twilight. A pale gold moon presented itself, called forth an army of stars. She hit the side of her fist into the tree trunk next to her. 'Bugger you! Bugger you. Bugger you. Bugger. Bugger.' She slid down to the base of the tree.

...

The sounds were of birds, a thump thump as a kangaroo made its way through the forest. Every direction looked the same—glimpses of grey sky through a net of leaves and branches.

She pushed her way through fern and cutting grass, there being no top to the hill, only an ongoing mess of scrub that scratched her, hooked her, tripped her. She fell and lay there among it all, her body given up to it until her will rose up biting and she was moving again.

She ran until her chest hurt and her breathing was hard. She stopped halfway up another slope. Around her damp rock leaked silence, preached cold, stubborn stillness. Wet shadows lurked in cracks big enough for someone, something, to hide in. Scraggly trees clung to the sides of rock, their roots pushing down into shallow dirt collected on ledges and in crevices. Their thin branches hung at queer angles, shivered in a whisper of wind.

When she stopped again she was in a gully, a rock wall behind her, a trickle of water running down it. Opposite her the slope was dense with trees, dark playing around their trunks. Her dress was torn, there was a gash on her leg, blood stuck to the shredded stocking around it. She licked the water then sat down against the dry end of the wall. Above her clouds laced with pink and orange drifted, the day out there taking its time to die its pretty death.

She ate a piece of damper, pulled her knees in close to her chest.

...

Morning light crept over her face like a spider, and then again the scrub grabbed at her, stroked her, pawed at her like a many-armed monster. She fought it until she was too tired to fight and it bit into her, took her down into its dark bowels where she wandered again until she must have found her way back to the creature's mouth because there below her was a plain with a flock of sheep grazing on it. She hurried down the slope, falling, grabbing onto tree trunks as she went. Sheep stared at her with their queer round eyes, their dirty arses retreating. She walked, trying to find something the sheep belonged to. Must be. Must have been something, someone.

A cloud approached the sun, slid over it. Rocks turned dull, blue hills faded to grey, the grass lost its shine and the wind grew cold. Another cloud moved in, silent and steady, a massive grey hand reaching out and suffocating the sun until it was nothing but a weak and passive glow. The landscape cowered. A gust came up that almost pushed her forward.

The sky continued to darken and then a few large drops fell and seconds later a curtain of rain came down. She stood under a tree while the rain pounded the ground like a child in a tantrum, and then stopped just as quickly as it had started. The clouds churned and rolled and turned a thick dark grey. Sodden sheep looked up from their grazing, ran through a sheet of water that sat over the land. She trudged over the wet ground while the cold wind ruffled the sky and blue appeared like something new and daring.

In the darkness she sat in a hollow tree, the shawl pulled tight around her.

Sea. Sea until there was nothing but sea. Until it had stolen everything that had come before so that all of life might have been a dream brushed away, painted over by strokes of blue and green. Cold rough sea, sea ironed flat by a baking sun; the sameness, the stillness of it like hands over a person's ears.

Bridget had crawled up the ladder out of the darkness and stood on the ship deck squinting, looking around at the tree-clad hills flanking the river. They were anchored in a bay, at the head of it a beach, and beyond that a cleared area of land in which there was a smattering of buildings. Beyond the clearing, a mountain; a lump of a thing like an animal lying sleeping, back to the sky, cloud clinging to it, a skirt of hills around it.

It wasn't what she had expected. She didn't know what she had expected, but not this. Emily Reid, a small birdy-looking woman, said she'd heard it was a good place, that a convict woman could marry a gentleman, that there was plenty of food.

A few weeks into the trip the girl in the bunk above Bridget had died, open eyes staring straight up, stunned, as if she'd seen God as she died and was surprised by the look of him. Sarah Merchant's baby cried all night and after a week of diarrhoea it died too, was thrown overboard wrapped in white cloth. Bridget curled herself up opposite the bunk where Sarah Merchant was quiet. Up on the deck she hoisted her dress out of the bucket. Salt water dripped onto her boots as she stared at the quivering horizon.

...

The ship sat in the bay for two days, the third morning like the one before: cool and overcast. Fog hung over the river and a fine drizzle fell, the shouts from the shore dulled, muffled by the kerchief of moisture that waved across the bay.

As Bridget stood on the deck a colder breeze came up, turned the shiny surface of the river to matt. There was a break in the thin cloud, a patch of sunlight on the water where white gulls bobbed under rays of gold light, grey turning an eerie brown all around them. She crossed her arms against the breeze, looked around at the forest-cloaked hills that followed the river all the way up and then spread out from the bay in any and every direction. She had never seen anything like it. Was this it? The good place?

On the beach two soldiers pushed a boat into the water and three men stood on the beach watching, each of them dressed in black. Two of these men wore high hats, appeared lifeless there, black sticks in the muting grey. There was a wave from one of the soldiers and then the sticks came to life, walked down the beach and climbed into the boat.

Across the ship deck women stood in groups, their chatter rising.

'Quiet! I said *quiet*!' The ship superintendent, gold buttons crawling over his red coat, shining like rare beetles. 'When your name is called you are to come forward.'

'Catherine. Adams.' The superintendent's voice strained to reach out over the deck.

When Bridget's name was called she looked behind her, seeking Beth, an older woman who had been in the bunk above Sarah and whose company Bridget had kept for most of the voyage. Now Beth met Bridget's gaze, nodded, her face solemn.

...

The town square was full of waiting men and their carts. In the middle Captain Marshall stood with five other gentlemen who were chatting about the price of this and the value of that. At the sound of the women coming up the slope from the bay the men ceased their conversation and turned to look. 'Yes, indeed,' said Captain Marshall, cutting short the conversation with the man who stood next to him.

The superintendent appeared first, followed by a motley group of women. They stopped in front of the commissariat building and Marshall noticed one of them in particular—she stood a little to the side of the group, her head raised slightly as though she was smelling the air, testing it for a scent. The superintendent was speaking but this girl appeared not to be listening at all. She had now turned her head to one side and was looking down towards the bay—not at the bay, but beyond it, and it was as though she was looking at, or seeing even, a world that lay far beyond the landscape in front of her. A breeze came up and flicked at the waves of light brown hair around her face and it seemed to be that tiny movement, that almost imperceptible flurry, that triggered the girl to return from whatever she gazed upon—for she now turned her head forward and in that split second of the head turning her eyes regained their former sharpness. And her gaze, when it fell on him, was full and direct. It was because of all this that Marshall did not hear when the superintendent called his name, and it was only when he repeated it, his voice sharp with impatience, that he stepped forward. Another name was called, and to his surprise the woman who had caused his momentary lapse of concentration stepped forward also.

The superintendent held out a quill and a book. 'This one's yours, Captain Marshall, if you'll sign here.'

...

Marshall stood aside as the girl climbed up onto the cart. Once seated next to her he took the liberty of glancing sideways at her face. She was seated looking dead ahead of her, her back held straight and her head tilted slightly so that the side of her jaw met the world fractionally ahead of the rest of her. Marshall shifted in his seat, cleared his throat and took up the reins. 'Bridget, is it? Your name?'

The girl seemed to look towards him and then look again, as though the first time she might have thought her senses deluded her. She recovered quickly, however, as he had already come to see was her habit.

She nodded.

On the side of the road two soldiers were speaking to a filthy, stumpy man with long dark hair that hung in clumps around his face. He opened and closed a gummy mouth, jumped up and down on one leg, arms swinging wildly. One of the soldiers pushed him and the man fell back into the dirt. The two of them stood laughing as the man tried to scramble to his feet.

Marshall saw her watching the scene. 'It's not altogether like England but some things don't change—not really,' he said, and laughed. He heard the strange and fake sound of his laugh, almost as though he had not himself generated it. He'd no idea what had set him so on edge.

He looked forward at the horse's head, which remained quite steady while the black mane flung upwards and then rested again on the neck in rhythm with its gait. They were headed up Elizabeth Street to New Town and to his home, Rosebury House. 'There is another girl already,' he said. 'She cooks principally, and assists with the children. It's the cleaning I believe she needs help with.' He drew a breath and waited, strangely nervous of her reply.

She only nodded once again. It was a slow nod, quite thoughtful, as though throughout it she were considering what she might say if she had not chosen only to nod.

'My sister is the children's governess,' he said, 'but she is not at home a lot of late. She has her own interests.' He leaned towards her slightly as he said it as though sharing a secret, or a joke with a companion and gave a short laugh. He saw that she removed her hands from her lap, where they had both been resting palm down against her thighs. Now she crossed her arms and then pulled herself up a little higher in the seat.

...

The house sat at the top of a rise looking down over the bay. It was two storeys high, stone steps leading up to a wide, decorated front door and muslin curtains framing the windows.

Bridget got down off the cart, relieved to be away from the man and his nervous laughter. A girl appeared from around the side of the house.

'Ah, Mary, thank you. If you would take care of Bridget.'

'Course, sir.'

'Come with me,' she said, 'round the back.'

From London, Bridget thought. The girl was short and walked quickly but with small steps.

'Only found out yesterday we was getting a new girl, don't tell me nothing only a convict I am, not like I'm running the place or nothing. Be lost without me they would. It's me what's in charge 'cause the missus trusts me and now that Jane's needing more time—sick of the children, she is,' the girl said. She looked back at Bridget, conspiratorial. 'Still, don't blame her none for that. They're so spoilt I'd tan their backsides if I could, only you can imagine the stink the missus'd kick up if I so much as touched 'em. Edward likes his milk warm but if it's too hot, he won't drink it . . .'

The woman talked on while Bridget walked behind her around to the back of the house, where there were two stables as well as two other timber buildings off a yard. The door to one of the buildings was open and she followed Mary in. The ceiling was low and the room dark, a fireplace in the corner and a table in the middle. 'This's the kitchen then.' Back out in the yard she pulled open the door to the other building. 'Sleep in here. Not too bad really; a bit cold this time of year, but I've seen worse. I mean, you shoulda seen where I had to sleep in the last place. Get a wool mattress here, only straw at the other place, and not just gaps like this, but bits of the wall missing and only one blanket with all that.'

She motioned to a pile of clothes on a stool. 'Those are yours. The water in the bucket there's warm. When you're clean come back to the house.'

Bridget pushed the door shut. There was no window but the gaps between the boards let in shards of light. Through the gaps she could see flickers of movement in the yard, heard Mary walk past. She stood there in the room, waited until there was stillness outside, then pulled the dress over her head, paused before taking off the petticoat. She dropped it on the floor, a slight breeze on her breasts.

When she tipped water over her head the taste of salt was sharp in her mouth.

...

'This way,' Mary said, leading her down a wide hall. She opened the first door they came to. 'This's the dining room. That there is a portrait of the master's father. Distinguished-looking, isn't he? But they all are in those paintings, aren't they? I mean, you wouldn't pay someone if they did a terrible picture of you, would you? And even if you did you'd most likely not put it on the wall, so in the end you can't tell a lot from them really at all—unless you believe the likeness, that is.'

She shut that door and continued down the hall opening and shutting doors, and then on up the stairs. 'The master's alright, he is. Not like *her*. She's more annoying than hives, I'll grant you, and there's no relief—not like with hives, what at least you can itch. He's an officer, you know. He's in with the gov'nor, helping find the bushrangers. I mean, he's not *that* important, but . . .'

Mary opened another door, the room inside spacious and light. On a rug in the middle there were two children, one boy about four and a girl, younger, as well as a lady who was struggling to get the boy's boot on. She looked up at the two people in the doorway.

'A new girl,' Mary said. 'Bridget her name is, missus.'

The woman stood up. 'Hello.'

'These two here are Edward and Sophie,' Mary said, and the boy who stood on one leg holding on to the woman's shoulder looked blankly at Bridget while the little girl kept focused on the doll in her lap.

Mary pulled the door shut behind them. 'That's Jane, the master's sister. We'd best get back downstairs, there's visitors coming.'

...

In the kitchen Mary gave her potatoes to chop, prattled at her the entire time.

Bridget put the knife down on the table. She had to get out of the room.

'Where are you going? Come back here, you—'

But Bridget was out the kitchen door, into the yard, where over the roof of the house the mountain towered. It had been hidden in cloud before, but now the cloud had cleared to reveal the columns of rock that decorated its face.

A man appeared around the corner of the house. Short already, he was made shorter by the hunchbacked way he carried himself and his gait took him almost as much from side to side as it did forward, making his progress painfully slow. He rocked his way along, looking at the ground, muttering to himself.

'Not daffodils there, for blarney's sake, pansies. Pansies, pansies, pansies. "*Oh, no pansies under the rosebush, I find the look of it quite common.*" She finds the look of it common. I'll give her common. Should put my hand up under that dress, give her a bit a this crooked ole finger, eh? I'll give her common.' The man chuckled. 'See how she likes a bit a freshly turned soil up her royal pinkness. Pansies, hmph.' He spat on the ground next to him and finally looked up. 'What are you doing?'

'What?'

The man squinted at her. 'Who the hell are you?'

From around the front of the house she heard the sound of horse's hooves on the gravel.

'She sent you out here, did she? What's she want now? S'pose she'll want birds next—the right birds, not the birds that live here, no, no, them's no bloody good. You wait and see: she'll make him ship over a whole load of sparras. You wait and see, she will.'

He pulled a plug of tobacco out of his pocket, broke off a piece and put it in his mouth. 'Want some?' Held it out to her between callused fingers crisscrossed with dirt-filled cracks.

She shook her head.

He shrugged. 'New are ya then? New, I s'pose.'

'Bridget! Bridget!' Mary had her head stuck out the kitchen door hollering.

The old man smiled and his eyes got lost. 'Oh, don't keep

her waiting; she'll claw your eyes out that one will. Possessed she is, possessed.'

...

Mary put the knife down and pushed a loaded tea tray across the table. 'Take this. In the dining room.'

She took her into the house and along the hall and pointed at a door on the left. 'In there.'

The door was closed but Bridget could hear voices inside. She jammed the tray between her waist and the doorframe, turned the door handle with her right hand, then used her foot to push it. The teapot and cups slid but stopped before the edge. She tipped the tray back the other way slightly and went into the room.

When she came in, Marshall, who sat at one end of the big table, looked up. The other man glanced at her then back at Marshall as though waiting for him to speak. For a moment Marshall said nothing.

She crossed the room to the cabinet, where she placed the tray.

'Well, I don't see how that can possibly be the case. I saw him just yesterday and he said they had been seen only a few miles west of Coal River.'

'I hardly think Mr Brewer would make up a thing like that, Captain, and he is not blind. And the description Linley has given of the men who robbed him matches the description of the banditti perfectly.'

'Yes, but they were seen near Coal River, Colonel. Only days ago.'

'Well, they can't have been at Coal River. They were at

Linley's last week, at the other end of the colony, Captain. There must have been some mistake.'

Captain Marshall sighed. 'Well, I'm told they have found a route through the mountains.'

Bridget leaned over and placed a cup of tea down in front of him.

'Thank you.'

The captain's politeness towards the servant did not escape the other man's attention. Bridget saw surprise light his eyes and flicker there before fading into a hazy question supplanted by the topic at hand. 'Perhaps so, but regardless, whoever made the report at Coal River must have been mistaken. The governor will not be made to look like a fool, Captain.'

Marshall lowered his head and when he spoke, he did so quietly. 'No. However, perhaps . . .'

She put a cup down in front of the colonel, who continued with the conversation. 'Pardon me, Captain?'

'He's making mistakes, Colonel.'

'Mistakes? I see. And what are these mistakes you would charge him with?'

'I am not sure precisely. His manner.'

'He is mistaken in his manner?'

Marshall sighed again. 'Look, I will pay a visit to Mr Brewer. I would like to hear what happened there for myself.'

'I don't see how you can comment on his manner when—'

Bridget pulled the door shut behind her. As she did, a woman descended the stairs. 'You'll be the new girl then.'

The nose was beaky and her eyes a rare ginger-brown, rimmed by darker circles. Freckles a shade or two lighter than her eyes stained the bridge of her nose, continued out towards her cheekbones.

Bridget nodded.

'I beg your pardon?'

'Yes.'

'*Yes?* You will address me as Ma'am and Captain Marshall as Sir, thank you very much. What is your name?'

'Bridget. Bridget Crack. Ma'am.'

'I see. And I trust Mary has shown you around?'

'Yes, Ma'am.'

'Speak up.'

'Yes. Ma'am.'

'Good.' She turned and, in a rustle of material, went up the hall.

...

The rock of the mountain was pink in the dawn light. A few yards away from where Bridget was milking, a creek flowed through a gully and the cleared land stopped. When she finished she left the bucket and walked over to the creek. A flock of black birds flew over uttering plaintive cries, their wings beating the air slowly. It had rained in the night and the air was still moist and the spicy smell prickled Bridget's nostrils. Trees with smooth dark green leaves that tapered at the ends crowded the creek and further up grew more closely together, a mess of shrubs below them, no light in there at all. In Suffolk there were some woods on the Harringtons' property. She had gone there a few times with her brother when she was little. But her father didn't like Harrington and said they weren't to go on his property. She remembered a carpet of bluebells, patches of sunlight, birds flitting from tree to tree. The rest of Suffolk was grass and hedgerows and villages.

She stood there a moment in the dark under the canopy with the rushing creek, inhaled the sharp fragrance. Not like the smell of Suffolk—flour and hay. Those were the smells she remembered.

...

In the town there was the occasional grand building made of pale, soft-looking stone, and then cottages, fenced gardens around some of them, rosebushes growing along the fences. Bridget walked along a wide busy street full of carts and bullocks and horses, people ducking and weaving through them to get from one side of the street to the other. A group of men stood out the front of a timber building yelling and laughing. A blacksmith worked under an awning, hammering and clanging, now and then a red-hot hiss, like a sigh, puncturing the iron ruckus.

Bridget found the store and delivered the note as instructed, had just arrived back at the house when there was a knock at the kitchen door. The red-haired woman she opened the door to regarded her. 'You new?' she said.

Bridget nodded.

'Just in then? Eliza. Servant the next place up there.' She pointed up the road. 'Note for the missus, from mine.' She held out a piece of paper, looked Bridget over. 'Where you from? London, me. Wexford really, but I been in London before here. Gotta go,' she said and hurried off around the side of the house.

'Saw you met, Eliza,' Mary said. 'Other servant at that place, Dan—Eliza *goes with him*. I don't know what I've done but she doesn't talk to me much anymore. She's Irish though and you know what they can be like,' she said, and laughed.

...

The next night Bridget woke to a knock on the wall. Her name hissed. 'Bridget!'

It was the red-haired woman, Eliza, standing there in the dark. 'Come on, get dressed.'

'What for?'

'Going down to town, to the public house.'

Paul was standing behind her. He and the old man Kelly were the male servants at Marshall's place; she'd met Paul the afternoon she arrived, from Devon with thin hair, a high forehead and a tendency to look away when he spoke.

'Daniel's waiting down the road,' Eliza said. 'He'll buy you a drink.'

Bridget looked behind her at the shape of Mary sleeping. 'Don't worry about her,' Eliza hissed.

Out on the road Bridget slowed, looked back at the house.

'Won't be long,' Eliza said. 'They'll never know you were gone. We do it all the time.'

The three dark shapes went ahead of her down the dirt road, laughter and banter rolling off them into the night sky.

'You coming or not?'

...

There were only a few cottages along the road, one grand house, but as they came down the hill the buildings were more tightly packed. They crossed a timber bridge over the creek and then Daniel turned into a muddy lane at the end of which was a brick building, double storey, but thin. Even from outside the place was noisy.

He opened the door and the four of them stepped into the din.

Inside the room was packed full of bodies and hazy with smoke. 'Well, well, Mr Rooke, what have you got here? Sharing, are we?' The gnarled man next to Daniel cast his eyes over Bridget and winked at her, then turned away and raised his arm. 'Paddy O'Doherty, get yourself over here—our man Rooke has been doing a wee bit of fossicking and I'll be damned if he hasn't turned up gold.'

A man with wrinkled skin and bright eyes came over. 'So, are you going to introduce me, Daniel?'

Daniel, in a flat, offhand way, told her this was Paddy.

'He's charming, he is,' Paddy said sarcastically.

Someone put a pitcher of brown liquid in Bridget's hand then. 'The finest brew in the colony, without a doubt.'

A man had just come in and was standing inside the door looking around. When Paddy saw him the smile left his face and he excused himself, pushed his way over to the man. Daniel joined them and a minute later the three of them disappeared out a side door.

Eliza, who had been talking to another woman, turned to Bridget. 'How do you like Mary then?'

'She talks a lot.'

Eliza tipped back her head and laughed. 'Talks a lot? You could say that. And most what she says ain't true. She cries too, mostly to get her way.'

Paul leaned in towards Bridget. 'At first I thought I'd strangle her, but now I think I'll shove her head in a bucket of water and hold it there till the bubbles stop.'

'You'll be holding for a while,' Eliza said.

Another man came up beside them. 'Just in, then? Eliza here said you was just in,' he slurred. He held his cup in the air. 'Welcome to Van Diemen's Land.'

...

Jane Marshall was different to most ladies that Bridget had met—not that she had met many, mostly seen them from a distance or across a room, and usually even if she did meet them their gaze hovered above her and they turned as quickly away from her as they would an uncomfortable truth. Jane was unmarried but not young, was sensible instead of frilly and was scornful of gossip. It was Jane who Bridget took her instruction from, and Mary. The house was one of the biggest in Hobart Town, sat on a street called Elizabeth that led uphill away from the bay. For most of the days she cleaned, did the jobs Mary didn't want to do. Every few nights Eliza knocked and Bridget got up and dressed, went out into the dark, down into the town to the Bird in Hand—something to look forward to, to break the tedium of her days.

There was a place behind the dairy that Bridget had found where she sometimes went to get away from Mary, from the house. There was a tree there; its leaves like fronds, hundreds of tiny leaves arranged along a series of stems, pale, washed-out green. She would stand there, pull a twig off the tree, comb the leaves through her hand, hear the house door open, Mary calling her name. Sometimes she would take the letter out of her stockings and read it, fold it back up and put it back in.

From here she could see out over the fields behind the house, but with the dairy behind her, and trees in front and on either side, she was fairly well hidden. She could sometimes see Paul or Kelly, ploughing or planting the field, saw Jane cross the field with the book she drew in. There was a room downstairs that was Jane's. Bridget had seen Jane come out one day, the door left ajar, had put her head around and looked. Pictures—the room full of them. She had stepped inside. The pictures were mostly of plants, a few of animals, queer-looking things. A huge bird or something like a bird, long scaly legs and black feathers, a yellow beak and nasty little dark eyes. A flower like a pine cone or a brush, but yellow. She had been standing there looking when she heard Jane come back. She had thought to hide but, finding Jane generally unthreatening, she stood there and let her come in and discover her.

'What do you think?'

Bridget shrugged.

'They're not very good,' Jane said.

Bridget pointed to the long-legged thing. 'What's that?'

'Emu, it's called.'

'The door was open,' Bridget said.

'That's alright.' Jane dipped a brush into paint.

...

A few days later she had been sitting behind the dairy, had heard someone coming and stood up to see Marshall walking towards her. She'd expected to be told off but he'd asked her how she was settling in, was everything alright. 'Jane said you were interested in her paintings.'

'The door was open,' she said.

He'd stood there looking like he wanted to say something,

but then Paul had appeared on the other side of the creek, walking in their direction.

'Yes, well. Alright . . .' the captain said before he walked off.

There was no reason she knew of for him to be down there. The dairy was the servants' area, the *female* servants' area. She didn't know what he wanted—didn't think it was the usual thing, but she wasn't sure. Eliza had told her that Marshall's was a good place to be assigned to. 'Likes to stroke himself over his goodness, the captain does,' she said. 'Prob'ly up there now: *Oh, I'm so good*,' she'd moaned, running her hand down her imaginary shaft. '*I'm sooo gooood*.' They'd been at the public house and she'd gone so on with it that people had turned to look.

...

Snow covered the mountain and then the hills above the town. Upstairs in the library Bridget ran a cloth over the gleaming timber of Captain Marshall's desk. Behind her on the wall was a shelf of books. She left the cloth on the table, picked out one of the books. *Mathilda*.

> Florence. Nov. 9th 1819
> It is only four o'clock; but it is winter and the sun has already set: there are no clouds in the clear, frosty sky to reflect its slant beams, but the air itself is tinged with a slight roseate colour which is again reflected on the snow that covers the ground. I live in a lone cottage on a solitary, wide heath: no voice of life reaches me.

She heard someone coming up the stairs, went to put the book back in its spot, but as she hurried to get in, it fell.

Captain Marshall stood in the doorway.

She picked the book up. 'It fell out. Sorry, sir . . . I was just dusting and the book fell.'

He regarded her. 'Do you like to read?'

She shrugged.

'You may borrow a book if you would like to.'

Bridget shook her head. 'Mary'll be needing me downstairs,' she muttered and hurried past him.

...

She was polishing knives in the dining room when he came in. 'I thought you might like to borrow it,' he said, and put the book on the table.

Bridget left the book there until after he had gone.

Later, when she leafed through the pages, she remembered her father perched on the stool, leaning forward and watching her intently, the dim light of a candle thrown over the Bible page. 'Again. Read it again,' he'd say. He'd rest his chin on his hand and stare at the floor while she read, then, when she'd finished, there might be a pause before he looked up, his brow furrowed, his eyes showing concern. He'd shake his head then, as though she had just performed a miracle—a somewhat troubling one at that. Once, her brother Steven went off fishing with Timmy instead of going to school. When her father found out he whipped him like he'd never whipped him before. He was always telling Mr Moore, the farmer he worked for, how well his children could read and write. 'Bridget's the best speller at the school,' he told Mrs Moore. It wasn't true;

but Samuel Owen wasn't one to let the truth get in the way of his fantasies, certainly not when it came to other people's opinion of him and his family.

...

Captain Marshall had been away, had just arrived back that morning. Bridget was walking along the hall when she heard voices coming from the sitting room, arguing. 'Oh, I understand the situation alright. I'll tell you what I understand. I understand that it was your idea that we come here in the first place when we were quite fine where we were. I understand that you would put your . . . your high ideals over the safety of your family, over your responsibility as a husband and as a father.'

'Eleanor, please—not this again.'

'No, Richard, don't you "please" me.'

'I am doing my best.'

'Your best?' she scoffed. 'We are all doing our best.'

'Are we? Are we, Eleanor?'

'Yes. We are.'

'And you choose to assassinate my character and tell me this is your best. Is that correct?'

'I am not assassinating your character.'

'Their children are dying, Eleanor, being killed. You talk about innocent people being killed . . . We have some obligation to protect them. Surely you agree?'

Silence.

'Come on, Eleanor, surely. I mean, imagine if—'

'No, Richard, don't. Don't say it. Don't you dare say it.'

'You are always talking about sides, Eleanor. Why does it

have to be about sides? We must stop looking at the situation in terms of sides.'

'No, you are wrong. You want me to imagine? I already imagine, Richard. Every day I imagine. I lie in bed at night and imagine them coming down out of the hills, coming here to this house. You are off away half the time and I do little but imagine. I imagine until I am almost ill and you tell me it is *my* attitude that is causing the trouble. No, Richard. The trouble is there's a horde of savages out there who would kill us as soon as look at us and all you can do is make excuses for them.'

'I don't believe this conversation is getting anywhere. I will see you later when you have calmed down.'

'I am not going to calm down!'

Bridget ran as quietly as she could along the hall. She heard a door slam and the missus go up the stairs. A few minutes later Captain Marshall went out the front door.

...

Mrs Marshall stood in front of Bridget, a dry rag from the line dangling from her thumb and forefinger. 'Do you call this white?'

'They're clean.' All morning Bridget had been in the washroom, her arms in water brown with the little boy's shit as she scrubbed his rags. She'd rubbed them against the washboard until her back ached.

'I beg your pardon?'

'I washed them, they're clean.'

'You will take all of those rags off the line and wash them again and they had better not be soiled the next time I see them.' She flicked the rag at Bridget's chest, turned and walked away.

Bridget swore under her breath and the woman stopped, turned around. 'What did you say?'

'Nothing.'

Mrs Marshall's face red, eyes bulging. Then she disappeared inside and the door slammed behind her.

Bridget stood there by the line near the row of rags and then walked away, away from the house to the place behind the dairy.

She heard the house door open, heard Mary calling her name. She moved back closer to the dairy wall. Mary called again and then the door shut.

She sat down with her knees up watching a line of ants go up the tree, drops of amber sap dry on the bark.

...

Winter settled in and Mary began complaining about Bridget's outings to the Bird in Hand. She threatened to tell Marshall that Bridget was going out at night, to which Bridget replied that if she did, she would kill her. Mary stopped talking to her for a while after that; only spoke to tell her what to do and it was in a clipped but sulky tone. Then one morning Bridget woke to Mary ringing a bell next to her head. She jumped up and tore it out of Mary's hand, pushed her against the wall, the handle of the bell across her throat. She saw the fear in Mary's eyes and her anger ebbed. She let go, stood holding the bell while Mary ran to the house.

Two quiet days followed, Mary not talking to her. Knowing that Mary would have bawled to her, Bridget expected the missus to say something, but she didn't. Then, on the afternoon of the third day, a constable came to the kitchen, the missus and Mary with him. 'Tell him,' Mrs Marshall said to Mary.

'She tried to kill me, sir.'

'There you are, as I told you,' Mrs Marshall said.

'I didn't try to kill no one.'

'Take her away, please,' Mrs Marshall said. 'Take her away now.'

...

The constable took her down through the town and to the gaol. She was charged with 'insolence and disorderly conduct', sentenced to time in the stocks, then to be reassigned. For two swollen hours she stood in the middle of the town locked into a timber frame, her jaw tightening against pain, ladies moving slightly closer together as they passed, lengthening their step. She was a few weeks in the gaol then, taken every day to the hospital to wash blood from sheets and bandages. She had just grown used to the haemorrhage of women that was the women's wing of the gaol—or the Female Factory, as it was known—when the matron told her one morning she would not be going to the hospital that day. Instead, she was sent down the hill to Johnson's—to the pale slug and his stolid, watchful wife.

...

Johnson was fat and oily-looking, his house when she arrived there sparse and tidy, cold with no fires burning in any of the hearths. The walls were thick and the curtains heavy and it smelled of stone. The kitchen at the back was as scrubbed and dustless as the rest of the house. His wife, with one child clinging to her hip, another looking up at Bridget from next to her, thumb in its mouth, was young and nervous.

When Bridget came up from the dairy on the first afternoon and into the yard he was there. He watched her, big eyes in a fat head, the skin under the eyes pulling away from the eyeballs and hanging in puffy sacks, exposing wet red skin below the whites of the eyes. The woman was at the kitchen door. When Johnson turned and walked towards the stable the woman stood there in the doorway watching him with crossed arms. She watched until he had gone then turned around and went in.

In the night Bridget snuck out of the small room adjoining the kitchen and went down into the town, back to the Bird in Hand, where Eliza pushed her way through the crowd, swore as someone bumped her and her drink sloshed down her front. She settled next to Bridget. 'Johnson, master at that new place you're at—girl who were there a while back got took back to the gaol, his bastard in her belly,' she said.

...

The little girl Hannah had just finished breakfast when she vomited all over the floor. Bridget cleaned it up. 'What've you fed her?' Johnson wanted to know. He was at her about everything then.

'You don't want to stay there,' Eliza said, and Bridget burned the potatoes nearly black, put them on the table in front of the missus, who looked at them, then only turned and walked out of the room. The next day she burned the lamb, was surprised to see a film of moisture over the woman's eyes.

...

On the day she had arrived at the gaol from Marshall's place she had been out in the yard when the door had flown open and a woman had run out, thrown herself on the gravel, wrapped her arms around her head and lay there on her side, knees pulled up toward her belly, wailing. Three others had come behind her and one of them grabbed her arms, tried to pull her up. 'Come on, Lottie, get up. Come on. It's alright now, get up.'

'Leave me alone.'

The woman let go of Lottie's arms and squatted down next to her, whispered something, but Lottie only continued to cry. Bridget found out later that she'd had her hair cut off, a punishment for insulting her mistress.

The day the constable came to Johnson's and took Bridget back to the gaol and they did it to her she sat stone-still staring at the wall in front of her.

Later, in the dark, she sat up and ran her hand over the rough stubble.

...

Bridget walked to the far side of the gaol's yard, sat down on the gravel and scraped at it with a rock. The sounds of the town came over the wall, the cries of gulls carried up from the cove. A few of them circled over the yard. She looked up at their white bellies, the stretch of their wings.

She was sitting against the wall staring at her boots when a shadow appeared over her. A woman with wide hips and thin shoulders stood in front of her. 'Matron's watching you. They'll lock you up for a lunatic and you'll never get out.' She looked over towards the door on the other side of the yard that led into the gaol. Bridget followed her gaze, saw the matron standing there with folded arms.

'I'm Anne,' the shadow said.

There was a scar that ran from the side of her eye in an arc down to her mouth. The sun was behind her, creating a glow around her head.

Bridget looked down at the pattern she'd scraped into the gravel. 'Bridget,' she said.

...

Ellen Cotton was loud. Her voice rose above everything, nasal and cracking. 'You, Mary-Ann Salter'd take the Devil's hot prong in ya mouth if you thought you'd get anything by it.' A chorus cackle rang through Bridget's head. She stood up from the table, took the bowl of soup. Poured it over black hair, Ellen Cotton's head. Ellen stood up fast. 'Crazy bitch! You crazy bitch!' She grabbed and clawed at Bridget, soup dripping onto her shoulders.

...

The walls and the low ceiling were made of stone blocks, the floor dirt, the only light coming in from a small window up high in the thick timber door, three bars through it. There was a bucket in the corner, the smell of shit and piss wafting through the suffocating dark filling up the whole cell. Twice a day keys rattled, the door opened and light flooded in. The matron brought bread and water, swapped the bucket for an empty one. Other than the bucket there was a blanket, coarse wool, a small hole in one corner. Between the cold stone blocks moss grew, the wall wet to touch on one side.

Sometimes the sound of a laugh a long way off, a scream, someone yelling.

Long days of darkness. She crawled to rays of light that fell over her like gold dust then were gone. Punishing dark again. Dark and more dark. She sat holding her knees, sometimes rocking without knowing she was.

...

The light was like nothing she could ever have imagined. It jabbed into her eyeballs like sticks. It hit her eyes and exploded there and all she saw was white. She put her arms up to shield herself from its violence. A whimper came from her throat. She couldn't see a thing.

...

The police magistrate sat in a room with high, decorated ceilings and furniture of polished timber. He read out something about her refusing to work at Johnson's. She hadn't refused to work, but she didn't get to say anything. He ordered that she be sent to the Interior. 'Up-country,' Anne said. 'Where they send the hard cases.' She didn't care; didn't give a damn what they did with her. They could go to hell.

...

The matron came into the workroom in the middle of the morning. Bridget got up from the spinning wheel and followed her to a small room near the street. The door was open and there was a man standing in there, black hair receding away from the rounds of his forehead, his eyes as dark as his hair. His jaw was angular and the bottom of the chin almost flat. His nose was large and, like the rest of his face, appeared bony rather than fleshy. It was a face that drew the viewer's attention to its structure, to the underlying frame. The matron said he was to be her new master, that his name was Mr Charles Pigot. He looked at Bridget and nodded. The matron was polite with him, eager to please.

He was a tall man with square shoulders and carried himself in an upright way. Outside on the street she kept her distance behind him, as both his posture and his manner demanded.

When they came to the corner of Elizabeth and Liverpool streets he stopped next to a black carriage, four horses harnessed to it. 'Wait here.' He went into a brick building the carriage was parked near.

On the other side of the road two women in fancy dresses, both holding parasols, walked past. She watched the people, the horses and bullocks and carts coming and going, cart wheels rolling over dried-up shit that was being broken up, pressed more and more into the gravel until eventually there would be nothing left of it but tiny pieces of grey grass that would be blown away. Bridget leaned against the shiny carriage.

She was standing there a long time before Pigot came back. He opened the carriage door. 'Get in.'

There were two seats facing one another. She sat in the one that faced the front of the carriage and moved into the corner by the window. He came in behind her, sat on the same seat near the other window.

They sat there in silence and then the door opened and a man with little glasses and an orange beard put his head in. 'Ah, Mr Pigot! Fancy that.'

'Mr Lloyd,' the dark-haired man said, his tone flat.

'We'll be travelling together then.'

'So it seems.'

The man got in and settled himself in the middle of the other seat, glanced at Bridget, wiped one of his hands along his thigh then sat with both hands on his knees. He cleared his throat, looked out the window.

Outside, a man came out of the building Pigot had gone into, climbed into the seat on the front of the carriage and a minute later they were moving.

Mr Lloyd seemed to ready himself, looked at Pigot. 'Quite nice weather, isn't it?' The day was sunny, a cool breeze.

Pigot didn't reply.

'I suppose you've heard about the trouble up at the Wilkinsons' place.'

'I heard something.'

'And you know Mr Clarke lost twelve sheep last week. Slaughtered by natives. Terrible waste.'

'Hard to believe, isn't it?' Pigot said.

Lloyd was silent for a moment, glanced at Bridget again. 'No one in their right mind would set up out our way. No one.' He laughed awkwardly.

The carriage was headed up the main road and a moment later they passed the turn-off to Marshall's place.

She could feel Lloyd's eyes on her even though he was trying to be furtive. She wondered how long she was going to be stuck in here with him and with Charles Pigot.

'It's rather close in here, isn't it? The air I mean, warm.' Lloyd spoke the words as though they had been building up, as though he had been contemplating speaking them for some time.

She nodded and Lloyd, who seemed disappointed with that response, looked down at his laced fingers in his lap.

Pigot's eyes were closed, but now a slight grin tugged at his mouth.

...

The carriage travelled through an open area of land, the river visible out the window on her side. They passed a chain gang, the men digging close to the road, the overseer walking back and forth in front of them. Some of the men stopped digging and looked up as the carriage passed.

The road became bumpier and for the next mile or so she could see nothing but trees on each side of the carriage, some of them close enough that the branches scraped the windows.

'Where are we going?'

Pigot said nothing although his eyes were open now. Lloyd looked from Pigot to Bridget and back again, leaned forward slightly. 'What, she doesn't even know where she's going? Good God. No, no, that's not right at all; they should at least be told where they are going. At the very least. Goodness gracious me.'

Pigot sighed.

Lloyd turned to her and spoke slowly as though addressing a child or an idiot. 'Mr Pigot, your new master—well, I gather . . . Yes, well, Mr Pigot has a property near Jericho, don't you, Charles?'

'Yes, Mr Lloyd, I do.'

'And that is where you are going,' Lloyd added. He glanced at Pigot. 'It is a . . . it's a nice place.'

'There's worse,' Pigot said.

'Oh, absolutely. Absolutely there is. There definitely is. I didn't mean there was anything wrong with it. Not at all.

Everyone has to start somewhere and it all takes time, doesn't it? You know what they say—Rome wasn't built in a day.' He laughed, but when Pigot didn't say anything the smile fell away from his face and he sat back in his seat again.

After a while the rough road evened out and followed close to the river where the land was flat, the river glassy, shallow for a good part of the way across, reeds growing up close to the track, the air smelling of mud. The smooth surface reflected the blue and white of the sky and the murky green of a hill on the other shore. Black swans carved tracks through the mirage of shiny colour. To her left the mountain, a light dusting of snow.

Further on they stopped at the river, where they drove onto a ferry, one of the horses snorting, picking its feet up and putting them down again, the carriage driver standing on the ferry's deck talking to the horse to calm it while the ferryman made small talk with the man.

On the other side of the river they jostled on, crossed a timber bridge then went up a hill and past a cottage and then the horses were pushed into a canter. They stopped outside a brick building where a fair woman in a peach-coloured dress got in, wearing matching gloves that she constantly adjusted. She seemed to know Lloyd, asked about his wife. Pigot she glanced at with a look of fear and distrust. She had looked at Bridget once when she got in and then adjusted her position as though trying to get further away from her, hadn't glanced her way again.

The road went up a hill and they passed a cottage and then a couple of huts off in the distance. For a long time after that there was nothing but trees until they came to a house and then just beyond it a group of buildings that was, as she discovered from another conversation between Lloyd and the woman, a town called Bagdad. They drove on and in the late afternoon stopped in front of a double-storey stone place built close to a creek. Pigot, Lloyd and the woman went into the house, Bridget following. Pigot spoke to a woman who took her upstairs to a small attic room with a set of drawers, a wash-bowl, a jug of water and a bed. 'You'll find a chamber pot under the bed.' She left and a key turned in the door.

The bed had an iron frame, a mattress and two blankets on top of it. There was a small window that Bridget could reach by standing on the bed. She tried to open it but it was nailed shut. Through it she could see only a grassy plain, blue hills beyond it.

...

Outside the hills were pink in the hurrah of dawn light. The woman brought her stew that was mostly water with a few small pieces of meat floating in it. She took Bridget downstairs and then out and along the road, pointed down a lane that ran alongside a building, said she was to go down there.

Pigot stood in a yard next to a bullock cart loaded with crates and barrels. He was talking to another man. A few yards away from the men there was a boy playing in the dirt with some wooden soldiers. The boy looked up at Bridget where she stood waiting and then went back to his game. One of the soldiers knocked the other two over and then one of the fallen ones got up and knocked down the offender, who then got up again and knocked down another one. The boy threw his arms around—'plah, plah'—spitting as he made the noise of spurting blood. He looked up at her again, left the toy soldiers where they were, came over and stood in front of her. He used his fingers as a gun, aimed it at a tree not far from where they stood, pretended to pull a trigger and made the sound of a gun going off. He turned to her. 'My brother is too small to hold a gun, but I can do it. I can shoot and everything.'

She didn't say anything and he aimed his fingers at the tree again. 'Boom. Die, you black bastard. Boom. Boom.'

'Joshua.' The man who had been speaking to Pigot was looking at the boy, who grinned at Bridget and then ran over to the man. The two of them walked to a bullock that was tied to a post. Pigot got up on the cart, told her to get on the back.

It was a bleak morning, her face and hands smarting from the cold. They travelled a long time through open woodland, past a cottage that sat alone a few yards back from the track. About half a mile after that the track led into dark forest. In the cart's wake darkness and trees closed off the world behind her.

The river roared, flowed through a narrow canyon, water curled silkily over rocks and then exploded into angry white below. Bridget lay on her stomach on a flat rock and scooped water into her mouth. From a ridge she had spotted the trail of white running between steep forested slopes. She had fought her way into the tangle of bush then slid for yards, the rush of the river audible way below.

She tried to follow the river downstream now, around her a labyrinth of sticks and logs and leaves. Branches and tree trunks arranged in every which way—vertical, horizontal, diagonal, some hanging from the branches of another tree, caught part way through their fall. The ground wasn't that at all but a trap of timber and bark, half rotten and freshly fallen about a yard or so deep, and then underneath that out of view were rocks and holes.

She sat among the mess of plants, wished she had more damper. She'd picked the last crumbs off her dress that morning. If she could, she'd go back to Pigot's. But she was nowhere. She'd walked and walked and she was nowhere. She put her hand down to feel the shape in the top of her stockings, the letter folded and folded again to make a small rectangle, the paper soft with wear against her thigh. On touching it she saw her sister, saw her niece walking on plump legs, falling backwards onto her bum and then smiling up at Bridget as though she had just done the cleverest thing. Something unreal about the memory, as though it were a far-fetched story someone was telling her, or a picture on a piece of paper disappearing into water.

A small brown bird hopped up onto a branch in front of her. She watched it. Was it lost? Are you lost? She picked up a rock from next to her boot, chucked it at the bird. You're not lost. Bugger of a thing.

Bridget scrambled towards the ridge again. There had been no sun all day, only a bright white sky behind slow grey cloud. The scrub relented, thinned, but she walked slower and hunger worked at her mind, brought thoughts she didn't know. The Devil followed her, waited behind trees.

She no longer cared much for direction. Walked carelessly without knowing why she walked.

Once she sat down and cried like a baby. Got herself up. Up and walking.

...

This was no ordinary rain. It came across the sky in dark grey sheets, the drops barbed with ice. It punished the canopy, the ground, without mercy. This was weather of a new kind—weather with no name. Whatever it was it grabbed the trees and shook them with an unbridled madness that had them groaning, their smaller branches scribbling in panic while strips of bark were ripped from their trunks and flung to the ground.

She scrambled up a slope, her boots bloated with water, the dress sticking to her. A rock jutted out from the hill to form a shallow overhang, a space under it that she wedged herself into.

Daylight faded into pitch-black. Thunder pressed the hills. Lightning spilled across the sky, for a moment exposed the abused, bedraggled world below. Then everything was claimed by darkness again. She lay folded into the hole, watching, shivering. Somewhere close by there was a crash and her heart hammered her chest bone. The silence, when it came, was so thick it seemed to buzz.

For a while she slept then woke suddenly. Something near her shoulder, something there. The knowing of it sharp in her body. She didn't breathe, kept perfectly still. It was close to her face now, blackness, darkness, whispering its ugliness. There was another clap of thunder. She pushed herself back against the dirt wall.

...

At dawn she unfolded herself from the hole, stood shaky as a foal. The sky was a soft mewing grey, the air fat and ripe with the stink of life—the sharp perfume of plants, the heady sweetness of soil. The trees were still and quiet, humble after their drenching. She wandered a way, licked water off bark, laboured uphill.

Another ridge. Tree-covered hills all the way to eternity. All the way to eternity and up its arse. She stumbled along the ridge and stopped. Far off, a trace of something rising into the sky above blue hills. Smoke? Was it? Smoke or just the wish for it?

She stumbled along without feeling. Her mind freed itself from her body like a rock from a hillside. Thoughts tumbled. Thy will be done. Timmy Crack. Bloody Crack. Others who sin against us. It's a child's job to rave at the unfairness of life. A child's job. Where did you get these coins? Your name. What is your name? Feel this. What? A feather. Shh. Shut up. Shut up!

Amen. Amen. Please, Amen.

It was just past dawn and rays of light fresh from heaven sloped through the trees, licking frost from the ground. She was hunched over next to the coarse brown trunk of a tree, head on her knees, the leaves of the lower branches leaning down as if to tickle her back, to wake her or offer advice.

She had stumbled through dawn, didn't remember stopping, only the suck of sleep, sinking down into it like a boot into thick mud.

Something filtered into her darkness now. A sound swam nearer. Something close. The sound found its name—dog. A dog bark. Dog barking. Bridget opened her eyes. There were two dogs running straight at her. She was on her feet in seconds. A man yelled at them to stop, another man behind him. The dogs stopped, turned and looked at the man who had yelled, then back at her, stayed where they were.

Bridget froze.

One of the men walked up to her. He wore tan cord trousers, a shirt with a fur vest over it, a hat squashed down over straw-coloured hair. A gun in his hand hung by his side. He stood there staring at her like he was trying to work out what she was. The other one stood behind him, shorter, skinny, also with a gun.

She seemed to come back to herself for a moment then. 'Do you have any food?' She shoved her hand into the dress pocket, held out a small, wet piece of tobacco. 'Please.'

The fair one in the vest one frowned at it, looked around. 'Where'd you come from?'

'I . . . I was just resting,' she mumbled.

He looked around at the hills, squinted at her.

'Can eat me,' the skinny one said. His hand was working at his belt. 'Eat this if she's fucking hungry.'

The fair one turned around. 'Get that out, I'll shoot it off.'

He turned back and stood there staring at her again. Irish. There was Irish in his accent.

The other one stopped playing with his trousers, rounded his shoulders, kicked at the ground with the toe of his boot.

'Alright, come on,' the fair one said, turned around and started walking.

'Wait on a minute, we—'

He spun around, spat words into the scrawny one's face. 'I am waiting for nothing!'

Bridget stepped back.

The scrawny one looked at him, bug-eyed. 'He'll kill ya. He'll kill ya, ya know.'

...

She followed them up a slope, lost sight of them as they wound their way around the base of outcrops of rock, some of them as big as a hut. She caught flashes of them as they pushed their way up the hill but they were too fast—she couldn't keep up. She stopped, leaned against a tree. She took a few steps again but her legs were shaky. She thought she was going to vomit, stopped again. Heat prickled her back, the trees ahead of her went out of focus and her knees gave way.

Bridget opened her eyes and sat bolt upright. There was something on her—an animal smell to it. A skin, fur. In front of her a big man sat on a rock, a dog asleep at his feet, another dog standing to attention next to him. She was lying near a fire in a dirt clearing. A man squatted next to the fire. She looked around and saw there were two others sitting behind her, both of them watching her. She scrambled to get up. The big man on the rock laughed. 'Well, how about that, she's alive.' His voice rumbled out of him like a wave out of a cave. He was both tall and solid with a thick beard and moustache, fat pink lips among the nest of black hair like something naked and newborn. His coat and trousers were animal skin, raw skin to the outside, the colour of the rock around him. Near where he sat there was a knapsack on the ground, stitched-together skins like his clothes, a gun leaning against the rock he sat on, another one on his belt.

The fair one by the fire—she remembered him now; she'd asked him for food—told her to sit down. He pulled a chunk of damper out of a knapsack and threw it so it landed on the fur next to her. She picked it up and stuffed it into her mouth, hardly chewed before she swallowed. He walked over with a flask, handed it to her. She guzzled, had only just started when he grabbed it off her.

'Drink it all at once, you'll be sick,' the big man on the rock said. 'Wouldn'ta lasted much longer, would ya, out there, he hadn't found ya.' He motioned with his pipe to the fair man, who had gone back to the fire, was prodding coals.

She stuffed another piece of the damper into her mouth.

The big one on the rock sat back, blew smoke, watched her, a trace of amusement in his face.

'Told him not to bring her here. Told him.'

The whiny voice belonged to the skinny ratty-looking man, the other one who she'd seen earlier. She remembered him undoing his belt. Her mind scanned her body—she'd been asleep, she thought. 'How'd I get here?'

'Knight in shining armour over there carried ya, didn't he.' He looked at the fair, sinewy man by the fire, who ignored him.

'Convict,' the big man said, nodding towards her, part question, part statement.

She concentrated on getting the damper down her throat.

He relit his pipe, took a short, sharp draw and exhaled. He watched the man by the fire and then her. He repacked his pipe, smoked. 'Matt here reckons we should feed everyone, don't ya Matt? We oughta be a bit more charitable. Keeping everything for ourselves like this ain't right. Is it, *Sheedy*?'

The sinewy one was squatted next to the fire arranging a billy of water over the flames. He didn't look up. His face was serious.

'Ain't that so, Budders? We should be more generous.'

'Yeah,' the ratty one behind her said. 'Yeah, we should be more generous.'

The one at the fire—Matt—spoke slowly, his voice steady. 'Fuck off, Henry.'

'*Fuck off, Henry?* That's bloody nice, ain' it? *Fuck off, Henry.* Worse manners than a whore, he's got.' He stared at Matt's bent back, his ice-blue eyes steady. They showed no trace of the amusement that was in his voice. 'He says you was lost. Tell ya what, I'm lost too. What's he gunna do for me, eh? We're all bloody lost.'

She stuffed another piece of damper in her mouth, fixed her eyes on the flask of water Matt had taken off her.

The ratty one behind her—Budders—got up, stood with his arms limp by his side. 'Wouldn't let me fuck her. Said I couldn't fuck her.' He glared at Matt, who was still by the fire.

Henry laughed. 'Did he now? Most uncharitable of him.'

'Lost,' Henry quipped though a haze of smoke. 'Well, fuck me.' He eyed her quizzically. 'Better be warned, he's hard to get on with.' He grinned down at Matt, who ignored him.

After a moment Henry lifted himself off the rock. 'Leave youse to get acquainted then. Knight and his fair maiden. Not that she's all that bloody fair. Quite filthy, actually. What happened to ya hair?'

She didn't say anything and he laughed again, the laugh low in his stomach. The other one—younger than the others, maybe about her age—who hadn't spoken yet stood up too. Then he and Budders and Henry and the two dogs walked into the scrub.

Matt squatted by the fire, looking into it with a frown that caused a deep crease like an upside-down Y between his eyebrows. The muscles of his thighs pushed against the fabric of his trousers. Hair the colour of dirty straw stuck to his forehead, a kink just above his right eye. At the back it curled up stiffly below his hat. He swallowed and a large Adam's apple tracked up his throat, settled again.

Steam rose from the billy. He picked it off the fire, poured tea into a cup, passed it to her. He poured one for himself and sat sipping it slowly.

She was suddenly very tired. She could feel her eyes wanting to close but kept them on him. He wiped the back of his hand across his cheek. He poked the fire, sipped again.

She looked around their camp. A pocket of dirt and rock in front of a shallow cave, above it more rock and either side and below it steep slopes of trees. She wondered which way she should go. There was no sound except bird calls, a slight wind in the trees and the crack of the fire.

She would go in a minute, would get up and go, after a little rest, just a bit of a rest. How long she had been walking for she had no idea now. There were four nights—no, five—hunger had made everything blurry.

...

She woke to see Henry drop a kangaroo in the dirt on the opposite side of the fire. She sat up quickly. Matt was sitting by the fire exactly where he had been before.

One of the dogs licked at the wound on the side of the roo's neck. Henry kicked it in the side. 'Out of it!' The dog slunk away.

Budders pulled out a knife and started hacking at the roo. 'Not here, for Christ's sake,' Matt grunted. 'Take it over there a bit.'

Budders dragged the roo off and Henry pulled tobacco out of his pocket, stuffed it in the pipe.

...

Smoke rose into the dark sky. The smell of cooking meat filled her nostrils and saliva welled under her tongue. She swallowed, tried not to appear too hungry. Off to the right of the fire the dogs jerked parts of the animal's insides down their eager throats. Budders had sat down next to her. A persistent trail of snot came from his right nostril, crawled like a slug towards his lip. Now and then he collected it with his tongue, sniffed loudly without taking his eyes off the meat that hung over the fire on a thick stick.

Matt passed a piece of meat to her.

Henry looked over at her. 'What's ya name again?'

'Bridget.'

'Bridget. So, ya ran away, Bridget?'

She shrugged. Had she run away? She wasn't sure.

'And where are you going now then?'

'Jericho.' She was trying to concentrate on the meat, on getting it in. 'Is this near Jericho?'

'That where you were going, Jericho?'

She nodded.

Henry grinned. ''Fraid you gone the wrong way.'

Next to her Budders giggled.

'Are you going there?' She addressed the question to Matt but it was Henry who answered.

'Are we going to Jericho?' He spoke slowly, paused. 'Are we going to Jericho, Sam?'

'Nah.' It was the first time he'd spoken—the younger one, his gaze on the dirt.

Henry sucked on his pipe, blew smoke. 'No. No, we're not going to Jericho.'

'What are you doing here?' she asked, looked around the clearing.

'Now *that* is a good question,' he said.

She didn't look at him, chewed the meat.

'What are you going to Jericho for?'

She shrugged.

'Don't know?' Henry said. He looked over at Matt. 'She don't know.' He watched her. 'Bit hungry, aren't ya?' He leaned forward, met her eyes over the fire. 'Food can be a bit hard to come by out here, can't it?'

'Leave her alone,' Matt growled.

Henry sat back. 'Just trying to be helpful,' he said, putting his feet up on a rock. 'Just trying to be fucking helpful.'

Later Henry sat smoking, watching Matt as he rolled the rest of the cooked roo tightly in a sack. 'Matt and I had a fine idea once, didn't we, Matt?'

'Doubt that,' Matt said.

'See, he's a smart bastard. What was it? Lemme think. Freedom. Freedom it mighta been, or some bloody grand idea like that.'

Matt shot Henry a look of warning.

Henry stood up. 'Told ya, can't say nothing to him. Worse than a bloody woman he is.' He walked past Matt, knocking him as he went. A few yards from the fire he climbed up onto a rock, pulled a fur over his broad shoulders.

Matt pulled a blanket off the top of a knapsack where it had been rolled and tied. Henry's voice came from the rock he was sitting on, gun by his side. 'You ain't rutting where I can hear ya. Don't wanna listen to your pig grunts. Piss off somewhere.'

Matt ignored him, spoke to Budders. 'Give her your blanket.'

Budders looked surprised. 'Ain't giving her my blanket. Give her yours.'

'Give it to her, I said.' He reached behind Bridget and smacked Budders on the side of the head.

Budders rubbed his head. 'Piss off.'

Matt grabbed Budders' blanket.

'Give it back!' Budders jumped to his feet.

Matt stood next to her. 'Get up.'

'I'll be cold. Give it back, I'll be cold,' Budders snivelled. 'Stupid whore,' he muttered.

Up on the rock Henry chuckled.

She followed Matt around the side of the overhang to a patch of dirt between two rocks. He put his blanket down, a gun next to it. She stood there, holding the blanket he'd given her.

'I'm going to the main road, to Jericho.'

Matt had lain down and now rolled onto his side towards the gun, facing away from her.

She sat down. It was cold but she couldn't bring herself to pull Budders' blanket over her.

'It won't kill you,' Matt said, still with his back turned.

'I'll go in the morning then. Can you show me the way? To the main road?'

No answer.

She left the blanket on the ground, but after a while the desire for warmth was stronger than her repulsion. She pulled the blanket over her knees but stayed sitting there, looking out into the dark, the sky a great bowl of stars, cold pouring down out of it. His back was still to her. He was breathing deeply. Henry was still up on the rock. No sound from Budders over by the fire, or from Sam. Eventually she lay down. She lay there awake, her body stiff, waiting for any movement from Matt, from the other side of the rock.

...

Bridget woke to light, to the four of them talking. She lay still and listened.

'She can come with us till we get to Jacobson's.' Matt's voice. 'Take her out to the road from there.'

'You ain't taking her to the road. Don't be bloody stupid.' Henry, she thought, the voice deep.

'She's gunna slow us down.' That was the young one, Sam.

'Stupid bitch got lost—she can deal with it.' Budders.

'Who asked you?' Matt. Then: 'Told you: I'll deal with her.'

Henry said something that she couldn't quite hear.

She heard them all move and then Matt came around the rocks. She was shivering, the morning cold enough to split brick. He threw her a coat. 'Get up, we're going.'

'Can I have something to eat?'

'Sam, get something.' He called it over his shoulder.

Bridget went around to the fire and Sam gave her a chunk of meat and a piece of damper. She swallowed it all as quickly as she could.

Matt was kicking dirt onto the coals. She pointed to the water flask that was over by a rock now. 'Can I've some of that?'

'Get it yourself,' Matt said.

She walked over next to Henry, who was tying a rolled fur to the top of a knapsack.

She gulped down water from the flask. Matt took it off her, shoved it into a knapsack he held. He and the other men hoicked their full knapsacks onto their backs. Then he turned around and started to walk down the hill, the two dogs and the three other men following him. She stood there by the ring of rocks where the fire had been. Around her, endless hills like ocean.

She went past the fireplace and into the trees where the men had gone.

...

A frypan, the rolled blanket and a coil of rope were all tied to the outside of Matt's knapsack. The skin on the back of his neck was dark with dirt. She could smell him: sweat and dirt and something else—personal and undefinable, slightly sweet but sickly. She hung back to avoid the intimacy of it.

Matt moved fast down the slope. She lost him, heard a dog bark and headed in the direction of the sound.

She found him stopped, waiting. As soon as she saw him he started again and she ran to catch up.

'Where are we going?'

He didn't turn around, didn't answer.

They came out of the trees and crossed a slope strewn with rock. The rocks slipped out from under her feet. Matt was ahead of her, about to enter the trees on the other side of the slope. She had to run not to lose sight of him again.

'Is this the way to the road?'

'If you'd stop talking and start walking, you might get somewhere.' He walked off again. She stopped, watched him until he was almost out of sight.

When she next caught up to them they were standing together talking, all four of them. She could tell by the way they looked at her that they had been talking about her. Henry gave her a long, dark look before he turned around and started walking again.

...

Henry walked in the lead, Budders behind him, then Matt and then Sam. Bridget yanked her dress off a twig where it had snagged, swore, and hurried after them. They were coming down a hill, holding on to trees to keep their footing. The going was hard with the ground wet and the bush dense. Ahead of Matt, Budders slipped and fell, banging into Henry, who turned sharply.

'Fuck me, if you're not the most useless bastard . . .'

'Ain't my fault it's muddy.'

'I'll tell you what's fucking muddy—your brains. Your brains is the muddiest thing round here by a long shot.' Henry hauled the man up by the back of his shirt.

'I can get up meself.'

Henry laughed. 'Judging from what I seen you can't even wipe your arse yourself. Hey, Matt—Budders here reckons he can get up himself.' Henry reached out a hand and pushed Budders hard. The man slipped, hit the ground backside first, and slid some distance down the bank before getting his feet underneath himself. 'Well, and so you can. Ain't that lovely, Matt? He can do it his self.'

Matt shook his head. Bridget could see that he was not amused.

Something moved in the bushes nearby then. Henry drew his gun, pointed it in the direction of the sound, his eyes narrowed over the barrel. He slowly lowered the gun and Budders giggled nervously. 'Stupid roo.'

The other three men said nothing, resumed walking.

'Stupid roo,' Budders persisted.

Henry's eyes were slits of razor-sharp readiness primed for a target. He turned the cool blade of them on Budders, who fell in quietly behind.

...

They crossed the creek where a log lay across it, followed a track up a hill, fat drops falling through the canopy, her and the men smelling of wet wool, the dogs' hair wet and flat against their skin.

The rain came down harder, smacked through the canopy. She felt as though they'd been walking through this forest forever; there was no end to it—it was a wet, cold blanket of moss thrown over her. She needed the walking for warmth now.

Finally they stopped, stood under a shallow rock overhang behind a tree. Darkness flowed into the spaces between the trees, filled the forest from the ground up, expanded into the whole of the sky. And still it rained. Blades of water stabbing down into the shadows of the forest, the five bodies lined up against the rock wall like prisoners waiting to be shot.

The rain eased and stopped. Light flowed into the sky like blood returning to a limb, a tingle of sun through the trees.

...

They walked along the side of a lake. A cold wind raked its grey surface. Drizzle turned to rain that needled Bridget's face as she walked. She felt the insistent prickle of cold as the moisture seeped through the woollen coat. A hill rose up on one side of the lake and most of the landscape was obscured by low cloud. She had the sense of walking further and further into nowhere. Again panic rose in her guts. What the hell was she doing following these men to God knew where? Stupid. Fucking stupid, Crack. Henry and Budders had been moving fast and were now out of sight, Matt about thirty yards ahead.

She slowed even more and then stopped, walked away from the lake into the scrub that bounded it in the direction she guessed might be south. It got thick quickly and she pushed into it, felt it scratch her thighs through her dress and petticoat. She pushed until the scrub's canopy got higher and by crouching she could move through it a little. She stopped to rest and at her feet saw a pile of bones, damp fur melding into the ground around them. She stayed there staring and then pushed back out the way she had come, grateful for the openness of the lake.

She caught up to Matt. 'I'm going back.'

'Don't be stupid.'

'Where is this? There's no road here.'

He stopped walking and faced her, flicked his arm at the lake. 'Go on then. Go back.'

She watched him walk away and then hurried after him again. Bastard.

...

She smelled the smoke and then the meat. Next to the fire they'd made was the fresh carcass of a scraggly-looking sheep, flesh having been carved off it, flies settling on the wounds.

By the time darkness arrived the smell of roasting lamb filled the air.

...

Matt was up and down in the night, prowling through the dark, gun at his side. Bridget felt Budders stir, felt him peering through the dark towards where she slept. She lay awake, heard Matt come back. The fire had died down, but she could still see the dark shape of him among the trees. He came back for the fourth or fifth time, this time stood close to where she lay. The blanket was no match for the frigid night air. Fingernails of cold reached through it, through her clothes, scratched at her skin.

...

They walked through deep mud enclosed under a canopy thick enough to block the sun. Light broke through in a patch where a tree had smashed through the canopy and now lay rotting, as peaceful in its death as it was thunderous in its dying. In other places light slipped through gaps in the canopy, highlighting droplets of water that held shakily to fern fronds. Small birds twittered and hopped, their tiny eyes live, tails flashing. Their chatter formed a layer of sound underneath the dogs' hard rhythmic panting, underneath the squelch of sodden ground.

All morning Matt had been surly, had spoken in clipped grunts. One of the dogs hesitated at jumping a fallen log and he picked the dog up in one swift movement and threw it to the other side. The trunk of the tree was high enough that Bridget didn't see the dog land, but heard its yelp. The next time she saw it, it was limping.

She walked behind Matt, watched the back of his calves until they were not calves anymore, were nothing more than motion. His legs had become two things that slid past each other in a steady rhythm. Not muscle, not human, but movement. Mud flew up behind his boots. A drop of water sat on top of a leaf, shivered as his boot caught the stem of the leaf and pushed it down, the drip slid down the leaf onto the damp ground and was gone.

...

A fern-fringed creek, sun filtering into the gully. Matt and Sam stood on rocks in the middle of the creek, crouched down, cupping their hands to scoop water, rays of sunlight on them. Henry laughed. 'Ain't that a sight. You boys look ever so pretty with that light on ya like that. Like a pair a bloody angels.'

Matt let out a long '*laaaa*', heavy with sarcasm.

Henry frowned, looked confused. 'I'd be bloody hoping angels can sing better than that.' He stepped across rocks onto the other bank. 'What *was* that noise?'

'It were a fucking la, weren't it? You deaf or something?'

'La?'

'Yeah. La.'

'Do it again.'

'Piss off.'

'Do it again.'

'For fuck's sake, we don't have time to be la-ing.'

'Well, now you say it. Now you say we don't have time to

be la-ing when just a second ago you was standing there doing it. Wasn't he, eh, Sam? He was just la-ing then and now he says, "Oh, we've got no time to be la-ing." Bloody confusing, ain't he? La-ing then no la-ing. Well, fuck me.'

Matt stepped over the rocks and brushed past Henry, went up the hill, Sam following behind him. For a second Henry didn't do anything, then he put his head back and laughed, his great mouth open to the sky.

...

She followed them along a creek through more forest, where grey light permeated down into the humus-y murk, black soil and wet tree trunks, no horizon. She tripped on tree roots, slipped on wet logs. Her heels were so painful that she clenched her jaw to stop herself crying. Her whole body ached, the bottom of her dress was even more ripped and was muddy all the way up to her knees. Uphill again. She sat down against a rock. Didn't care what happened—they could leave her there. She wasn't going any further. She took her boots off. The backs of her heels were a mess of broken skin; the skin where her stockings were shredded was decorated in black leeches fat with her blood. Bridget sat there on the wet ground. She heard the sound of him coming back.

He stood above her. 'We're going up to the mountains,' he said. 'Be there a while, come down to the road later on.'

'Isn't this the mountains?'

'No.'

He offered his hand to help her up. She took it, let him pull her to her feet.

...

Henry made his way jauntily through the open undergrowth, whistling, the dogs at his heels. His form was flooded with sunlight then coated in shade, light and then shade, light, shade until they headed downhill again and the ground got damp and the flickering stopped. They crossed a small creek and began another ascent. Bridget's boots were sopping, her heels raw, and walking hurt like hell.

...

They spent the night sheltered against a rock wall, in the morning trudged uphill. From the top of the hill there was a view of the country all around. Rolls of hills washed in blue, small lakes glinting like coins and, in the distance, jagged mountains capped with snow. A cold wind blew across the ridge. Henry stood on a slab of rock, took the telescope away from his eye. 'Looks like pickings.' He passed the telescope to Matt.

'Gimme a look. Gimme a look.' Budders danced around next to Matt.

Matt lowered the telescope. 'Who do you think they are?'

Down below them were two small lakes. At the far end of the biggest there were two tents, just visible, pitched close to a cart. Smoke rose up from near the tents. As Bridget watched she saw a figure come out of one of the tents and walk across to the cart.

'Well, they ain't redcoats,' Henry said. 'And there's one way to find out, ain't there? Reckon they might like some visitors, whoever they are.'

'Yeah,' Budders said. 'Yeah, reckon they might like some visitors.'

...

Matt grabbed one of the dogs, put a rope around its neck and tied it to a tree, then tied the other one with it. He turned to Bridget. 'Stay here. Don't move.'

She was glad; sat down on the ground near the dogs and watched the men wind their way down the hill through the trees until they were out of sight. She could just see the tents at the end of the lake.

One of the dogs started whimpering and then sat down and stared at her, wagging its tail expectantly.

There was a shout and now there were five figures in view. One man stood a few yards from the tent while four men faced him—Matt, Henry, Sam and Budders. Another man came out of the tent, joined the first one. Then Budders went into the tent, came out with something that he gave to Henry.

The smaller dog Higgins barked. Bridget turned to see two men coming down the hill straight towards her, guns by their sides. The dogs were jumping, howling, straining at their ropes. She got up and took off down the hill, the men running after her.

Matt and Henry—they were standing at the bottom of the slope, guns pointed through the trees.

The two men stopped on the slope above her.

'Put them down and walk down here, slowly.' Henry's voice, deep and gravelly.

The men squatted, put their guns down. They walked past her and Matt came up and grabbed her, pushed her ahead of him, and they followed Henry, the two men in front of him, his gun pointed at the middle of their backs.

There was a bullock behind the cart, tied to it. The back

of the cart was laden with goods. Matt was pulling things off, going through sacks and crates.

Budders came out of the tent again, held up a knapsack. 'Got one.'

Henry said something, pointed behind him to a pile Matt had made on the ground.

Matt and Henry had tied up the men who had surprised her on the hill and the two others, were now forcing them to drink rum from a barrel. One of them said something to Matt who put his gun close to the man's head. 'Do you want to die?'

Matt came over to where she stood and grabbed her wrist, 'Let's go.'

She pulled her arm away from him.

She knew. She'd already known. But now there was no doubting it. Bushrangers—they were bushrangers.

The sun hit the water, spat and sparkled there. Tiny bits of shell in the sand shone silver. Water rushed in and spread itself over the sand then withdrew only to return again in a splish seconds later. It would do this all day. And all throughout the night in the dark the rhythmic splish would ripple the silence, again and again. An eternity of persistence without achievement, Captain Marshall thought; wondered if his own life was much different. What futility. Absolute and *pure* futility. He could not see the point in anything today.

There were five horses and carts parked above the beach, the ladies all sitting on blankets at the top of the sand, their parasols held above them. Mr Bainbridge and Mr Humphrey walked along the beach, deep in conversation, both of them with their hands behind their backs. Jane sat alone on the rugged rock point that headed out into the bay, looking out over the water and then back at her canvas. Always painting. 'She'll never get a husband, always painting like that,' Eleanor said. Marshall had said that he didn't know that securing a husband was Jane's aim, particularly. 'That is just what I *mean*,' Eleanor said. 'What does a woman want with all that painting?' She gave him a confounded, irritated look and walked away.

Marshall stood behind the women on the rocks at the top of the beach. The boats in the cove were still today, not a trace of rocking in their hulls. Mrs Bainbridge moved her parasol to the side, leaned back. 'It's a darling little sandy bay, Mr Marshall. Wouldn't you say? I am most glad to have come upon it.'

'Yes, indeed. Indeed it is.'

He looked over at Jane again, walked over towards the rocks.

...

In the afternoon cloud came in and turned dark. Splotches of rain fell onto the women's parasols. They squealed and hurried to the carts, Jane coming over last and smiling her lovely conspiratorial smile at him. *They are silly, aren't they?* her smile said. *We know they are silly, you and I. We are not like them. We are not silly.* This was, he knew, one of the things that had turned Eleanor against his sister; her constant affirmation of their difference from Eleanor, her insistence—communicated in these small ways—that she and her brother were a team that Eleanor was not on. And it was true, Jane was not like Eleanor at all, but Richard himself was not nearly as much like Jane as she thought he was; he lacked her will and courage entirely, but if she had not noticed that, he was glad, for he sometimes felt that her good opinion was the only one he had. Everyone else saw him as lacking, saw his weaknesses, he was sure. And they were probably far more correct than Jane. Jane had always loved him. For no good reason. She just did. And for that, he was immensely grateful.

The sky had turned darker, a cold breeze lashed at them from the water, where the waves had turned messy, the water gone from blue to dead grey. Loose bits of brown seaweed slewed back and forth near the shore. 'Goodness me,' Mrs Bainbridge said, hauling herself up onto the cart among her skirts. 'I do hope no one catches cold. We shall all be needing a bath!'

...

Eleanor pulled impatiently at the ties on her dress, steam rising from the bath beside her. Marshall could feel the accusation in her body. It was almost always there. Everything that went wrong, any discomfort of hers was his fault. All of Eleanor's hurt seemed to become anger, and her anger a fire. He could not for the life of him work out how to get behind the hot wall of it.

...

In his study he stood by the window, held the curtain aside. Down below he saw the servant girl, Martha, cross the yard with a pail of water. He wondered about Bridget—she had been reassigned to the Interior, he'd been told. He recalled how sometimes he had sat here at his desk and found himself drawn to get up and cross the room and look down into the yard. Even now that she had been gone some time she continued to enter his thoughts. He did not know at all what had caused his interest in her. Had it been the unsettling sea-green eyes? The mole that sat teasingly above her lip near the side of her mouth, which might have been ugly but instead was—he had to admit—enticing? She'd been sharp, he thought, clever.

'The wonderful thing about women of lower classes is that they can't ask anything of you.' He recalled his cousin

Laurence, pouring whiskey. And then Jane: 'If I can do something, one little thing to leave the world better than when I found it, I will be happy.'

Marshall let the curtain go, walked over to the bookshelf and balled his fist, put his head against the flat of it. He wished he had not come here. It was supposed to have been a blank slate. In his mind he scoffed at that idea now. How stupid of him. What slate was ever blank? One took one's marked and damned soul with one wherever he went. He had been unhappy in England. His father was critical of him and his marriage to Eleanor was like a fur: an adornment missing its animal. It had been his mother's idea, of course—their *union*. Eleanor's family had good social standing and, his mother said, she was 'a fine-looking girl'. She had then reminded him of his age, that he was no longer young.

It had been his father's idea that he join the army and it had never suited him. He had joined at sixteen and was thirty when, after the end of the war, his battalion was disbanded. He'd lived on half-pay in his father's house then, filled his time with reading. Jane had become involved with the Society for the Abolition of the Slave Trade, passed him abolitionist literature. Perhaps it was all the death he'd seen, perhaps the new ideas stirring in him—he found himself increasingly uncomfortable in his own skin. Thinking his discontent in part due to the excess of time on his hands, he took an administrative post in India. However, he was not there long before he became very ill and returned to England.

After he was married and the children born he was still living with his father (who regularly pointed out how well his older brother George had done as a merchant, and that

Alfred, the next oldest, was now a colonel). So when Alfred told him that George Arthur had been appointed governor of Van Diemen's Land, that the man was an acquaintance of his and he could write to him regarding the possibility of a position there, Marshall agreed. Their cousin Godfrey was already in Van Diemen's Land, had written that he'd secured a land grant, found the climate agreeable.

At first Eleanor had said no, that she wasn't going to Van Diemen's Land. Then Jane had said she would like to go, that she thought it was a wonderful idea. He told Eleanor he was going; it would only be for a few years and she could remain in England. Once it had become clear he really was going she came to him one night and said she wanted to come too. At first he'd felt disappointed, had quietly hoped she might stay. But then he'd thought it might be a new start, a chance for them to begin anew. Yet ever since they had been here, she had complained endlessly of her dislike for the place.

His position in the colony as commissariat officer was dull and required little of him in terms of time and effort. Still, though, he found himself often tired and even more unhappy than he'd been in England. The thought came to him—as it often had before—that whatever was wrong with him was the fault of his middle name: Ferdinand. He'd never liked it. But that was ridiculous, he thought. *Ridiculous.*

He reprimanded himself now for his self-pity, stood up straight and went and sat at his desk, folded his hands, stared at the door. He would do something in a minute, he thought. But for now, he would just sit here. It seemed as good a thing to do as any. For all of a sudden he felt entirely lost. Quite, entirely lost.

Henry shrugged the load off his back and let it fall. 'Home, sweet home', he said. They had come down a broad and wooded valley, the understorey open and grassy, a river running down one side of it, a chorus of mountains surrounding it. The men and the dogs splashed through a shallow part of the river, Bridget behind them. There was a track leading through scrub that after about twenty yards opened into a clearing. In the middle of it was a circle of rocks, a rope slung between two trees and, at the back of the clearing, a rock wall with a rough lean-to built against it, only barely visible among the bushes growing around it.

Sam dropped his knapsack, walked up to the lean-to and went inside it. He came out with an axe and walked off into the trees.

Matt sat on a log, unlaced his boots, pulled one off with a groan.

Budders went into the lean-to and came out with a sack, tipped it upside down on the ground and sat by the ring of rocks that marked a fireplace, sorting through the contents. Among them was a doll, a small silver tray, a handkerchief, a knife, a watch and a lump of jewellery, all caught up and tangled. He picked up the doll, lifted its white dress up to its neck and turned it over, examining it.

Bridget went over to the tree where Matt sat and stood next to him, conscious again, as she had been for days now, of where and how she stood, how she spoke. 'How long are we going to be here?'

'Got somewhere to be, have ya, Bridge-it?' Henry called over. He had taken to saying her name: *Bridge-it.*

The sound of Sam cutting wood came from the scrub below the lean-to.

Matt got up, walked in bare feet back towards the river.

'Don't know about anybody else, but I could do with a feed and a drink. Make yourself bloody useful,' Henry said to her, laughed.

Budders put the doll down, shoved everything else back into the sack and took it up to the lean-to. On the way back he walked past Bridget deliberately close, grinned as he went. Henry crossed the river with the dogs, Budders following behind him.

She took a few steps towards the shelter. It leaned up against a bare rock wall, the mountain rising so high above it that from the camp she couldn't see its top. The lean-to was made with the boughs of trees, these covered in branches, all the leaves on them dead. At one end there was a door of kinds, an animal skin hanging from the bough above it.

She pushed the skin back. Inside a smattering of light came through the branches and dead leaves that formed both the wall and roof. Water dripped down the black rock wall that the structure leaned against.

...

After the robbery at the lake they had spent the night in the hollow of a huge tree. Matt had been standing so close to her that she could feel the pressure of his arm against hers. She'd wanted to move away but Budders was on the other side of her. Matt and Henry had argued about having a fire, Matt saying it was too risky; if there was a party after them the smoke would give them away. Henry said, 'You worry more than a woman. There's not going to be no one after us, and if there is, it won't be for days.' He said that they'd forced the men at the lake to drink so much rum they wouldn't even wake until morning, and when they did they wouldn't have a clue which way they'd gone. In the end smoke filled the cramped inside of the tree, the struggling fire impotent against the cold, and she sat shivering until Matt threw her a dry woollen coat, part of what they'd taken from the men at the lake. She took the damp one off and put this one on, the sleeves coming down over her hands, the wool full of the smell of a stranger. The men emptied out everything they had taken onto the ground. Salted pork; flour; tobacco; three candles; a tin, a few pennies in it; a leather pouch containing a letter and a brown curl of hair; a pipe, the letters RP engraved into the wood.

Bridget eyed the pipe. 'Can I have that?' She had lost the one from Pigot's; it had come out of her pocket somewhere.

They all turned to look at her. Henry shrugged, looked at Matt. 'Can she have it?' Matt picked it up and chucked it to her.

Bridget turned it over, inspected it, closed her hand over it.

Henry passed a letter to Sam. 'What's it say?' Sam read it slowly, tripped over the words.

She put her hand out for it and all four of the men stared at her. She read it out. It was to dear Mr Price, about someone called Miss Lacy having died.

Bridget sat and listened as the men talked. The men they had robbed were a government surveyor and some convicts in his service. 'Mapping Van Diemen's Land,' Matt said. 'Settlers and sheep up here soon. Stick a sheep on a pimple on a black's arse if they thought it'd live there.'

Their clothes steamed with the heat from their bodies and stank as they started to dry out. She felt Henry looking at her, kept her gaze on the ground. The smoke stung her eyes and the air was too thick, the silence too thick also. She stepped over Higgins, who lay across the entrance, and he stood up suddenly so that for a moment she straddled him and almost tripped over. Laughter came from inside the tree. She turned around to see Henry and Budders laughing. But Matt was not laughing. He was looking straight at her, his face serious and puzzled.

...

In the morning Matt squatted near her feet, picked them up and looked at her heels. He pressed salt into them while her eyes watered. Then he cut two pieces off his skin blanket. 'Put it over them.'

They trudged through flat, cold country, the ground rocky and covered with clumps of dry grass, prickly heath and low bushes that grew between gums with twisted limbs, their trunks as fat as ten men. Snow had fallen, the day becoming strangely quiet, as though all the birds had vanished. The snow stopped and the sun broke through the thinning cloud but the wind had teeth. The men had been slower since the lake, were loaded like donkeys.

...

A ridge. Miles and miles of wind and cold and space. No road. No houses. Nothing. All day traipsing across a plateau, shimmering and still, a dusting of bird calls. They went down into a gully and when they broke out of the darkness of the forest the mountain she had seen in the distance earlier in the morning was close enough that she could see the shine on the wet black rock, the thin cloud that swept over its peak. The next time they had come down into a valley they had come here, to this place.

...

Henry went down a skinny track and came back with five bottles of rum. He and Sam and Budders had come back earlier with a good-sized roo and they'd eaten well. Sitting on a rock near the fire, Henry opened the lid of one of the bottles. He passed it to Sam, who swigged, passed it to Bridget. She watched Henry pack his pipe, asked for tobacco. He handed it to her across the fire, watched her as she dragged smoke into her lungs. Her knees were warm and her face was warm but behind her the cold curled against her back. Orange sparks from the fire raced off into the dark sky and smoke filled her eyes.

By the time Henry opened the fifth bottle his speech was slurred and he was unsteady on the log where he sat. 'What was her name? I can't remember her bloody name now. From bloody Norwich, ugly as the day is long, but fuck me she could sing.' He laughed. 'She were just about old enough to be my mother.'

'Did ya fuck her?' Budders stood on the other side of the fire. He thrust his hips back and forth.

'Jesus Christ, do you have to cheapen everything?' Henry looked over at Budders, his eyes bleary. 'It were pure bloody love. I'm telling you about pure love.'

'Pure fucking,' Budders said, and did a dance on the spot, his face almost splitting with excitement. 'Pure fucking!'

Henry shook his head. Next to Bridget, Sam was scribbling on a rock in front of him with a piece of coal.

Budders sat down, picked up the doll that he'd had earlier. He grinned at Bridget, lifted the doll's dress and started rubbing between its legs with his forefinger. Matt stepped around the fire, ripped the doll out of Budders' hands and threw it into the bush.

Budders stood up. 'What you do that for?'

'Get some manners,' Matt snarled, sat back down.

Henry drank. A bead of rum escaped into his beard. He passed the bottle to Budders, considered Sam sketching on the rock for a moment then moved on to Bridget. His gaze was foggy with drink. 'So, what happened to you then? How'd you end up in good Van Diemen's Land, Bridge-it?'

She shrugged.

'Don't flaming give me that bullshit.' Henry shrugged, mimicking her. 'What is that bullshit?' He cocked his head towards Matt. 'Why's she do that all the time?'

Matt drank from the bottle that Budders had just passed him, held it out to her. He wiped his mouth. 'I don't fucking know.'

Henry turned back to Bridget. 'Why do you do that?'

She shrugged.

'See? Did it again.'

Matt ignored him.

'Come on, aren't you gunna tell me?'

She tipped the bottle, felt the prickle of rum in the back of her throat. It heated her stomach. She drank again.

'Come on,' Henry said, 'fucking tell me. Why's everybody so fucking touchy? Eh? Fucking touchy this, touchy that. Why don't you just fucking tell me?'

Bridget looked up at him. 'What did you do?'

'What did I do? I hit a bloke who deserved it. When he fell a rock got in his way. Nothing to do with me. I didn't put the rock there.' He looked over at Matt, who was exhaling smoke, looking up at the dark top of the mountain. 'Not like Matt over there. Smashed a bloke's head in with a log of wood. Didn't ya, Matt?'

Matt slowly turned his head, landed his dark gaze on Henry. Then he stood up and walked away.

No one spoke then, not even Henry.

Budders was looking at her. She stood up. She wasn't going to sit there with Budders there and Matt gone. As she walked away she heard Henry: 'Going after her beau.'

Bridget walked down the skinny track where Henry had gone earlier, stopped near a big tree, messy with dangling bark. Above her the top of the escarpment was visible in the pitch-black—the rock in the night blacker than the sky. The river was running fast, chatty as a drunk priest.

She heard the sound near the river, someone coming through the bushes. The dark shape of a figure approached the tree where she stood. Matt. He stopped where he was a few yards away. Both of them stood still, the moon shining on one side of his face. He approached slowly, bark cracking under his boots. He stood close in front of her, his hand going into her stubby hair and gripping. His hand went to the inside of her leg and he shoved her dress away. He pushed her back and she was against the tree. Overhead a cloud smothered the moon.

Marshall sat alone in the sitting room, blue evening light coming in through the muslin curtains, his ears full of the sound of crickets. Eleanor was unwell—or so she said—and was in bed already, and Jane was upstairs putting the children to bed. Marshall picked up the book that Jane had been reading earlier, opened it at the marked page.

I wandered lonely as a cloud
That floats on high o'er vales and hills,
When all at once I saw a crowd,
A host, of golden daffodils;
Beside the lake, beneath the trees,
Fluttering and dancing in the breeze.

Continuous as the stars that shine
And twinkle on the milky way,
They stretched in never-ending line
Along the margin of a bay:
Ten thousand saw I at a glance,
Tossing their heads in sprightly dance.

The waves beside them danced; but they
Out-did the sparkling waves in glee:
A poet could not but be gay,
In such a jocund company:
I gazed—and gazed—but little thought
What wealth the show to me had brought:

For oft, when on my couch I lie
In vacant or in pensive mood,
They flash upon that inward eye
Which is the bliss of solitude;
And then my heart with pleasure fills,
And dances with the daffodils.

He put the book down on the arm of the chair. What came to him was the smell of dry oak leaves after rain, so clear and certain that he may have been standing in his father's garden right then, a thick carpet of shining leaves at his feet. Next to the oak tree there had been an acorn tree. He and Jane used to collect the little hard casings from the acorns and put them on the tops of their fingers, make little puppet shows with them. Marshall smiled and a small sound came out his nose. But the feeling that was left when the smile faded was a terrible emptiness.

Outside the window a veil of darkness settled over the land and for a while everything seemed to pause, entranced by its whisper-black touch.

Marshall sat in the dark. Then he hauled himself up out of the chair, closed the door to the sitting room behind him and went slowly up the stairs.

Bridget was so itchy she'd scratched until her skin welted and bled. She pulled all the animal furs out of the lean-to, dragged them to the river and dumped them in. Later she threw them over tree branches to dry. Matt had shown her how to make a pair of soft boots from roo skin and the skin on her heels was finally less raw. He took her other boots and fixed the gaps between the leather and the sole, sewed them up with sinew.

Budders sat down next to her by the fire. She adjusted her position to move away from him. He had been watching her. Slits for eyes, always following her. Matt watching him watching her. Now Budders sat with his arm around Higgins, who tried to lick his face. He grabbed at the dog's flicking pink tongue with his fingers. As he got hold of its tongue the dog yelped and Matt glanced at Budders. He put his foot on a branch that was lying next to the fire, pulled one end of it. It cracked. He put the half he held on the fire, looked up, straight at Budders. 'Leave the dog alone,' he said, his voice rougher and darker than she'd heard it.

There were two tracks off the clearing—a faint one that led to the river, and the one she'd gone down the other night. She followed that one again now, past the scraggly tree.

A few yards from where it stopped there was a hollow tree, the opening covered with a flap of sewn-together skins. She pushed it aside. Inside there were more skins over the top of a crate, three caskets, two full sacks, a bayonet leaning against one of them, and four more guns sitting on top of the crate.

She dropped the flap, stepped back.

In town there'd been stories about bushrangers—they'd killed settlers and and a soldier. But there'd been stories about everything.

Now Henry's laugh came from up near the fire, the realness of it echoing off the escarpment.

...

As the sun skulked away behind the mountain and the camp was taken over by shade, Henry produced bottles of a stringent-tasting drink. 'Cider,' he said, when she nearly spat it out.

'Blacks get it. His black woman showed him how to get it,' Budders said. 'She were the one what brung us up here.'

'That she was,' Henry said, drank. 'That she was.'

Bridget looked over at Matt. He didn't say anything, didn't look up.

...

In the morning Bridget came out of the lean-to to find Henry, Sam and Budders asleep by the dead fire, their blankets over them. On the ground near them were three empty bottles, a pipe lying in the dirt next to one of them. Henry's feet were near a squarish rock—the rock that Sam had been drawing on again. Sketched in charcoal, clear enough to make out what it was: a figure with a rope around its neck. A man hanging. She looked over at Sam who had just sat up, now rubbed his face.

...

Bridget picked her way to the river and put one foot into the freezing water, pulled it back out. She could feel Matt's gaze on her back from where he lay under a tree near the bank. He'd brought her down here to a deep bend.

She crossed her arms over her breasts and looked up the river towards the camp.

Matt was propped up on his elbows. 'They're not going to come.'

She gasped as the cold sucked the air from her lungs, scrambled back to the bank.

...

Matt sat on a rock at the edge of the river, his boots off, his trousers rolled to the middle of his shin. He'd hacked his beard short and now he held a razor close to the side of his face, the bottom half of which was lathered with soap. She sat on a rock a couple of yards from him, watched the soapy hair fall into the water, a rainbow-coloured slick forming around the clods as they washed away.

'What do you think?' he said.

He grinned and it shocked her. She realised she had hardly seen him smile. It was a boyish grin, a shy tug of the mouth, and now with the beard gone the deep dimples either side of it showed. His eyes appeared brighter. Everything he felt showed in his eyes, every change of feeling in him registering in them. It frightened Bridget—this transparency, and the dark hole of need that seemed to open in his eyes sometimes. In his body there was always the sense of something bound, loaded, as though the muscle mass was packed too tightly, his body humming with readiness. But now as she looked at him sitting here by the river he was smiling and he looked almost relaxed.

...

She left the camp alone with him. They walked through slow-moving fog into the bottom of a valley and then headed uphill onto a ridge. The fog cleared to reveal a sea of blue dips and rises, a blanket of silence hanging over it prickled by birdsong. Any speech at all cracked through the silence, settled with the same ominousness as a crude word in a church. They were going to get sap to make cider, he said. Take it back to camp, he said.

They slept the night in a lean-to. Inside, the timber frame had circles and some other shapes—figures, perhaps—cut into the bark. 'What are they?'

'Blacks did them,' he said, nodded at the circle. 'Moon.'

'They're here?'

'No. Soon. In the summer.'

...

The lake was surrounded by loose black rock most of the way around, a creek entering it at one end, a huddle of gnarled trees crippled and leaning from the constant abuse of wind. Fog crawled down over the rock and over the top of the lake, the lake gone all of a sudden, then wind took the fog, ripped it away again. The sound of wind and the light tink-tinkering of the lake.

They crossed land covered in giant green plants, round but flattened on the top. They were hard and dense, and she made her way by stepping from one to the other when possible, the mud between them so deep that at times she sank to her knees. The ground began to slope and they made their way down a steep hill covered in a thick stand of pines. At the bottom of this hill was a small creek in a valley jammed with ferns. They stopped to drink, then began the climb uphill, reaching a boggy grassland that stretched about a mile to a spot where a thicket of tortured-looking gums grew. 'Cider gums,' he said. He pointed to a tree that already had a wound in the trunk like the one he'd just made.

...

Back at the camp they drank and rain came in and stayed. Matt cut branches and piled them on top of the lean-to, which did little to keep the water out. The other men worked in the rain cutting trees and branches, building an A-frame shelter on the other side of the clearing which they then piled into.

Bridget sat in the wet and dripping lean-to next to Matt. He wore trousers and no top, the scarring over his back caught by the weak light. He sat with his knees up looking out of the lean-to, passed her his pipe. There was a tattoo on the top of his right arm, a heart with the initials EF in it. 'Who's EF?'

He paused before he spoke. 'Wife.'

'Where is she?'

'Dead. Ask a lot of questions.'

'How'd she die?'

'She just died, alright?' He turned and glared at her, pulled his shirt on, got up and walked out of the lean-to into the rain.

...

The rain eased and they crawled out of their shelters into the rich fug of wet plants. It was dusk when Bridget walked down the track and into the bushes. She had just stood up again when she heard someone coming through the scrub. She saw him and ran, but he grabbed her, hand over her mouth.

The sound of her yelling was muffled. She couldn't breathe, his hand closing off the air to her nose.

The shape came out of the half-dark and grew large behind him. Suddenly she sucked air. Matt threw Budders against a rock and drove his fist into his face. Blood sprayed out of Budders' nose. Matt hit him again and Budders went to the ground, Matt's boot driving into his gut. Then someone running, Henry there, pulling Matt off Budders.

Budders was up off the ground and crashing through the bushes. Henry let Matt go and he strode off in the direction of the camp. Henry stood there and then he looked over at Bridget, his gaze saying: *It's your fault. This is your fault.* He turned around and followed where Matt had gone.

'And so, let us sing.' The reverend spread his thick rosy hands.

Captain Marshall rose from his pew. The convicts who stood up the back accounted for more than half the people squashed into the church and they sang with vigour, the volume of their voices dominating the congregation. The fabulous sound they produced always surprised Marshall—he consistently forgot to expect it. Next to him Eleanor stood with her neck long and her mouth round. Marshall had never been much of a singer himself. He had always found it rather like the process of getting a shy child to kiss its churlish aunt. The whole thing was quite tainted with reluctance. He just preferred not to. It was an aspect of himself over which he felt interminable shame; the enjoyment of singing was natural. No one ought to trust a man who did not like to sing. And so he employed now the strategy that, as far as he knew, had served him well over many years—his lips made the shapes of the necessary words and he emitted a little bit of noise, enough that it might pass as singing to anyone who should glance in his direction, while all the while keeping his voice to himself.

The reverend read to them now, paused over the book and, looking out over the pews, considered them. 'A man shall not be established by wickedness, but the root of the righteous shall not be moved.' The reverend read this same passage nearly every week—for the sake of the convicts, of course. However today Marshall sat wondering: was he righteous? 'A virtuous woman is a crown to her husband, but she that maketh ashamed is as rottenness in his bones.' Eleanor looked down at her hands, which were folded in her lap.

They sang and then the reverend read again. 'A river went out of Eden to water the garden; and from thence it was parted, and became into four heads.' He motioned to the window and when he spoke his voice was grave. 'Here now, through the goodness of God, the Lord hath given us Van Diemen's Land, delivered her unto us that we may take her riches and with them build good and prosperous lives.'

Marshall looked up at the bright red of the stained-glass window. Dust motes hovered high in the light.

'And now, let us pray.'

There was loud shuffling as the congregation went to their knees.

The tea-coloured river roared through the forest. A waterfall ran down over rocks like stairs, a wash of white. Sunlight leaked through the canopy and down into the water, where it dazzled the rocks at the bottom of a pool. Fish sat in the current, the bigger dog, Caesar, seeing one and barking at it so the thing darted under a rock.

They came out into the shock of light. Bridget wasn't sure how long they'd been at the camp. Her heels had scabbed then healed but were sore again already. Her legs ached and she wanted to stop but it was only the middle of the day.

...

A dry ridge, hills veiled under a hush of light cloud. A wide river in the distance, snaking through the landscape. The rowdy squawk of a flock of white cockatoos, far off at first, like pieces of paper floating in the sky, then closer, argumentative. Then a loud crack, sharp and sudden. Budders stood with a musket pointed to the sky.

Matt grabbed it off him. 'What the fuck are you doing?'

'Shooting the noisy bastards. Get one of 'em to eat.'

'Don't be bloody stupid. As if you can shoot one of them from here. Jesus, you're a stupid bastard.'

...

The hut was among wattles beside a fast, shallow creek. Smoke rose from its chimney in a thin and almost straight line. It was late afternoon; the gullies were full of shadow and cold was rising from the ground into a dark blue sky turning darker. As they came up through the damp clearing in front of the bark hut Matt called out. 'Smith!'

The door opened slightly.

'It's Matt, ya sly bastard.'

A tall, gaunt man stood in the doorway, a gun by his thigh. He squinted. 'Who's that you got with ya?' he said, trying to see behind Matt. 'Jesus!' He spoke over his shoulder. 'They got a woman.' One of his green eyes looked at Bridget, the other one looked off to her right. In the hut behind him a man sat at a table smoking.

She looked away from the tall man's bung eye.

'Missed us did ya, Smithy?' Henry pushed past the tall man into the hut, Matt behind him. Budders, who had also stepped inside, grinned.

Smith saw him looking. 'Get up.'

A girl who looked not more than twelve rose slowly from where she squatted in the dark corner of the hut. She was naked, her hair cropped close to her head.

Smith pushed the man in the chair hard on his shoulder. 'Dennis here just finished. Didn't ya, Dennis?'

Matt turned to Bridget, who was standing just outside the door with Sam. 'Stay there,' he said.

Budders walked over to the corner, cupped his hand around the girl's dark, barely formed breast and pushed it up. He had just dropped his trousers around his ankles, his naked arse cheeks clenched, when Matt grabbed the back of his shirt, pulled him backwards and chucked him out of the hut so he went sprawling on the ground a few yards from where Bridget and Sam stood.

'Get her out of here.' Matt growled the instruction to Sam, pushed the door shut.

Budders was banging on the door, 'Lemme in, lemme in, it ain't fair.'

'Come on,' Sam said, walked away from the hut.

She followed him along a faint track through trees. He sat on a log, bent forward, jamming a stick into the ground. There was shouting coming from the hut.

Sam pulled a water flask from his knapsack, passed it to her.

He looked over at her and then back at the ground. 'What was you doing up on that hill?'

She shrugged.

Sam fiddled with the top of the flask. 'Bide your time sometimes, that's the thing I never knew. All these blokes what reckon Matt and Henry's some kinda heroes.' He scoffed. 'What you wanna be is smart, know when to do something, know when to shut up. Seen blokes taking all kinds a shit, shutting their mouths and copping it, not saying a fucking thing. I thought they was gutless, but they wasn't—what they was, was smart. Biggest mistake I ever made.' He shook his head. 'Biggest mistake.'

He threw the stick away, sat looking towards the creek.

'Bloke at the island where we was, Pinky Farrell, got blokes to lay bets: how many strokes Henry could take before he made a sound—cried out.' He looked up at her then, like he wanted to see if she knew what he meant.

She looked away.

'Only man to silently take a hundred. And everyone reckoned that made him great. S'pose it did.' He picked up a stick from next to his boot, twirled it in his fingers. 'Criers—Misty Symmons first time on the triangle begged at only thirty lashes. Seamus Fogherty made a killing that day, said he'd picked Misty for a crier straight off. Two days later Misty Symmons drove a nail into his own head. They dragged him out of the cell next morning, took him out to Dead Island.'

Budders came through the trees, stood a few yards from them kicking at the ground, his face still puffed and scabby from Matt's fists. The night Budders had grabbed her Matt had pinned him to the ground, held the burning end of a branch near his face. 'Look at her again, I'll burn your fucking eyes out. Understand? . . . DO YOU UNDERSTAND?!' The boom of his voice had the trees around the camp standing taller.

The three of them waited now, not saying anything, wet trees calling to the sky all around them.

Matt strode into view, Henry behind him.

Matt didn't pause, kept walking fast along the track. 'Told you we couldn't trust them.'

'Well, who else is going to do it?'

'Plenty of people.'

'You find them then.'

'Take stuff in, sell it ourselves.'

'Fucking great idea, just walk into Hobart Town.'

Matt stopped then. 'Yes. We will. We'll walk into Hobart Town.'

He walked off again then, Henry standing there swearing.

...

They were a long time following the track before they veered off it and crossed a creek, a rock wall on the other side of it, a wide cave with a low roof. There was a rope tied to the side of a tree that one at a time the men used to pull themselves up into the cave, Matt reaching down for Bridget's hand and hauling her up while her boots scrabbled at the rock, the dogs the last to find their way up.

...

They had just eaten when Caesar started to bark furiously, Higgins joining him, both of them looking out into the dark, growling then barking again. All four of the men picked up their guns. Matt got up first, told Sam to stay there with Bridget.

'Why do I always have to stay with her?'

She listened to the sound of them going down the slope. Someone slipped and swore.

Sam drew in the dirt on the cave floor—the same thing he had etched onto the rock with coal up at the camp: a figure, a person hanging from a scaffold. He saw her looking at it, caught her eye in the firelight. Neither of them said anything.

They came back a while later. 'Wild dog,' Matt muttered, leaning the gun against the cave wall. She had seen them in the night, the brown dogs with stripes and a long snout. Once one had come close to her. She'd sat completely still, willing the thing to go away. It sniffed her boot, looked behind it into the night then walked off, her breath coming out of her as it went.

...

She lay in the cave next to Matt, Henry and Budders asleep on the other side of him, Sam sitting up with his back to them at the front of the cave, gun across his lap.

'Who were they?'

Matt's back was to her. 'What?'

'The men.'

'Shepherds.'

'Who was she?'

'What?'

'The girl. Who was she?'

'How the fuck should I know?'

'Where'd they get her?'

Matt turned his head towards her. 'What?'

'Where did they get her from?'

He turned away, looked into the darkness. 'Her people used to pass through this way.'

'They took her?'

'Maybe. They might have bought her. Now shut up.'

Caesar lay by the fire, a flick of light over him, his head between his paws. When she looked at him he whimpered, beat his tail against the cave floor, his glassy round dog eyes sad but hopeful. He got up, scampered over to her, ran his rough tongue up her cheek.

...

The man was bent over in a garden in front of a hut as they came up the slope. When he saw them he picked up the gun that was on the ground next to him, raised it and then lowered it again. 'Jacobson,' Matt said.

The man looked them over, looked at Bridget then looked again. 'Heard you had a woman with ya.'

Bridget glanced over at Matt.

'Taylor was out here day before yesterday, been in Norfolk Plains, said he heard it there, and that you robbed some government bloke up the lakes.'

'That right?' Matt said.

Early in the morning from the top of a hill she'd seen flat land in the distance, patches of it cleared—a sign of human life, but as the day went on they'd only traipsed through more forest.

Now they'd arrived here—another lone hut in a damp valley.

Inside the hut the man Jacobson gave them bread and butter then Matt took her down into scrub near the creek that flowed about fifty yards below the hut. Here there was a small A-frame shelter. 'Wait here,' he said, went back up to the hut.

She sat on the ground by the spattering creek, thought about what Jacobson had said—someone had told him there was a woman with them. She remembered a day, not very long after she'd arrived at Marshall's, when she'd gone into the town to deliver a note for the missus, had walked back past the gaol where a group of people had gathered on the street opposite and stood looking. Inside the wall of the gaol was a scaffold, the top of it in view above the wall. Two bodies hung side by side, limp, their heads covered with sacks. Both spun ever so slightly on the ropes that were around their throats. Next to Bridget a man turned to the man next to him: 'If they leave them up there too long, their heads'll fall off.' People around him laughed.

'What did they do?'

All heads turned at the sound of a woman's voice. 'They're Beasley and McGuinley,' one of them said.

'Who are they?'

'Are?' The man laughed and the sound came out of his nose. 'Were. Don't you mean, who were they?'

'Yes. Who were they?'

'Bushrangers.'

The next time she'd been in the gaol, another two men had been hung. The yard of the men's gaol shared a wall with that of the women's and in the morning she'd heard yelling and then cheering. One of the women said the noise was coming from a group out on the road. They were there because there was going to be a hanging. When Bridget went out into the yard later, there on the other side of the high wall were two bodies, white sacks covering their heads. It was windy and the rope that held them creaked against the timber scaffold. A few days later they were still there. The white sacks were black with flies and the breeze brought a foul stench from them.

Bridget sat for a long time and then walked up to the hut. The door was shut. Inside Henry's voice was raised. 'They know now that she's been with us. She knows where the camp is.'

'Never find it,' Matt said.

'Slows us down,' Henry said. 'Told you we should never have picked her up in the first place. Bloody stupid idea.'

...

Inside the hut she sat on a log close to the fire, her body soaking up the warmth. Later she lay next to Matt in the dark in the shelter by the creek. She wondered where this place was, how far it was from here to the road.

Matt had said he was going to take her to the road from Jacobson's but she knew he wasn't going to. Earlier she'd seen a track that went around the side of the hut, disappeared into trees behind it. It might go to the road. She could follow it and see, try to find her way to the road on her own. But what would she tell a constable? Who would believe her? No one was going to believe her. They'd put her back in the stocks, or in that cell, then send her wherever, and to whomever, they wanted. Or worse.

At first light Matt rolled over, took something from his pocket, held a necklace out in front of her. Silver, the pendant with a light pink stone in the middle surrounded by diamonds. 'Put it on.'

She hesitated. She had never touched anything so valuable. He watched as she fumbled with the clasp. She felt the coldness and foreignness of the pendant against her skin.

Matt lay back again, arms behind his head, looking at the top of the A-frame. 'We'll get a boat, go to China,' he said. 'Live like kings there,' he said.

'Live like kings.'

...

The men came down the slope, knapsacks on. 'Mighty pleasant down here, ain't it?' Henry said.

They crossed the creek, the morning overcast and still. Bridget went last. As she reached the other bank she paused there, looked back at the track that snaked around behind the hut.

2

THE ROTTENNESS OF BONES

Days chucked on top of days—a pile of time, everything made of walking. Wood, dirt, sky and water. The dogs and the men. Her own smell and theirs. Rain. Rain so that it was all there was: a curtain of water dropped over the world. Stinking wet. And then: a field. A hut. They circled around behind it among the trees. She smelled the river before she saw it—wide and flat. The hut they stopped at was built close to the bank, a boat tied up to a narrow jetty. The man they called Doyle, pallid and bony with a sneer for a smile, eyed her suspiciously.

Matt said they would be back within a day. She was to stay there. Stay put. Don't go out, keep the shutter closed, don't open the door to anyone.

In the pre-dawn darkness the men left the hut, Doyle with them. She heard the dogs barking; the men must have left them behind, tied them up with the other dog that had been there when they arrived. Then nothing. Bark of a dog, crack of the fire, the thuck thuck of the cocky.

There was a dried sinew tied around the bird's leg then tied to the leg of the table, the sinew about ten inches long. A white cocky. Now and then it would have a fit, flap its wings making a thucking sound, jump up and down, pull at the sinew. Then it would go quiet again, stand still by the table leg, only to start the thucking and pulling again. All night it had done it, Bridget awake in the dark listening to it.

There was a knife on the table. As she sat there she thought about cutting the sinew, taking the bird outside and letting it go. Dawn light was leaking in under the door. It would fly out into the morning. If it could still fly.

She wondered what this river was, where it would take her if she followed it. If it might go to Hobart Town, how far it would be. She thought again about that man Jacobson saying he'd heard she was with them. She wondered where China was, what it was like there. Maybe it would be a good place. She wondered then how far it was from there to England, felt the pendant. It would be worth enough to get back to England. She was sure it would be.

The bird had stopped for a while, started up again now, this time thwacking against the table leg that was a cut tree branch. Her gaze fell on the knife on the table again. But she didn't move, only stared at the knife, sat listening to the bird tugging against the sinew.

...

She did go outside. Walked down to the river's edge and looked up and down. The sky was dirty white and low, the surface of the water grazed by a cold breeze. All the dogs were barking and crying, jumping and pulling on their ropes. She took wood from the stack at the side of the hut, added it to the simmering fire inside. Ate Doyle's meat and bread, smoked his tobacco. Sat watching the line of light under the door. Wondered if they would come back. What she would do if they didn't. After a while of sitting, getting up, walking around the hut, picking things up and putting them down again, she lay down by the fire.

...

She woke to the sound of the oars on the side of the boat, heard them coming to the hut, stood up. Then the men all barrelling in, the dogs with them, Higgins rushing at the bird, Doyle's boot connecting with him before he got to it, sending him sprawling across the hut floor. Not long after they were leaving, walking fast away from the hut into the trees behind it.

Walking again, ceaseless trudging, pushing into punishing scrub. A flea, a flea trying to get through the bristles of a massive beast, all the jump worked out of it. A worn-out, staggering flea.

...

Damp white breath of God, clinging to the hills. The hiss of His exhale. The flat lands behind them, the expressionless faces of black rock mountains.

...

The river ran wide, steep and shallow over smooth brown rocks, the roar of it loud enough that the men had to yell to hear each other. The forest they had come through was open, blond grass growing between the trees. They crossed it on a log and soon after came to a hut surrounded by tall gums. Immediately in front was cleared, a few fat black stumps sticking up out of the ground. As they walked towards it a pack of dogs came rushing at them, barking. Caesar and Higgins were welcomed into the crowd with wagging tails and noses shoved into their arseholes. 'Some bloody welcome,' Henry said, watching them. 'I wouldn't be putting up with that. Would you, Matt? Would you put up with that?'

'Depends who was licking my arse.'

Henry's body jiggled as he walked. 'Dirty bastard.'

The hut was dark and low to the ground. At one end of it was a smaller hut, this one open-fronted, timber with a shingle roof. Inside it hung a mass of kangaroo skins. A shot went off, the bullet passing Henry's right shoulder. 'Bloody oath. What the . . . ? Stupid old bastard. Nearly bloody shot me.'

'Sully, you old bastard, what the bloody hell are you doing?' Henry yelled.

The hut door opened further and a man stood in the doorway, wild grey hair and beard obscuring most of his face. 'Oh, it's you. Heard the dogs making a bloody racket. What do you want?'

'Just passing through.'

Sully eyed the group, looked over at Bridget and nodded in greeting.

'Matt picked her up,' Henry said.

Sully looked at Matt, who seemed to be blushing as he stepped into the hut.

It was crowded inside, just one room, a fire going up one end, a hammock in one corner, barrels stacked under it, a wide shelf piled high with all manner of tins and rope and bottles and leather. Near the fire there was an armchair, upholstered in green fabric with pale pink flowers through it. It was faded, ripped and worn on the arms and the seat of it was sunken.

Matt squatted next to the fire.

'S'pose you want tea? I'm not making it for ya. You know where everything is. Make it yourself.' Sully sat down in the armchair.

'No water in the bucket here,' Henry said.

'Whole bloody river full of it out there. Go and get some, ya lazy bastard.'

'Budders,' Henry said, 'go and get water.'

'How come I have to?'

'Go and get some fucking water.'

Budders went out. Matt sat where he was, played with a knife, turning the blade over, while Henry looked for tea.

Bridget stood awkwardly behind the chair where Sully was.

'Sit down, for God's sake, you're making me tired,' Sully said without turning around.

She looked for somewhere to sit, found a drum and sat on that.

Budders came back slopping water on the floor, earning a clip around the head from Matt.

Later, with his tea, Matt leaned against the window frame while Budders sat on the floor next to Sully's chair.

Sully looked into his cup then drank. 'S'pose you heard the reward's gone up?'

Matt glanced at Henry. 'Who said that?'

Sully got up, walked over to a crowded bench, picked up a newspaper and threw it down in front of Matt.

'How much?' Henry said.

'One hundred guineas,' Sully said.

'One hundred guineas?' Budders stood up. 'We's worth one hundred bloody guineas.'

He stood over the paper, close to Matt. Matt looked up at him, a warning in his eye, and Budders moved.

Sully sat. 'Gov'nor swears he's gunna be rid of the lot of ya. Talking about some new law that all shepherds have to have a supervisor, make sure they're not helping bushrangers.' He looked up at Henry, across at Matt.

'Bullshit,' Henry said. 'He can't do that.'

'He's the bloody gov'nor, can do what he likes just about. Fixing to make an example of ya.'

Matt looked at Henry. He appeared to be growing more uncomfortable. Henry was serious, not a trace of a grin on his face now. Matt went over to the open door. 'What about a boat?'

'What about one?' Sully said.

'Steal one. Find a bloke that can sail.'

'S'pose you could. And go where?'

Matt didn't say anything; he was looking out the door.

'Yeah,' Budders said, 'a boat. We'll get a boat.'

'Go to China,' Sam said.

'China?' Sully said, a trace of mocking in his tone. 'Tell ya what I'd do if I were you.'

Matt looked over at him. 'What?'

'I'd wear out me frigging knees.'

Sam looked up, confused.

Henry laughed a bit. 'Fat lot a good that'll do us.'

Sam looked to Henry for explanation. 'Pray,' Henry said, a slight grin again, but gone quickly now. 'We should pray.'

'Men like us don't pray,' Matt said.

Sully stood up. 'Just an idea.'

'Well it's bullshit.' Matt snapped.

Sully turned, challenge in his eyes. They stood about a yard apart.

'What would you know, anyway? About any of this? Who do you think you are? Do you think God's going to listen to me? To give me any bloody thing? Or him.' He pointed at Henry. 'Or him.' At Budders now.

'Gived me a big dick,' Budders said, grinning. 'A big fat dick.'

Matt's gaze was on Sully. 'What the hell are we to God? You shoot a man, that's it, you have no fucking God. You are on your own. You are on your fucking own.'

'Then get a fucking boat,' Sully said, and he pushed past Matt and went out the door.

Matt turned and drove his fist into a crate behind him. The thing shattered.

'Alright,' Henry said. 'Easy. Take it easy.'

Matt and Henry stood close enough to inhale each other's breath, their eyes glimmering.

Matt sat down heavily in the chair by the fire, one fist curled around the other, his chin resting on them.

One of the dogs stood outside the door looking up at Henry, wagging its tail. Henry squatted down. It came forward and he rubbed under its jaw.

...

A Proclamation

By His Excellency Colonel GEORGE ARTHUR,

Lieutenant Governor of the Island of Van Diemen's Land

and its Dependencies

WHEREAS Matthew Sheedy, Henry Evans, Samuel Merriweather and William Budworth (for whom Apprehension Rewards have already been offered) yet remain at large and have lately added to their Crimes of Murder and other Personal Outrage and Plunder by an unprovoked Attack on the Premises and Property of William Effingham Lawrence at Lake River: NOW THEREFORE, for the Protection of the Settlers at this Important Time, I DO HEREBY PROCLAIM, that, instead of the Rewards already offered any Persons who may apprehend any of the Offenders before named shall immediately receive from the Government the sum of One Hundred Guineas, or (at their election) One Hundred Acres of Land, free from all restrictions: And if the Offenders shall be apprehended by prisoners, such prisoners shall receive a Free Pardon: AND I DO HEREBY FURTHER PROCLAIM that any person who may apprehend Bridget Crack (5 ft. 3 in. light brown hair, green eyes, 21 years of age, arrived per *Faith*, native place Suffolk, absconded from Black Marsh, October 7, 1826) having absented herself from her usual place of residence and lately suspected to be in the company of the before named Offenders, will immediately receive from the Government the sum of Fifty Guineas, or (at their election) Fifty Acres of Land, free from all restrictions: And if the Offender shall be apprehended by prisoners, such prisoners shall receive a Free Pardon.

...

Bridget went outside, stood on the bank looking down into the flow of the river. She heard him coming, flicked around to face him as he got within a few yards of her. 'Get away from me.

Get away!' The screeching ripped out of her and he stopped in his tracks. He stood there staring at her and retreated; turned around and strode back towards the hut.

...

That night she lay on the floor of the hut, unfolded the letter. By the light from the fire she could just make out the words.

> Dear Bridget
> if I ever see timothy crack again I will kill the cur   you will come bak   I know you will   you must have faith in God Bridget   you must never give up hope   we will see each other again   father has took sick   he has not been hisself since he herd about you   I am praying for you
> Your loving sister
> Kate

It had been delivered to her in gaol in Manchester. She held it as a flame jumped up from the log, burned blue in the middle, wavered and then was gone. She put the note away, lay her head down on the floor.

'Gentlemen, as you are aware, the colony finds itself in a delicate situation. The seriousness of the threat posed by both the bushrangers and the natives is one I believe you all understand. We are concerned here with correction and punishment, indeed. But we are also building a colony—an ordered and civilised society of which Britain may be proud.' Governor Arthur cast his gaze around the table at which the twelve men were seated, settled it on Marshall. 'Is that not correct, Captain Marshall?'

'I believe it is, sir.'

A number of months ago two native men had been hanged for the murder of a stock keeper, Arthur hoping that the hangings would act as a deterrent to others. Since then, however, the conflict that had been building in the Interior had only intensified with natives recently killing three stock keepers and a settler. And the Sheedy gang had now been at large for more than twelve months. The governor had called a meeting to discuss what he had described as an 'inadmissible' state of affairs.

Marshall had only been half listening. Some weeks ago now he had been informed that Bridget Crack had taken up with Sheedy. At the time he had been unable to contain his shock and had questioned the governor about the possibility of it being a mistake. 'I hardly think it is a mistake, Captain. The description of the woman given by the surveyor's men matches the description in the woman's convict record. On what grounds do you assume it mistaken?' Marshall explained that the girl had been in his service and that . . . what? He had petered out then, unsure what he'd been going to say. That he couldn't imagine her taking up with bushrangers? As he'd started to say it he realised he was no longer sure. Perhaps he could imagine that. Sitting at the table now he wondered—was he sure? It seemed no one and nothing ever turned out to be what he'd thought. He no longer trusted himself. If he ever had.

'It is imperative that the settlers are armed and ready to defend themselves,' Arthur said.

Captain Marshall stared at the wave of grain in the wood of the table as his thoughts went from Bridget to Jane. She had become friends with a Quaker woman in Hobart Town, an older woman, Mrs Potter. The two had become almost inseparable. And with the blossoming of this friendship had come Jane's letter-writing endeavours; she had taken to writing to England about any and every matter that she saw as an injustice, and that Mrs Potter pointed out to be so. She had written about the conditions in the women's gaol, in the orphanage, about the natives.

Just last night he had again urged her to curb her letter-writing. Yesterday Arthur had been speaking to him about his troubles with Britain. No one there had any idea what he was dealing with: the type of country, the mountains and dense scrub—they were, he said, issuing orders that were quite inappropriate. At the end of the conversation Arthur had been quiet a moment, then said: 'And how is your, sister, Captain? Jane, isn't it?' From the way he had asked the question, Marshall suspected he knew about Jane's activities.

A couple of weeks ago he and Jane had argued. He had simply said that life was not always fair; that you could not always know God's plan.

She had stood there staring at him with what he thought was dislike blistering in her eyes. When she said, 'Really, Richard?' it was in a tone she had not used with him before. 'So we are to turn a blind eye to suffering, to accept it and not try at all to do anything to help, to right a wrong? How *dare* you attempt to sedate me with such a platitude. What a convenient excuse. We may be completely lazy then. To do nothing at all. Is that right?'

He said he just meant that you couldn't fight everything.

'God's plan,' she said, 'is not for me to be a coward.' And then she walked out of the room.

He could hear himself saying it now, 'Life is not fair,' and he wondered all of a sudden what on earth he had been talking about. Of what had he been trying to convince her? A few days later she had gone up-country to Macquarie Plains. She had been there since, staying with a friend of Mrs Potter.

Arthur's voice crashed into his consciousness. 'What do you say, Captain Marshall?'

...

Marshall sat beside the lamp in the sitting room. The house was quiet, everyone in bed. He had gone that day to look at Bridget Crack's convict record. She had been sentenced to seven years' transportation for having in her possession counterfeit coins. Arrived April 1826. Assigned to him, then charged with insolence and disorderly conduct and put in the stocks for two hours. Assigned in August to Nathanial Johnson. He'd winced internally over that. Knew the man. Her hair cut then, and solitary confinement. He had been surprised by the strength of his response on reading that her hair had been cut, had felt it somewhere in his viscera. September, assigned to Charles Pigot in the Interior. October, absconded. Ship surgeon's comments: Behaved Tolerably Well.

Tolerably well. What did that mean? he wondered again now.

He read another document, put it down on the table in front of him, sat back. Eight of them had left Macquarie Harbour, it said, stole the ship they had been building, sailed her around the south-west coast and then up the east coast, where they were reportedly caught in bad weather and abandoned her. Three of the eight men were apprehended at Cartwright's property after they had robbed him; one had been shot dead, and the other two, Beasley and McGuinley, had since been tried and hanged for bushranging. The body of another, a Brian Ruthers, was found by a farmer months later in a gully near Crooked Hat Hill. The rest of the document outlined who the remaining four had robbed, on what date, what they had taken, how much it was worth, who had been hurt and how—the house of a Mr Raynor was robbed and he was shot in the shoulder; one soldier was killed.

He was already acquainted with these events. Nine months ago the bushrangers had robbed his cousin at his property at Elizabeth River. His cousin's wife, Sally, had been most shaken by the experience and had been unwell for a time after it, his cousin set back quite a few pounds. Marshall had consequentially taken an interest in the hunt for the gang. He had read over the document again, he realised now, looking for something in it that would help to explain why Bridget Crack was now in their company. These were the men she had taken up with. He still found it inconceivable.

Marshall tapped his fingers on the arm of his chair then picked up a letter from Jane at Macquarie Plains. He reread one of the paragraphs.

> Time does not heal all wounds. Kindness and beauty are the only real healers and they are like butterflies—brief visitors whom you may see or not; sometimes it depends on which way you are facing. Then again, if they don't fly your way—well, you may have to run for them. Who knows how far?

Marshall put the letter down. He looked up at the portrait of his father that his mother had insisted he bring. Then he leaned back in the chair and closed his eyes.

The flames were as tall as Bridget, the front of her body hot. A man threw another log onto the fire and she stepped back. Sparks raced off into the night sky. The men cheered, held their cups in the air. They had arrived at this hut in the late afternoon after three days on the move since Sully's, had come back down out of the mountains again, apparently—from what she'd overheard—towards a place called Jacob's Sugar Loaf.

There had been four men here when they arrived. One of them, Cole, had said there were others coming later: sawyers who were working nearby. Four of them had turned up and then a man and a woman on a cart after that. Matt had watched the cart coming along the track. Cole walked over to him. 'Connor, the shepherd from a new land grant over the way, and his wife Essie, bringing supplies. They're alright, nothing to worry about.' Matt had nodded but continued to stare at the approaching cart, frowning.

Matt had gone inside the hut a while ago, someone laughing loudly in there now. One of the sawyers came around the fire to where Bridget stood. 'Alright there, darling?'

She nodded, sipped ale.

'Bloke left ya on your own has he?'

'I'm fine on my own.' She'd heard Henry talking to Cole before. 'Told him he should of left her at Sully's. But he won't bloody listen.'

'Are ya?' the sawyer said. 'I'm not. Get pretty bloody lonely sometimes, can tell ya that.'

Bridget looked up at the hut. People laughing then someone singing.

'Hey, where you going? I was just chatting.'

The small hut was cramped with nine bodies in it, full of the smell of stale sweat, smoke, bullock fat and damp from the dirt floor, made to feel even more cramped by the shouting and carousing going on. Light came from the fire and from two candles on the table, the shadows of Essie and the boy Nimble, who were sitting at the table, appearing huge and ghoulish on the timber wall behind them.

Matt, Henry and Cole were by the fire, cups raised. Nimble called out one, two, three, go! The three men threw their heads back and poured the rum into their throats, Henry the first one to raise his cup in the air declaring it empty, the other two holding their own cups up with one hand, patting Henry on the back with the other. The woman, Essie, caught Bridget's eye, gave her a small tight-lipped smile.

Matt passed Bridget without acknowledging her, disappeared out the door.

'Come on, Sam.' Henry looked over to a log in the corner where Sam sat gazing into his cup. 'I'll give ya a go.'

Sam shook his head.

'Come on,' Henry said, motioning for Sam to get up.

Sam reached out for the bottle on the table in front him, filled his cup.

'What's eating him?' Henry said to no one, to himself. 'Something always bloody eating him,' he mumbled. 'Misses his bloody mummy.'

'Yeah,' Budders said. 'Misses her tit.'

Bridget saw Essie dip her head, look down into her lap over the belly that protruded in front of her.

Bridget wondered where Matt had gone. Cole produced more tobacco and she went over to the table, helped herself to some and repacked her pipe. The man Connor poured her rum, handed it to her. 'Drink up there, girl. Come on.'

Connor and another man picked up fiddles, started to play. Essie slapped her thigh. One of the sawyers got her up on her feet then to dance with him. Still no sign of Matt. Sam was still sitting on the log, fiddling with the handle of his cup. Cole grabbed Bridget's hand. 'Come on, dance with me.' She shook her head, but he reached for her hand again, grabbed it. Just as he did, Matt came in, strode towards him. The man dropped Bridget's hand, took a step back, put both his hands up.

Matt grabbed her arm, dragged her to the door and outside. 'Let me go!' She ripped her arm from his grip.

He turned to her. 'What were you doing in there? Huh? I leave you alone for, what, ten minutes . . .'

'It wasn't ten minutes.'

'Like him, do you?'

He was drunk. Glaring at her. She wasn't answering his stupid questions. She turned around to go back in. He grabbed her arm again, then squeezed her chin in one hand, pushed her head back. He stood there holding her head like that, looking at her like he was going to say something, then he let go, stalked off. Bridget watched him, her face hot where his thumb and finger had been. What the hell? Bloody cur. Something wrong with him. Something the hell wrong with him. She went back inside, downed an ale. Everyone silent.

'What?' She turned around to face the middle of the room. 'What are you all staring at?' She looked over at Connor. 'Are you going to play that thing? Play it!'

Connor surprised, started to play.

Bridget pushed past Henry to where Sam sat. 'Get up. Dance.'

His soft face creased into a frown.

'Get up and dance!'

'Alright, alright.'

He got soggily to his feet. She took hold of his sweaty hands, all of him limp. Useless. She let go of him, stormed back out.

Around the side she stood fuming, staring into the dark hole that was a track going into trees behind the hut.

It wasn't planned. Matt saw the boy through the telescope from the top of a hill, said it looked like his cartwheel was broken. They went down into the valley, watched him from the trees. Matt went out into the clearing to talk to him and then called to the others. When the boy saw them his eyes widened with alarm. 'I know who you are. I know who you are—you're bushrangers and you're going to kill us, you're going to kill my mother and my father and my brothers and kill me too. I know who you are.' His young freckled face streamed with tears.

Henry sighed and Matt stepped closer to him. 'Stop your bloody blubbering.'

'Jesus Christ,' Henry said, 'he's a bloody girl.' He pushed past Matt and grabbed the boy's arm. 'Get going.'

The man was in a fenced garden in front of the stone house when they approached, Henry walking with one hand on the boy's shoulder, his gun loosely by his side in the other hand. The man was still, frowning, watching them come.

Henry stood outside the fence, a few yards from it, his hand still on the boy.

Matt stepped in front of them. 'Andrew here said you might be so good as to let us in for a chat, a bit of a feed maybe.'

'What do you want from us?'

'Just what I said.'

The door of the house opened now and a woman looked out. When she saw the boy with Henry her hand went up to her mouth. She came forward. 'Don't hurt him. Please don't hurt my son.'

'Stay there, Martha,' the man said.

She stopped, her hand over her mouth again.

'I'm alright, Mama.'

'Let him go and you can have what you want.'

Matt regarded the man. 'Take her inside. Then Andrew'll come in.'

He turned to Budders. 'Go with them'.

'Do what he says, Robert,' the woman said. 'Please, let's just do what he says.'

The man opened the gate and walked to his wife, who put her hand on his shoulder blade, pushed him ahead of her, looked back at the boy as they went into the cottage. Budders went in behind them.

'Stay there,' Matt said, looking at Bridget.

She stood near the fence while they all went into the house. A few minutes later he came back out, dragged her in and down a dark hall. He pushed her into a bedroom where the woman was standing uncomfortably at the end of the bed. 'Get her a dress,' he said to the woman.

The woman glanced at Bridget. 'I beg your pardon?'

Matt pushed past her then, pulled open a cupboard. 'Are you deaf? Get her a dress.'

The woman looked at Matt, confused.

'Do it!' His voice like a gunshot.

The startled woman grabbed at a dress.

He went out, shut the door.

The woman put her hands to the side of her head. 'I . . . I didn't realise . . . Here,' she said. 'Take them off.'

Bridget had put trousers on under her dress up at the camp, had left the petticoat behind. Her stockings had been destroyed and the trousers were warmer anyway. After Jacobson's she'd convinced Matt to give her his spare shirt and then she'd taken the dress off and left it in the bushes, sick of it snagging. Matt didn't like it; but he didn't like her being slow either and she was faster in the trousers. And who was going to see her out there anyway?

Bridget took the blue dress the woman held out to her and pulled it on. It was big on her in the front, the woman bigger-busted than her. The woman did the back of it up.

The door opened and Matt was standing in the doorway wearing a silk vest and black hat, a gold watch hanging from the pocket of the vest. 'Out here.'

Andrew and another two boys, younger, were standing against the wall in the dining room. Matt sat at the head of the table and made Bridget sit next to him. There were two servants at the table, as well as Henry and Sam. The missus came in with hot potatoes and more bread, the master with whiskey. The food was eaten in silence while the master and missus and the boys stood by the wall.

When they'd eaten Matt told the others to go around the house, see what they could get. He watched Bridget as she went out of the room.

The clothes she'd taken off were lying on the end of the big bed. She was pulling the trousers back on when Henry came in, yanked drawers open. He went out and then Matt came in, shut the door behind him.

...

As she went out the front door, she heard from down the hall behind her the sound of someone crying.

Matt filled a horn with gunpowder, picked up the gun. He motioned for Bridget to go with him across the river.

They had been on the move for over a week, all day, every day. When they did finally stop they were back at the camp in the mountains. Same river, same lean-to.

Matt stood about forty yards from a tall gum, aimed at the trunk. The shot lodged into the bark. He shot it about ten times then, only missed once, reloaded the gun after each shot. Bridget was leaning against a tree a few yards away from him. What was she supposed to do, stand here all afternoon and watch him shoot the tree? He hadn't spoken to her, hadn't looked at her, just told her to stand there.

He shot a few more times and then Budders came running across the clearing.

'Henry says he wants to sleep, you're to shut the fuck up.'

Matt ignored him, pushed powder into the gun.

'He said shut up.'

'And I said piss off.'

'Nah, ya didn't.'

'Fuck off or I'll shoot ya.'

'Henry said to come over and tell ya,' Budders persisted.

Matt turned to him now. 'I told you to bugger off, didn't I?'

Budders stood still where he was. 'He said to tell ya.'

'Good, so ya told me. Now, go.'

Budders started to walk off.

'Wait a minute.' Matt considered him and a grin crawled over his face. 'Come here.'

'What for?'

'Just come here a minute.' Matt walked slowly towards Budders.

'What? Budders took a step back but Matt lunged at him, grabbed both his wrists then, holding them in one hand, pulled at the rope that hung coiled at the side of his trousers. He wrapped it tight around Budders' wrists.

'Get off of me! Get off.'

Matt dragged Budders by his wrists to the tree he'd been shooting.

'What's wrong? It's just a little game.'

'Let me go, I ain't done nothing—it were Henry what said it.'

Matt pushed Budders roughly against the trunk. He passed the rope around Budders, behind the tree, across Budders' chest, around the tree again, pinning Budders' arms to the sides of his body. He tied the rope tight, stood back to survey his work.

Budders' eyes held the worried, dejected look of a kicked dog.

Matt walked back to the spot where he'd been standing before.

Bridget stood up from where she'd been leaning.

Budders opened his mouth to speak but as he did a shot lodged into the tree above his right shoulder, only inches from his head. 'I didn't do nothing. Henry were sleeping is all. I didn't do nothing.'

Matt shot again on the other side of Budders' head. Budders began to whimper.

'Come on, don't you trust me?' Matt shot again, this time low, the bullet only narrowly missing Budders' foot. Budders jerked his foot away. 'I didn't do nothing! Henry said you was to stop. I just run across there. I come running across there, 'cause Henry said to. I don't wanna do this. I don't wanna do it. Lemme go. Lemme go . . .'

Budders' screwed-up eyes streamed. The mouth was no longer a mouth but something red and wet and ghastly that had taken hold of the whole face and now a slow-moving, lost creature, morphed from one grotesque shape to another. Saliva-coated protests born from it ran down his chin.

Bridget had had enough, went to leave, but Matt lurched at her, grabbed her arm. 'Where are you going?'

'Get off me.'

'Why, what's wrong? Feel sorry for him?'

She glanced at Budders then looked away from his streaming face, tried to pull her arm from Matt's grip.

'What, you feel sorry for him now, do ya?'

'You made your point.' Almost a whisper, but he heard it.

'Made my point? *Made my point?*' The muscles in Matt's jaw tightened. 'Is that right? I've made my point, have I? And what the fuck would you know about my point, Miss . . . Miss Fucking Run Away and Play in the Bush? Eh? You want to know about my point? Fine. I'll tell you about my point. My point is that every single fucking day I wake up and I'm stuck out here with three brainless fucking no-hopers, and every pimple-arsed redcoat in the colony is after my neck, all because . . . because what? I didn't want to rot like a frigging dog. You want to know something? I'll tell you something—I've just about had enough. What am I supposed to do, huh? You tell me: what the fuck am I supposed to do?'

Bridget looked at the ground, could feel Matt's eyes on her, ruddy fury like a birthmark over his face. 'I don't know.'

'What?'

'I said I don't know.'

She sensed him relax a little and she looked up.

He said nothing for a moment, only held her gaze before he shook his head and began to walk away. Then he stopped. 'Anyway, why the fuck have you taken his side all of a sudden? How come you're looking after him?' He flicked his arm towards the wilted man on the tree. 'I saved you from his filthy cock and now you're his best friend. What, you want him after all, is that it?'

'No.'

'What?'

'I said no!'

She turned to go but he grabbed her elbow and held it hard. 'Where are you going? You're not going to just leave him there, are you? You seemed so worried about him and now you're just going to go?'

'Let go of me.'

'*Oh, let go of me, don't hurt me, you're hurting me*. Fuck you and your bullshit complaints. In fact, how about, seeing as you two are so cosy . . .'

He dragged her to the tree, Bridget kicking and hitting at him. He pushed her against the trunk next to Budders, pulled roughly at the knot near Budders' left arm. He shoved his hand in behind her back, pulled at the rope. Tied it once around both of them, and then a second time. His movements were efficient, unlaboured. He pulled hard on the knot. 'Hope you have a nice time there together then. Give you a chance to get a bit more acquainted, won't it?' He strode off towards the river without looking back.

Next to her Budders snivelled quietly. The rope dug into her upper arm on one side and the inside of her elbow on the other, her chest felt crushed where she was locked hard against the tree. Her left arm was touching Budders' arm, making her stomach turn. At least there were two layers of cloth between their skin, but still she could feel him. Could feel the creepy insipidness that was Budders. Could smell the dried stale sweat on his body, the oil in his hair, and something else: the unmistakable smell of human shit.

The smell of oils from the gum and of the ants at the base of the tree floated like fine notes over the stink beside her.

The sun inched towards the horizon and long shadows stretched over the rough, dry grass. An uncanny quiet clothed the day, held it still in light washed-blue anticipation. As night approached the edges of everything became sharper and the air clearer. The lowest branches of the tree reached out above their heads and smaller branches drooped towards the ground, bunches of leaves nodded in the light breeze, brushing the air. From the direction of the river came the sound of wood being chopped, the rhythm of it steady and certain. Crows moaned. Smaller birds whistled and twittered. Puffs of cloud turning yellow at the edges moved lazily across the sky.

Finally Budders had become silent. She couldn't tell now what he was doing, if his eyes were open or shut, didn't want to turn her head and look at him. Kept her gaze ahead and her body as still as possible.

'When I get off of here I'm gunna fuck you till ya can't walk. Gunna fuck ya real bad.'

The skin and muscles on the left side of Bridget's body flinched, tried to draw themselves in. In front of her a leaf fluttered quietly to the ground. Spun as it fell. Fell over, over, over, over. Landed on the ground with the pointy end of it touching another leaf—a brown leaf with a rise in its middle from where it had shrunk as it dried.

'You hear what I said?'

Next to that leaf there was a stick. No leaves on the stick. Where did the leaves go?

'Maybe you'll like it, eh? Maybe that's what you come here for. Henry says Matt don't like to share, but I don't care. I don't care, I don't, what Matt says. I ain't scared a Matt. You hear me? I said I ain't scared a Matt.'

Where did the leaves go? Where did the leaves go? Where did the leaves go?

'One day nearly had me a nice bit, I did. Black hair, real white skin. Nice little titties.' A foul sound came from his body; a laugh like a stream of fast, sharp hiccups. 'Titties like little buds. Had some book in her lap when we come in, she did. Read it, I says. See her pink tongue behind them fat lips. Read it again, I says. Just 'bout to make meself at home I were and in comes Matt. "Piss off over there. Piss off, Budders."

'Better when Ruthers were here. Didn't like Matt none. Gived me a go sometimes when he'd finished, Ruthers did.'

The rancid laugh again, his grunting chest straining against the rope.

The light of the low sun came straight at Bridget's face. The temperature was dropping quite suddenly and shadow spreading over the land.

'Got this little black one once, not even no titties. Whiny little bitch, she were.'

'Shut up.'

'Whimpering she were. Had to shut her up, didn't we?'

'Shut up!'

'Shut the little bitch up.'

He laughed and the sun quivered at the level of the horizon. Slipped away. A damp chill clamped the air. Bridget was losing feeling in her feet, her hands. Clenched her fists. Lifted one foot, the other. The delicate shape of the new moon appeared. Cut like a scythe into the darkening blue. Stars like silent sirens.

He was there. Undoing the ropes in the dark. Budders hitting at him. 'I'll kill ya, I'll fucking kill ya.' Then Budders was running.

The rope released her, her legs gave way and she slumped at the bottom of the tree.

He stood above her. 'Get up.'

'Piss off!' A shriek more than words.

Matt looked away from her, sighed. 'Just get up.'

'What do you want from me? What do you want? Go away! Leave me alone!' She was crying and screaming.

He walked off while she sat there on the cold ground hating him, wishing to God she had never seen him.

...

It was Sam who came to the tree in the dark, stood there and spoke quietly to her. 'Too cold, Bridge. Come on. He's calmed down. Wants you to come back. Come on, Bridget. Will you?'

She took his hand to get up.

...

Henry was sitting by the fire. No sign of Budders or Matt. Sam sat her down on a rock, put a skin around her shoulders, a cup of something in her hand. She sipped it. He put some meat in front of her but she didn't want it.

'Bit of a lovers' quarrel, eh?'

She looked up at him—Henry—sitting on the other side of the fire, his face dappled in orange, features made bigger by shadows. 'Got your hands full there, girly, I tell ya that much. Got your bloody hands full.'

'I haven't got nothing.'

''Fraid you have. 'Fraid you got Matty-boy there fancying you.' He looked over at the lean-to.

'Always show his affection like that, does he?'

Henry laughed loud. The night flinched.

There was a sound in the bush near the river. Henry turned around and pulled out his gun, Sam too. A figure stood in the darkness among the trees at the end of the clearing.

Henry kept his gun on Budders as he approached the fire.

Henry grinned. 'Missed us, did ya? Couldn't stay away?'

'Shut up.'

Henry laughed. 'Well. How about that? Bit a pluck he comes back with. Kinda language is that?'

Budders' eyes throwing hot embers of hate.

'You shouldn'ta done that, ya know. Shouldn'ta made me do that.' He stood over her. 'Why'd ya have to go protecting him? Whattaya expect me to do when you go protecting him like that, eh? Whattaya expect me to do?'

Behind her now, he paced. 'You should be more grateful. If it wasn't for me, you'd be dead. If I hadn't got you from up on that hill, fed you, do you think you'd of survived?'

She felt a surge of heat through her body, her stomach cramped violently and she leaned forward as the water she had just drunk came up into the dirt next to her.

Matt ran his hand across the back of his neck. 'Christ. Jesus Christ.'

'Alright!' She didn't care what she said. Just wanted him to shut up, go away and leave her alone.

He stopped pacing, stood still behind her. 'What?'

'I said, alright.'

...

Days floated out under her like water. She had no grip on them, no grip on anything. Time was lost. Meaning was lost. A sack only brown, rough to touch, rich grassy smell. The fire hot, orange, flickering. Words mostly meaningless—only the quality of the voice: soft, or harsh, throaty or high.

Damp gully, no fire. No stars, no moon. Night like a blackboard that had never seen chalk. Teeth-aching screech of dreams on it. Then the silent sneaking shift of cloud and the round face of the moon, staring, intent and menacing like the face of a school bully. Matt rolled over, caught her eye, held it. For too long. A look that reminded her of the river they were camped beside. Of the water close to the banks where it was cold, dark and hardly moved. She turned her head away from his shape. She lay awake listening to Budders sniff snot back up his nose. Without looking, saw it on his upper lip. Saw his quick tongue take it.

She couldn't sleep with him snivelling like that. Couldn't sleep anyway. Sleep belonged to the past. Everything did.

An owl started with its gentle hoot. Whooo . . . Whooo . . . Whooo . . . She rested on the sound somehow. Made it a boat. Drifted away on it. Didn't care where, just away. Away, away, away. Whooo . . . away . . . whooo . . . away . . . whooo.

Jane and Marshall left the house early in the morning. It was a beautiful day, summer having arrived in Van Diemen's Land. Jane was staying with their cousin at Elizabeth River and Marshall had called in on the way back to Hobart Town from a trip to Launceston.

Yesterday afternoon when he'd arrived she'd been down by the river painting a cliff and a splayed tree that grew up in front of it. This morning he followed her out in the other direction, away from the river and up a slope of gum and wattle. It was a dry slope, parched grey rock jutting out from the hill, the shallow soil around it littered with bark like old leather, dead leaves and pale grasses, the colour sucked out of them by the summer sun.

Jane stopped, wiped sweat from her brow then bent over the ground, lightly poking something with her finger. 'Isn't it beautiful?' she said. He went over to see what she was looking at. A flower. A small mauve flower growing up on a single stalk. 'How does it do that? All around it everything so dry and brown and dead and then this, this perfect little flower. A miracle, isn't it?' She had spoken out loud but the words had seemed more like thoughts of her own, directed to the ground where she was looking. Now she turned to Marshall. 'Don't you think?'

'Yes,' he said, 'I suppose it is.'

He had always felt comfortable in her company, but standing there now he felt rather awkward. She had been at the house less and less, most of her time spent with Mrs Potter. He wondered what he might say to re-establish the feeling of connection he was used to between them, to close the space that he felt. But he couldn't think of anything that wouldn't sound false and inane.

'Where shall I put this?' He had the basket with some lunch Godfrey's convict servant had packed for her.

Jane had settled her sketchbook on a rock, was rifling through the case of paints. She waved at a spot on the ground. 'Just put it there, thank you.'

When he left she didn't turn away from her paints.

They stood under a lone wattle on a slope crowded with gums, Matt in front of Bridget and focused on the scene below, where Henry could just be seen, standing in a field talking to a man. The man pointed to a house in the distance, turned his head and looked up into the trees where Bridget, Matt, Budders and Sam waited.

A few minutes later Henry came up the hill, panting. He put his hand on a thick branch, leaned his weight on it. 'Only the master and missus at the place, two young uns, no visitors expected tonight that he knows of. Three other servants.' He laughed. 'Said he'd heard of us, was pleased to meet me. Fancy that, eh?'

They had walked a long way, had been camped a week at a place called White Kangaroo River. Had walked again to this place, the settler they were going to rob a wealthy one.

They stayed on the hill until dark, when a faint light could be seen burning in one of the windows of the house. Henry put a rope around both of the dogs' necks, tied them to a tree.

As they came across the paddock the house was a dark square on the plain, the details of its shape becoming clearer as they came closer. They reached the stables first and pushed themselves against the back of the stable wall, Henry peering around the corner.

A dog barked and a door opened. The dog barked again. 'Rippa, here. Come here.' It was a man's voice, but soft, young-sounding.

Now a deep stern voice came from near the back of the house. 'What's going on?'

The younger voice again. 'I don't know, sir. Rippa seen a roo or something.'

'A roo?'

'I don't know, sir. Something.'

'Go and have a look.'

'Yes, sir.'

The door shut and then there was the crunch of boots on gravel coming towards where they stood. Henry looked at Matt, who nodded, and then Matt stepped out from behind the stable. He grabbed the man, pulled him back against the wall.

'Told you to put the dog around the front,' Henry said.

'I couldn't before—the master likes to feed him and were later than usual today. I were about to take him then.' The man looked along the back of the stable at the other three and saw Bridget there, a flicker of surprise in his eyes.

'You said I could trust you, Blakely,' Henry growled.

'You can, it's just that he's gunna know, ain't he? He's gunna know I were in on it.'

Henry sighed. He grabbed the man and pushed him towards the house, his gun on him. 'Get going.'

Matt dragged Bridget out from behind the stable, yanked open the stable door and shoved her inside with a horse that threw its head up in shock. Matt turned to Blakely. 'Keep her there.'

Henry, Matt and Budders went into the house and Sam went around the front to keep watch. Blakely stood there looking at the back of the house and then at the stable and back at the house again. He looked dumbfounded, like a man who had just been robbed of all his clothes.

Next to Bridget the horse was showing the whites of its eyes, tossing its head.

The back door of the house opened and Matt came out, opened the stable door. 'Let's go. You too.' He pushed Blakely ahead of him.

Matt walked behind them, stopped at a door that led off a wide hallway and knocked on it twice with the end of his gun.

Henry opened the door. Inside there was a long table, a dark-haired man sitting at the head of it facing the door. He eyed Blakely suspiciously as Blakely, avoiding the man's eye, went and stood against the wall where Matt told him to stand. Against the same wall there was another man, also a servant, and two maids.

Behind the dark-haired man, the master of the house, a fire burned in the hearth and a stout fair woman in a green silk dress with a glittering brooch on the bodice stood next to it, her hands folded in front of her. The woman's face was flushed and her eyes shone with the pleading fear of the trapped. Beside her stood two girls, both of them with long auburn ringlets falling out from beneath the bonnets they wore. One of them rubbed her fingers together nervously. The other one kept her eyes on Henry.

The woman by the fire settled her gaze on Bridget. For the first time in a long time Bridget considered what she might look like, what this woman might be seeing—dirty clothes, matted hair and a man's coat. Bridget moved further into the corner behind her.

Budders stood on the other side of the table opposite them, gun in his hand, his face glowing with excitement. A painting of a proud stag hung on the wall behind him. In the middle of the table sat a silver candelabra, the six candles in it burning brightly. Red velvet drapes covered the windows.

Matt crossed his arms and surveyed the room. 'Good,' he said, 'very good,' and sat at the end of the table opposite the master. Only the two of them occupied the table that Matt now put his feet up on. Henry closed the door and stood in front of it, behind Matt. The man kept his eyes on the soles of Matt's boots.

'I hear you have a boat, Mr Goodwin.'

The man continued to stare at Matt's boots.

Matt watched Mr Goodwin then leaned forward, lifted his right foot and looked at the sole of his boot.

Mr Goodwin's eyes flicked up then.

'Hear you have a boat,' Matt repeated.

'That is true.'

'Sails alright, does she?'

'Not at the present, no. She is in need of maintenance.'

'Really? I'm sure she is. You wouldn't lie to me of course, Mr Goodwin. I can't stomach lying, can't stomach it at all.'

'As I said, she is not in perfect condition at the present.'

'Not in perfect condition? I see. And where is this boat that's not in perfect condition?'

'She is at Port Dalrymple.'

'Is that right? Interesting. Very interesting.' Matt looked over at one of the maids. 'Can get that dinner you were fixing to serve now. Go with her,' he said to Henry.

Henry followed the maid out the door.

For a moment the room was silent. One of the girls dropped her head and looked at her feet. In the hall outside the door a clock ticked. There was the faint sound of wind outside. Budders' eyes roved nervously.

Matt took his feet down off the table. 'This is a nice set-up you've got here, Mr Goodwin. Nice indeed—couple of pretty daughters, wife, big place. Must be plenty of people 'round who want what you've got.'

'Perhaps there are.'

Matt stood up. He walked up the side of the table behind Mr Goodwin and stopped in front of the woman, who took a step back. Mr Goodwin went to stand up and Matt casually pointed his gun at him. 'Told you about standing up. Won't tell you again.' He looked down at the woman's hand. 'That's a nice ring you got there.'

Instinctively she covered her wedding ring with her thumb.

'Take it off.'

'Leave it, Margaret.'

Matt turned around and hit Mr Goodwin hard in the face.

The woman gasped, took her ring off and held it out to Matt.

Matt grabbed it off her, put it on the table in front of Mr Goodwin, whose lip was dripping blood.

There was a crash from up the hall. Matt looked over to Budders. 'Watch them.' He went out of the room.

Budders eyed the two girls, moved around the table towards them. Mr Goodwin stood up.

'Siddown,' Budders said.

The man stayed where he was.

'I said siddown. I'll kill ya if ya don't siddown.'

Mr Goodwin sat slowly. Budders stood close to one of the girls, fingered a loose strand of her hair. 'Got nice hair, ain't ya?' Over Budders' shoulder, the girl sought her father's eyes.

Budders looked down at the top of the girl's dress, moved closer. Mr Goodwin glanced behind him.

The male servant watched Budders, looked at Mr Goodwin and shifted his feet. Mr Goodwin stood up suddenly, grabbed the poker from the fireplace behind him. Bridget saw Budders turn, saw the man lift his weapon and strike. Budders fell. The door flung open and Bridget jumped back as Henry's figure filled the doorway. He hardly paused before he lifted his gun and fired.

The woman screamed and dropped to her knees beside her husband, who lay on the floor, blood pouring from his chest. She pushed hair away from his forehead. 'Oh my God, oh dear God, dear God.'

Matt was at the door now. He took a few steps towards Mr Goodwin and then went back to Henry, who still stood at the door. 'What you do that for?'

Henry was staring at the body on the floor. 'Bloody hell.'

Budders sat up, grabbed hold of a chair and dragged himself up from the floor.

'Let's go,' Matt said.

Henry stood there.

'Let's go!'

Budders stumbled towards the door. Matt grabbed Bridget and they went up the hall and through the kitchen where Matt picked up a sack from the floor and the frightened maid slunk back against the bench. They went out the door into the yard, Henry and Sam behind them now. Budders was slow and Henry half dragged him across the paddock, into the trees. He was bleeding from the side of his head and yabbering insensibly. Henry let go of him and he crumpled to the ground.

'A daft cur,' Budders said. 'Come here and let me get a look at ya.' His voice changed. 'I never done it, sir, it weren't me, I never done it.' He started to whimper and curled up on the ground, still gibbering.

'Leave him,' Matt said.

Henry stood over Budders. 'Can't leave him; they catch him he'll tell them any bloody thing they want to know.'

'What about a bit a whiskey, surely you can spare a drop. They call him Bobby Riser, he's from Norfolk. From bloody Norfolk.' Budders laughed. '*Rock-a-bye baby in the tree top, when the wind blows the cradle will rock, when the bough breaks the cradle will fall . . .*' Budders groaned now.

'Jesus,' Henry muttered.

Matt lifted his gun, aimed it at Budders' head. Henry sighed, shook his head and turned his back to Budders, looked towards the house at the other end of the clearing.

Bridget's ears rang from the shot. Budders was quiet.

Henry turned back around, looked at Budders' body. 'I met his sister once.'

'Come on,' Matt said.

Sam had already walked away. Matt turned, pushed Bridget ahead of him and they ran up the hill.

...

Six days of moving fast, Matt almost dragging her along, swearing at her for being so slow. On the second day they had been chased, shot at. Bridget heard the sound of the bullet close to her head, saw it lodge in a tree in front of her. In the night the men were up, prowling and pacing.

When they stopped again it was at Doyle's hut. The cocky was gone. Where was the cocky? 'Where's the cocky?'

Doyle looked over at her. 'I ate it.'

In the morning Bridget woke up nauseous as she had the last few days. Outside she was sick in the scrub, came back to the hut wiping her mouth, Matt watching her.

The next evening he packed two knapsacks, told her to put one on. Sam and Henry didn't look set to go anywhere.

'Where are we going?'

He opened the door, pushed her out. She almost fell, turned around to swear at him, then saw the hard shine in his eyes.

...

'Bloody stupid, chasing after some kinda bloody principle that'll never give you nothing even though you've piled your whole flaming life on its back.' Matt was pacing in the scrub. He flicked his arm out towards the dark forest. 'You know what they say—blokes like me, we have no principles, but it's just that; a fucking principle leading a man to his death half the time, a fucking principle that's dragged a man out here into this hellhole. And in the end everything's so that you don't even know what it was you were after, what you were chasing in the first place.' He drew breath, stood with his back to her where she sat on the damp ground, then turned, fixed her again with his frightened gaze.

He sat in the bush with his face in his hands, crying.

She sat a few yards from him, waited until he stopped. 'Where are we going?'

'Sully's,' he mumbled. 'Take you to Sully's. Sully's alright,' he said faintly to the bush, as though he were thinking about something else. 'Sully's alright.'

It was close to dark when she and Joseph Primrose—Primmy—and the donkey crossed a fern bridge to a hut that was barely visible, dark as it was in the shade of trees. As they arrived a man appeared from inside.

'Who's that?'

Primmy threw a sack off the donkey onto the ground at the man's feet. 'Who is it? Sheedy's woman.'

'Sheedy? What's she doing here?'

Primmy kicked the sack. 'Take that in.'

A boy came out then, stood there staring at her.

Inside, they ate soup in silence.

'You can sleep there.' Primmy pointed to a hammock strung between two poles. She lay awake, heard Primmy's rough whisper. 'Sheedy'll kill us if he has *any* reason to suspect anything. The man's full of his own imaginings and enough rage for two men. He'll kill you as good as look at you if he thinks you've touched anything that's his.'

...

Matt had taken her to a small cottage beyond Norfolk Plains, where the woman, Janet, tutted over the myriad small scars left from flea bites all over Bridget's arms, rubbed oil into her hair against the lice. Primmy had turned up one night and the transaction took place between him and Slip, the owner of the cottage and the father of Janet's three children—Slip gave half of the money Matt had given him to Primmy; he was to deliver Bridget to John Sullivan and tell Sullivan that he would be there to get her soon, that he was to keep her there until he came.

...

Branches etched mad and scattered stories onto a flat grey sky. Grey trees bent forward, cried out like a whipped man pleading. Boulders huddled together, let out a deep old sound that hummed under the wind. Primmy walked ahead, the donkey loaded with sacks again. The wind dropped and the sky lifted. They went up a dry slope and then followed a track along a ridge above a hurtling river. They cut away from a gorge up a dry rocky hill and for a while she couldn't hear the river, then the rush of it was back and they had come downhill and were travelling above the river again, following it upstream.

...

Sully stood watching them come, the musket hanging from his right hand. He wore a hat low over small squinty eyes that glared out of a face compressed by a frown, a small stick between his teeth.

The dogs ran at Bridget and Primmy barking and growling. Sully bellowed at them and they went back, grouped around him, hackles raised, snarling like the Devil's own guards.

Sully took the stick out of his mouth. 'Well. This's a surprise.'

'Sheedy's woman,' Primmy said.

'Know who she is,' Sully said, chucked the stick on the ground.

The hut was as she remembered it from before: faded chair; hammock; barrels and tins piled on top of each other, some with a layer of dust and grime over them, as though they hadn't been touched for years. It sat within a horseshoe-shaped piece of land that the river ran around, huge trees towering up all around it. A rock wall came straight up from the other side of the river, a high and vicious peak at one end. At the place where it met the sky clouds stretched and broke slowly, the dark rock spattered with snow.

The hut had been built from the trunks of the tree ferns that grew around the river. There was a flock of sheep between the river and the hut, a garden growing potatoes. Out the front a tree lay on the ground, half of it chopped up, logs strewn around it. 'Don't want you here,' he said. She watched him walking to the river, bowlegged but surefooted, a stream of dogs behind him.

Captain Marshall stopped, put his hands on his hips, and looked at the smooth hunch of rock growing out of the bush ahead of him, like a queer bald head lying half buried, face down. The others had just disappeared up over it and now their retreating voices were mingling with the gossip of the brook than ran below him. His lungs were straining. He had no idea why he had agreed to come on this . . . this *expedition*. He had, he recalled, allowed himself to be talked into it by William Watson, who had slapped him on the back and said it would be 'grand'. Marshall scoffed silently now. Not one for making friends easily, he had observed the popular and amiable Watson, had seen how well he made his way in Van Diemen's Land society, how quickly people warmed to him, and had wanted Watson to like him. He had wanted the man's warm, happy glow to extend over him and so he had reluctantly agreed. That was ridiculous—he was never going to be like Watson; the man was antithetical to him in every possible way. Watson was outgoing and in his demeanour, carefree. He was a joker.

Now, standing on a steep, wet slope, the sounds of slashing and talking moving further away from him as he dropped behind the group, he berated himself for his stupidity. The 'mission' that Watson had described was to 'find out what was beyond the mountains'. He had leaned over the map that Robert Price, the government surveyor, had just completed—the most recent, up-to-date map of Van Diemen's Land—pointed at a mark that looked decidedly like an old man's eyebrow drawn sideways. Next to it was written: *Very high rocky Mountains.* 'Beyond here,' Watson said, gesturing to the western side of the map, 'no one really knows.' He held up his finger. 'Not yet.' Then he laughed, slapped Marshall on the back. 'Don't look so afraid, my friend.'

They had brought horses, but had to leave them two days ago—the scrub had become too thick for the horses to get through. All day they had been trudging, the convict servant and Watson in front, slashing at branches and grasses, Andrew Carrington ready with his gun should any natives or bushrangers surprise them and Thompson peering at his compass. The so-called 'grass' they were in was tough and sharp and taller than Marshall, and he'd not been able to see above it for hours now. His trousers were wet to his waist and his hands cut to pieces. He had been in rugged country before, he had been in bush before, but nothing as wet and dense and suffocating as this, and never for a reason as seemingly pointless as this one seemed to him now—to see what was over the mountain.

In the late afternoon they finally began to climb out of the boggy sedgeland onto a slightly drier slope. Marshall found the five men stopped on an open rise. Thompson pointed. 'That lake over there is where the bushrangers robbed us. Out there somewhere'—he pointed to a spread of mountains and lakes—'must be where they hide.' Marshall remembered

Watson's words again: 'No one knows what's out there. That's the beauty of it. We will! Don't you want to be part of that, Captain? Who knows what we might find.' He remembered Watson's arm around him.

Marshall didn't care now what they found. He had found his own physical limit much more quickly than he had imagined he might. He did not have the endurance he once had. He had also found the limit of his tolerance for punishing vegetation. He looked back down the hill, wondered if the so-called 'track' they had made would be visible enough for them to follow back down.

...

Marshall reached his hand up and his fingers found the rough edge of rock, a groan coming out of him as he pulled himself up. The fog had crept down over the mountain so that he was within it now. He could hear nothing, no sound from the others penetrating the fog. He looked up at the expanse of grey rock above him, pushed the toe of his boot into a crack and found a chink in the rock where his fingers could take hold, pulled again. There was a rip in his trousers at the knee, blood soaking the fabric all around the tear, but the skin was numb with cold, no pain coming from the cut. His foot slipped and he grabbed at the rock, his arm shaking, the foot finding hold again. The fog was thicker again here. He continued to climb, no sound at all but the rush of the wind. Marshall felt his panic grow. He pulled himself up once again and now stood on flat rock in a swirl of white, his face smarting, his fingers red and raw. The fog cleared for a few moments to reveal columns of rock and then they were gone again, covered in a blanket of white.

'Captain! Captaaaainnn!'

Watson.

Marshall almost cried, rushed towards the sound.

...

Four of the horses were dead, the other two so close to it that they had to be shot. The vote had been five to one that they turn back, only Thompson wanting to go on in the fog with few supplies to last them. Marshall was confident they all would have perished had they not turned back when they did.

...

Over a week later the hungry, bedraggled group arrived at a house near the Western River. As they came up close to it Watson stood staring. He turned to Marshall. 'The grass,' he said. A bemused and faraway look occupied his eyes that stood out in a round face. 'It was too tough for them to eat.' It took Marshall a moment to work out what he was talking about, then he realised he meant the horses. Marshall nodded doubtfully. They both stood on the track in light drizzle, Watson squinting at the grey horizon as though he could see something miraculous there. Then he turned around and started walking and Marshall went too, the two of them behind the other four, all of them looking like tramps trudging up the long lane to the house.

Bridget was down at the river collecting water when she heard the dogs bark. She came up to see two men standing outside the hut talking to Sully. One of them wore nothing but a skin around his waist. In his right hand he held a spear. The other one wore trousers, had a leather cap pushed down over his hair.

As she approached them the one in the trousers watched her, amusement playing in his eyes. Sully said something to them and the trousered one said something back to him. Bridget hurried past them and went into the hut.

From inside she listened to them talking, couldn't understand what they were saying—a foreign sound, Sully speaking it. He yelled over his shoulder for her to bring out a sack of flour. Bridget pulled it from a barrel in the corner, stood in the doorway, held it out to Sully. Through the door she saw him give it to them. They stood there talking a while longer. The one who had taken the flour threw his head back and laughed, said something that made Sully laugh, the other one grinning wide.

Henry had spoken to some of them. There had been a group of them on a hill, men and dogs and women with children. He had spoken to three men for a long time, Matt with him. For the rest of that day Henry had seemed strange to her—that new sound having come from his mouth, having been standing with them.

The one in the trousers turned now and looked through the doorway. Bridget looked down into the bowl her hands were in. 'Bye, missus.'

Mute with surprise—she hadn't expected him to speak English—Bridget looked up. He laughed and the two of them left.

Trousers, Sully called him when she asked later. But then another name too, in more serious tones—one composed of the unfamiliar sounds he'd spoken before. 'Them and their people up there.' He gestured loosely towards the hut door, the gesture meant to extend beyond the mountain. 'Lived in Hobart Town with a white family. He's back out here now.'

...

The first morning she was there she had been sick into the ferns behind the hut. When she had come back in Sully had watched her, said nothing. For days she slept into the afternoons, woke to light sneaking in around the timber window shutters. Sully had given her his hammock in the dark corner of the hut, slept on skins by the fire. He hardly spoke to her. At night he lowered his weight into the chair, drank cider and watched flames draw up into the chimney. 'Met Matt when I first come to Van Diemen's Land', he said one night to the fire. 'Never going to settle to the life of a prisoner.' He drank again, considered the fire. 'Some people just are what they are, there's no changing them.' He'd looked over at her then, his gaze stern. She'd waited for him to say more, but that was it. It was the most he'd said to her in the time she'd been there.

...

Autumn. Winter and its freezing grey fingers close. In the mornings its cold breath floated over the river. For days it rained and hailed, an occasional sneak of blue then the hard cold kick of weather again, dark grey clouds like balled fists, the hammer of hail, wind that ripped shingles from the hut roof.

...

She was down at the river one morning when she felt it start. She squatted among the tree roots, tried to stand up, but the pain had her sitting back down. She sat by the cold river rocking and groaning and then made her way doubled over up the slope.

...

Sully had the door open. She lay and watched the dust drift through the sunlight in the middle of the hut. Outside the warble of a bird. There was then—there was outside. The smell of blood. That was what she remembered. All of the world had become the smell of blood. And then floating. Floating above herself, looking down at the girl in the hammock, at her sweating, grimacing and clenching. Feeling nothing. Just watching. But then back in the hammock, back inside the hollow vessel that was her body. Later Sully's face close, his hands large under her, lifting. Him lowering her again, his hands coming away from her. Bridget feeling there was no weight in her for the hammock to take.

Now she turned her head to the shelf next to the hammock, saw the cup. Her mouth was dry and her head felt swollen on the pillow. She sat up and drank. A flap of memory here, like a grey bird passing. So few of early childhood. But this one—her mother on the mattress, the cool grey of her face. The chilliness of her hand. Her aunt there—'Say goodbye, Bridget'—and Bridget had looked up at her, not comprehending. What could that mean? Bridget lay now, stroked soft grey feathers.

Sully brought her broth.

He waited there next to her while she drank.

'You should go back to Hobart Town.'

When he put his hand out to take the cup from her she didn't look at him.

...

Sully had brought a roo up to the hut, dropped it, shooed the dogs away. Bridget was still tired but sick of lying around in the hut. She took the roo and rammed the knife in under its fur, hacked at the sinew. She dropped a chunk of muscle into the wooden trough behind the hut, kneaded salt into the flesh, pushed and pushed the meat into the sides of the trough. Her hands were hurting but she kept ramming flesh against timber. She saw him walk past, heard him stop. He stopped there and watched her then he walked up to her and took her wrists. 'Stop it.' She tried to pull her hands away. Her chest heaved and her jaw clenched against tears. She tried again to get away from him but he wrapped his arms around her. He said it more quietly: 'Stop it.' Her eyes moistened and she stared up at the black rock of the mountain, stood stiffly in his embrace.

...

He'd gone down the valley towards Primmy's to hunt again. It had just started raining. She made tea, picked up a tin from the dusty shelf and looked through it. Behind the tin was a book, small, bound with rough leather, yellowed pages.

> i dont no what the date is mary other wise id rite it down here for you thing is i aint got much need for dates no more aint had in a long time now if you seed where i were you probly wuld not beleev it tis not a place youd wanta live mary id ner of brung you out here bloody beutiful tho a place like nuthin i ever seen out here no one comes here much sept Trowsers and his lot and matt and them passen thru some times most of the time mary i am left alone wich is all i want any more for meself i had enuf of peple a long time ago now mary all i want now is to be left alone peple ner did mak much sense to me mary probly you no that i warnt no good back then not much good to you i didnt do the rite thing by you i spose ya wulda found an other man to live with you take care of them childrun i thort bout that a lot you livin with an other man used to get rale upset bout it nowdays i hope ya did that ya got some one to help you get by with the childrun and that he done all rite by ya i hope you mite of forgived me mary but its all rite if you aint i probly dont daserve no forgivnes is nerly winta here now mary in the spring mary ya shuld see it i wish you culd see it mary all the flowers come out the rivers flo is a site for sore eyes mary like hevan i recon mary like hevan Trowsers nos what to eat what you cant eat youd meet him if youd come corse ya not gunna be comin mary I know that i thort for a long time mary id get some money

> and come back but then time went by mary and i thort youd have some one and i didnt no if youd want me and its a lot to get back ther mary   so I never come   but I thort of you i hope you can forgive me mary

Bridget put the book back exactly where she'd found it.

...

Snow blanketed the mountain, fell on the hut.

She squatted by the edge of the river. The top of it was frozen near the edge again and she reached for the rock she'd left there and hit the ice. It broke easily, making a round hole that sent water flowing over the top of the ice sheet around it. She cupped her hands and plunged them in, threw freezing water on her face. Now she took the billy and pushed it down, let it fill, then brought it up to her lips. She drank and waited as the vicious ache produced by the cold water spread across her forehead. Around her boots bunches of thread-like icicles stuck up between the grains of rock that fringed the river, fine little structures that had pushed up out of the ground in the night, some of them balancing the tiny grain of rock that they'd displaced on the top of their ice stalks. She stood up and looked into the brilliant green of the canopy. The sun had come out and quiet drops of water dizzy with morning light gleamed like tiny heroes.

...

The air in the hut was brittle with cold. The fire had burned down to coals. She could see the lump that was Sully curled under skins. Bridget climbed out of the hammock.

The heat from the coals warmed the back of her legs. She lay down with her back to him, close to him but not touching. She felt him wake but he didn't move. She shuffled backwards then so that her back was against him. She watched the coals breathe; bright and dull, bright and then dull, as though it were her own breath inside them. He drew closer to her, put the blanket over her. She could feel his hair, his coarse beard, smell the earthy smell of him. His rough palm went to her forehead and stroked her hair, brushed it away from her forehead, then rested there. For a while she could feel him awake, could feel that he was thinking about her, wondering something, but she didn't know what. Worried—he was worried, she thought. After a while his hand grew heavy on her head and he was breathing deeply, was asleep again.

...

Primmy came with supplies, the boy Sy with him. They had come before; this was the second time. Last time they had left with Sully's roo skins roped to the donkey. They took them into Norfolk Plains and sold them for him, kept a percentage of it for themselves.

Sy was a strange boy, talkative one minute and then falling into long silences the next. When they were here before he'd been out the front of the hut, jabbing at the air with an imaginary sword. 'Take that. And that. And that.

'One day I'll be famous in the whole of Van Diemen's Land. Sir Symon I'll be called, and I'll have so many medals I won't even be able to walk. Gold medals they'll be, won't they, Primmy? They'll be gold.'

Primmy didn't say anything, kept piling skins onto the donkey.

The boy was quiet for a moment and then he came and sat down next to Bridget. 'Have you ever seen one?'

'What?'

'A dragon.'

'No.'

'They're up on the mountain. Big ones, with eyes like this.' He opened his eyes wide. 'One come down to our hut one night and were outside breathing fire. Haaaaaa.' The boy's breath warm near Bridget's neck. 'Last time it come I went out and I were gunna stick it through its heart only it saw me and run off back to the mountain to its cave where it lives. But one day I'm gunna go up there and I'll get them all and then I'll be King of Van Diemen's Land and all the people who don't do what I say can go in my dungeon 'cept for the ones that are slaves.'

Primmy laughed then and Bridget smiled.

Sy had just turned up one day, Sully said. Primmy had been assigned to a bloke out near the North Esk River and 'one day this kid turns up starving and won't say where he come from, who he belonged to or nothing. Been with Primmy ever since.'

The two of them unloaded the donkey—candles, flour, salt, sugar, tea, tobacco and gunpowder. They stayed the night in the hut and in the morning she sat outside with them, she and Primmy smoking pipes. They ate damper and Trousers turned up. Primmy passed him a pipe. Sully brought cider out. 'Missus,' Trousers said, and grinned across at her.

The morning was sunny and cold and their smoke lingered around them. 'Your blokes,' Trousers said, looked at Bridget, 'that gov'nor say, go after them. Find them blokes.' He drew on the pipe. 'We take them out long way. Tell them, you go up there. That the right way. You find them blokes up thatta way.' He grinned. 'Them fellas gone way way away, not find your blokes, missus. We pull that colonel's leg.'

'Could've got yourself in trouble,' Primmy said.

'Trouble?' Trousers grinned. 'Already in trouble.'

'They're not my blokes,' she said quietly. Only Primmy heard, glanced at her.

'That gov'nor him mate come, he riding on that horse, say that one there, that one mountain—him called Brown Mountain. This other one—him called Table Mountain. What he know about that one name?' Trousers looked over at Primmy. 'I tell you—you name George.' Sy giggled. 'What you say then? You name George then because I say that one you name? You tell me bloody bullshit. "My name Joe Primrose. You bloody crazy fella?" That what you say.'

Primmy packed a pipe, nodded. 'I might say that,' he said. 'I just might say that.' He glanced across at Bridget, a smile on his face.

There was a long silence and then Sy stood up. 'There was these knights, twelve of 'em . . . I think it were twelve . . . Anyway, it don't matter. There was these knights and they was looking for something, something they needed to find real bad, only the thing were, they couldn't find the thing. You know why? 'Cause it's a mystery, that's why. A mystery is a thing where there's something what happens, only you don't know the answer and you might not never know the answer. Which is different to God though. God ain't a mystery.'

Sully laughed, ruffled the boy's hair.

Trousers had sat in silence, frowning, during Sy's story. After a while he got up and walked off.

'He wants guns,' Sully said. He spoke to Primmy, said Trousers had asked him to get guns for him. 'Told him I couldn't just get guns. "This hunting ground's not yours," he said. Told him I knew it wasn't bloody mine. He says its theirs, gov'nor probably says it's the king's, some farmer'll come out here one day with a piece of paper says it's his, and not long now neither. "I don't know whose bloody hunting ground it is," I said, "but I been giving you flour and sugar ever since I bloody got here, I do know that." So then he says again that I have to get him guns. "Whitefella kill plenty blackfella," he tells me. "Kill women, piccaninnies." I asked him, "Do you think they're going to stop killing you because you kill them?" He didn't say much then, buggered off. Today's the first day I've seen him since.' Sully chucked the stick he'd been chewing on the ground. 'They can't win this.' He used his boot to grind the stick into the dirt. 'Can't bloody win this.'

...

That night he sat by the fire drinking cider. 'This time,' he said—and his voice was quiet and he leaned down and put his drink down on the floor—'I ain't been in Van Diemen's Land long. Were out hunting roo, few mile upriver from town. It were a windy day.' He paused, squinted at the fire, and when he spoke again his voice seemed even more faraway. 'I remember it were real windy. I come up this slope. Come to the top of the rise and I seen them there. I seen them. I knew what I were seeing. I knew it alright, but . . . sometimes you can see a thing, you know what it is, but you can't *figure it out.* So I stood there. I just stood there.

Little kids and everything. The dogs sniffing at them. I turned round and just about run down the hill.

'Blacks,' he said. 'All of them shot.'

He leaned over and picked up his drink. He didn't look at her. Didn't move. Just kept sitting there staring at the fire.

...

The next day Sully was still quiet. He sat smoking his pipe on the log at the front of the hut, looking up at the mountain.

When he first came to Van Diemen's Land, he said, Hobart Town was just a few tents, mostly soldiers and convicts, hardly any settlers. The governor had sent him out into the bush to hunt kangaroo. He could have stayed out there then, he said, not gone back. In the years he'd been in Van Diemen's Land—and there were plenty of them—more and more settlers had come, more and more land granted to them and the Van Diemen's Land Company. He gazed into the trees. 'West, out beyond the settlement on the Clyde River. A river out there—the Shannon—magnificent place. One place a person might still be left in peace,' he said.

...

Winter in the valley had a face. A white ice face with no eyes. A voice that spoke through the cold mad blabbering of the river. The river flowed over rocks and played a tune of them, each one it touched a different pitch; it stroked and cajoled them and they told their musical stories that fell on all but deaf ears. The white face of winter felt nothing. It was a beautiful criminal. Adept. When the white ice face died, it would give off no smell.

...

Sully was bringing wood in when he dropped the logs, gripped his chest, put his other hand out to steady himself against the fireplace. When she went to him he pushed her away. 'Piss off.' He bent to pick up the logs and she saw the grimace, the stiffness in his movements.

A few days later, on a clear cold day, she sat with him and Primmy outside the hut smoking. 'People say all sorts of rubbish, how a man should live, what he should do, shouldn't do. They'll shake their head, give it some kinda fancy name—call it sin, or whatever fine words they come up with. Most of the time, they don't know nothing. In the end, it's living and dying what matters. That's it. Living and dying.'

'You can do whatever you want then?' Primmy said.

'No. You can do what you have to do. And then find a way to live with it.'

'Right.' He grinned and Bridget saw the cheek glimmering in his eyes. 'And what if you can't, John?'

'Then you drink, Joseph. You drink.'

Primmy chuckled and Sully was quiet a while then, smoking and looking into the trees. 'A good place to die,' he said, spitting a bit of tobacco out of his mouth. 'Nowhere better,' he said.

The next day, after Primmy was gone, he took her to the river downstream from the hut, said there was something he wanted to show her. He stood close to the edge of the river, pointed at the island in the middle. 'That's where I want to be buried!' he yelled over the rush of the water. Bridget made a face at him. Why was he telling her this? 'On that island. You see it?'

Of course she saw it.

...

Primmy and Sy came through snow with supplies and news—Primmy had been granted a Ticket of Leave, would be going. Beadle would take the skins into Norfolk Plains for Sully, bring back supplies. Sully said no, he wasn't dealing with Beadle. Primmy didn't say anything then, just that he was going, wouldn't be back. Sy was going with him.

The hut where Beadle, Primmy and Sy lived was half a day's walk from Sully's. The men were convict shepherds assigned to a sheep thief called Albert Little. Primmy and Beadle kept his sheep for him out there where the law wouldn't come looking. The sheep that grazed near Sully's had also belonged to their master—some arrangement between Sully and Primmy. But Primmy had taken the sheep now, took them when he left.

...

Sully sat in his chair smoking. 'Ain't been off this mountain in three years,' he said, 'maybe more. Ain't got no desire to. None at all.' His smoke disappeared into the trees that he was talking to. 'Don't fucking trust him,' he said about Beadle. 'Be going into Norfolk Plains myself. Don't trust that bastard.'

The first night Sully was gone she lay awake listening to every crack, every growl, every groan. He'd taken two dogs, three of them still there with her. 'No,' he'd said, when she said she wanted to go with him. 'Stay here. Be back in a few days.' With Sully gone the hut felt even colder. She'd sewn trousers and a coat, both from roo skins. She wore them now, more skins piled over her. Darkness and silence wrapped tight around her. So cosy they were, the two of them. Cheek to cheek, they danced a slow cold dance that sounded like, felt like, the waltz of death.

When she went outside in the night, she squatted, peering into the dark, the trousers dropped around her ankles, and then hurried back to the hut, shut the door hard and fast behind her, pushed the lock across. Then she took Sully's shotgun, put it in the hammock next to her.

Now and then through the night came the squeal of the animals they called devils, or the low growl of a possum. In the morning she opened the hut door and looked out at the rain, later the sharp black rock shining in dull light. In the long, cold afternoon she saw her own past in the dark between the trees, just as she had been for weeks now. Everything that had never been and could not be spoken hissed through the cold white air.

...

She didn't know how old she was when Barbara came to the small cottage with her three children, Philip, Maria and Susan, who, when food was low, were always fed before Bridget, Stephen and Kate.

'Stupid girl. Say sorry.' Smacks hitting her arms that were raised over her head. She tried to make it, tried to make the word *sorry*. Down at the river she threw sticks in the river, silently told her wish to the cool air. *I wish my mother would come back.*

...

Kate married Michael Knox, a wheelwright from a nearby village, Bury St Edmunds. The first baby, Alfie, came and then after the second one was born Bridget went to live with them. She helped around the cottage and with the baby Phoebe, who would sit on the floor and giggle, put out her fat little hand and pull Bridget's face to hers, put her whole wet mouth over Bridget's nose. A few years of peace there then, a few years to hold up to the light, see the sun shining through. Three of them, three years, and then the doctor writing saying Father's cough was bad that winter, saying you're needed there now, Bridget. That your father is asking for you. That perhaps he might not last the winter. But he did, and Timmy Crack came calling.

She had known Timothy Crack since she was a child. He had been her brother's best friend and had always been around. She was seventeen when they were married, on a rainy November day. They lived in a hut then on the property of Mr Rochester, the farmer who Timmy worked for. Bridget got work in the dairy. At lunchtime Timmy would grin at her across the table and at night they drank and he told her stories, his favourite an absurd tale about a one-eyed ferret. Then he started talking about Manchester. They would do well there, he said; have a good life. He knew someone there who could get him a better job. Bridget walked the four miles to Bury St Edmunds to tell Kate she wasn't going; she was staying there with her. 'He's your husband, Bridget. You should go,' Kate said. She didn't look at her, hoicked Phoebe onto her hip.

...

Manchester. A wet rag of a place, a world of mud and shit and smoke and clatter, everyone climbing on everyone else to get a view of something they called the future. He led her through rain along muddy lanes where packs of soaked, barefoot children ran up and down, sliding in the mud, to a makeshift two-room cottage where his friend, Andrew Potts, known to most only as Potts, lived with Maggie and their two little children. Potts with his big-noting, loud, fun-loving ways. She saw straight away how Timmy looked up to him.

It had been alright for a while. There were people around all the time: music, drinking and dancing. Everyone living in the muddy lanes knew Potts, patted Timmy on the back and liked him because he was Potts's friend. Then the baby came and three days later left again, her tiny face grey in the cold morning. Timmy, who'd been drinking with Potts, drank more then, was out all the time. Working with Potts, he said. And she knew by then what Potts's work was—he was a forger, forging coins. In the night Timmy turned away from her as though she'd done something to make it happen, as though it were her fault the small pink bundle had left them so soon. Soon she started to think maybe she had.

The new life sagged and drooped. The expectation drained out of her and reality set like drying mud in the bottom of her stomach. Timmy started getting round with Milly Robinson. Bridget knew he was; everyone knew he was. Then one day at the bakery the woman turned the coin Bridget had given her over in her hand. She had not long left the bakery when two constables appeared, grabbed her arms.

She had known what the coins were, but they needed food. She said she'd found them, only later gave them Potts's name. In the gaol she waited to see if someone was going to come, if Timmy would go to the constable, to the gaol, to tell them he'd given her the coins. No one had come.

...

'Van Demon's Land.' The name had sounded strange to her ears.

...

The days trembled then slipped into darkness. In the afternoon she heard a dog bark in the distance. One of the dogs Sully had left with her—Noah, his favourite—started hollering, a look of excitement and knowing on his face. Bridget stood up from the fire, fought the urge to run to the door.

Light of spring. Bright springtime angel. The sweetest voice. Now the river was fast. It spoke as though it had a sermon to deliver, a desperate message, but no time to deliver it. The river in its drunken springtime plight.

Sully took her across the drier slopes to collect seeds and berries, vicious red, that they ate back at the hut.

...

It was a clear and cold morning and Bridget was fumbling through the dark to open the door. Sully was usually up before her. She usually woke to him moving around the hut, the scrape of the door opening. She left him to sleep, went down to the river. When she came back up he still hadn't moved. Bridget went over to him. He was faced towards the dead fire, the fur blanket pulled up close to his face.

'Sully.'

Nothing.

'Sully?' She touched his arm then. Drew it back, fast and sharp. She took a step back. Noah came in and went over to Sully, whined and wagged his tail then sat down against him.

'Sully?' she said, quietly now.

...

Bridget stood over him, pulled on the arm furthest away from her and rolled him over. Then she pulled the fur up over his head.

Outside a light wind stroked the hut. She sat down next to him. Noah, excited by the strange snuffling noises, the sounds of human crying, came over and tried to lick her face. She pushed him off and he lay down on the other side of Sully.

...

In the morning she walked along the faint track that went to Beadle's. Didn't get far before she came back again. Sully didn't like Beadle; wouldn't want him here.

She took the spade from where it leaned against the wood stack, went down to the river, all the dogs following her.

On the little island she went into the bush and stopped in what seemed like the middle between two sassafras trees. The spade hit the ground and hardly penetrated, sent a jolt up her arm and into her body. She swore and threw the spade hard. She stood there, then went and got the spade, smacked it back into the unyielding ground.

...

Bridget held the needle in the fire, her hand shaking. The left sleeve of her shirt was rolled up to the elbow, the soft skin of the inside of her arm exposed. She dipped the needle into the gunpowder, pushed the dark tip of it into her skin until a tiny drop of blood appeared. Noah was whimpering by the door. She got up, let him out. The fire was lighting the shape that was Sully near his chair where she had moved him and piled skins over him.

She put the needle back in the fire, dipped it into the gunpowder. There were a lot of dots now, red around the steel-grey of the gunpowder, the dots joining up to form an arc. She sat pricking the dots into her arm long into the night, then she lay down and pulled two fur blankets over her head.

...

The sun was twinkling on the slow water upstream but where she stood opposite the island, the shallow river was rough and loud with rapids. She stood looking over at the island and then around at the trees. Behind her was a tree with a speckled trunk, wide dark green leaves. Bridget wrapped the rope around it a few times and tied it. She took the other end with her, picked her way slowly across the river, the water above her knees, the bottom covered with rocks. On the other side she attached the rope to another tree, came back over, one hand on the rope to steady herself against the rush and pull of the river.

...

She dragged him to the door. Noah watched and barked. She was a long time dragging him down there. Leaves gathered in his hair, he bumped over rocks. There was nothing else she could do.

...

He was lying in the leaves next to the river opposite the island. She took off his boots, left them on the bank. In the river she struggled to stay upright and hold on to the top half of him. His legs headed downstream. She fell, felt herself getting swept away, grabbed the rope, her head just above the water. She leaned out into the current, grabbed Sully's arm with her free hand, the other one holding the rope. Eventually she brought the body in tight against her, rested there in the middle of the river and then started again.

She nearly lost him again near the bank, grabbed him under the arms and dragged him onto the firm ground of the island. She rested a while then dragged him through the scrub to the place where she had pounded at the ground. It was more an area of disturbed moss and exposed roots than a hole, but she had dug there until sunset to make it. She lay him down on it then went back up to the hut, came back down with a crude cross made from two bits of wood cut and tied together with twine. She collected rocks and built them around the cross.

...

Sully's armchair. Sully's hammock, barrels and sacks and furs, Sully's guns and powder horn. Noah sat in the doorway watching her, wagged his tail.

She lay awake for a long time listening to the splutter of the night. There was salted meat—that would last a while. With the dogs she could get more. There was about a quarter of a sack of flour, a few handfuls of sugar. Not much left of one candle.

There was a growl outside. She had brought all of the dogs into the hut with her. They woke up now, barked. The dogs sat looking at the door and then lay back down. She threw another log onto the fire. The flames lifted and the shadow of her and the dogs grew large on the hut wall.

...

Sky raw ripping blue, a light falling of snow. The swelling went from the skin of her inner arm, the rawness and pinkness faded so that all that was left was the colour of the gunpowder. In the firelight she could see it: inch-long scythe shape, the outline filled. A dark grey new moon.

...

Bridget followed the track all day, Noah and Job with her, the other three dogs locked in the hut. It was dusk when she came to the frayed rope slung over the river, tied between trees on either side, the bottom of the rope brushing the water. A track led up the bank into the bush. She walked up and stood in the trees at the edge of the clearing. Close to where she was standing on the track were pieces of a broken water cask, the timber rotting into the soil next to a bottlebrush tree.

Smoke came from the hut's chimney. After a while a figure came from around the side of the hut. Beadle. She watched him go inside the hut, take the dogs with him.

...

Beadle looked at the tin of nails, knife and gun she'd put on the table. It wasn't enough for the supplies she wanted, he said. She said he could have one of the dogs. She knew that hunting dogs were worth a lot. The men had talked about it. Sam had found a puppy in a trap on their way to Norfolk Plains, the trap having cut its leg all the way through to the bone. Little brown puppy. It was lying there with its eyes half closed, whimpering. Henry said to shoot it but Sam had opened the trap and picked it up. Matt said it was probably wild, that there were packs of wild dogs around—hunting dogs that had got away and bred. 'Doesn't look wild,' Sam said. When he'd freed it, it had hardly moved. He wrapped it up in a fur and carried it all day. He tried to get it to take water from the creek off his fingers, to eat some meat, but it wouldn't. Henry laughed at him carrying it. 'Sell it,' Sam said, 'get a good price for it.' That night, after Henry and Matt were asleep, Sam sat up by the fire with the puppy. It was shaking. He had said he was going to find a cow in the morning, get some milk for it. Bridget was awake, saw him put his finger down to it, the puppy lick his finger. She saw it when it died there in his arms. In the light from the fire she saw the film of moisture come over Sam's eyes. In the morning he'd buried it, Henry shaking his head. That day Sam was quiet. But that wasn't new; Sam was mostly quiet.

'Not yours to sell,' Beadle said.

'They are now.'

'Not going to Norfolk Plains,' he said. Things he had more of a need for than dogs, he said, his gaze sliding over her body.

He kept the gun, gave her a sack with not more than a few handfuls of flour in it.

When she left he stood out the front of the hut and watched her go.

...

She ran out of wood. She cut more but it was too wet too burn. She went down the valley looking for drier wood, made her way back to the hut exhausted, scratched and muddy. The wood was wrapped in hessian slung across her back. She hoisted it higher and plodded on through the mud.

Finally, she could see the hut. She stopped.

Something wasn't right. Her stomach tightened and the back of her neck prickled. She put the wood down and pulled the gun out of Sully's belt she wore, held it firmly in her hand. It still felt strange. Matt's gun had looked like an extension of his arm. He handled it with familiarity, but she still felt almost as awkward with this gun now as she had the first time she'd picked it up.

She walked slowly towards the hut, and when she was close stopped behind a tree and listened. Hiss of wind, run of the river, caw of a crow. Her breath had become short and sharp and her heart knocked its distress against her chest. Noah and the other dogs were around her; they weren't barking or growling, only appeared curious about what she was doing, but still the uneasy feeling in her stomach remained.

She walked to the hut with the gun held out in front of her, unlatched the door and pushed it open. She stood in the doorway pointing the gun into the semi-darkness. Nothing: the fireplace at one end, everything around it just as she had left it. She went outside and looked behind the hut, checked the bushes all around.

This had happened a few days before when she had come back from the river. She had come up the bank and had that same feeling: that someone was there, or had been there.

On moonlit nights, when she went outside, rocks and stumps became animals and shadows morphed into people. Now she stood looking up at the top of the mountain and then down the other way towards the valley, towards lower land where the wind blew warmer. Then she went back down the hill to get the wood.

...

She lay awake listening to the hiss and growl of possums, looked around now at the dark shapes of the dogs on the floor. The fire was almost out. There was not much cut wood left again. There was only a stub of a candle. No flour, no tobacco, no sugar. She had eaten all the potatoes that had been left in the garden.

Early in the morning she took the dogs and shut the hut door behind her.

...

Spring had brought out the yellow flowers on the wattle trees that crowded the slopes of the lower valleys. The nights were less freezing and some days a warm breeze blew across the clearing. Bridget lay awake listening to the raspy draw of Jack Beadle's breath.

...

She woke to crisp air, scratched at her scalp. She sat up and Noah stirred. Over in the hammock Beadle didn't move. Outside a dog barked and Beadle sat up suddenly. Noah had started up a racket and Beadle grabbed his gun, pulled trousers on as he made his way towards the door.

'Primrose!'

The voice was outside the door. Bridget knew it. Knew it immediately.

She saw the door open, felt the cold come in, saw Matt standing there in the doorway, saw him glance at her then look straight at Beadle, who started to say something. The shot sent Beadle backwards. He lay half on the table, a gaping pulpy mess where his chest had been.

...

Matt pushed her hard. He pulled her up, pushed her along in front of him again.

Bridget faced him and he stood glaring at her. Back at the hut he'd looked at her belly, had seen there was no fullness to it. 'Where is it?' he said now.

She shook her head. 'Gone.'

He stood there glowering and she looked straight at him. 'It's gone.'

Sam was a few yards away down the slope now, arms by his side. He said nothing but his gaze was calm and even and he had a way of making Matt feel ashamed just by the way he was.

Matt walked past them into the scrub.

Marshall walked with Mr Blessington over the field. 'Broad daylight,' Blessington said. 'We were inside eating lunch when Riley, the servant, came running in and said there were natives here. They were standing over there.' Blessington pointed to a place where a flock of sheep grazed in front of a stand of trees. 'Ten or so of them. A couple of them with burning sticks. I fired a shot into the trees there. They just stood there, so I fired again. They went then, thankfully. But they could still be around here.' He looked around at the clumps of trees that skirted the field.

'You know they burned all of Carlow's hay a few months ago,' he said as they turned to walk back to the house. 'I never go anywhere without this now.' Raising his gun. 'And I'm very glad you and the other soldiers are here. I know you're here for the bushrangers, but, well, with all this business—' he nodded at the field—'I know Cathy is pleased you are here, and I must say, I am too.'

...

The governor had sent Marshall out here to Mr Blessington's large land grant on the Macquarie River. He had Lieutenant

Pullen with him and three privates. Colonel Gower had taken another group to a property near York Plains. Arthur was sending parties of soldiers out to be stationed on settlers' properties so that if the bushrangers struck, they would be there, ready. Previously it had generally taken up to a day for a settler to reach a constable to report a robbery, and then another day at least for the constable to gather men and reach the property, by which time the bushrangers were long gone, most likely on their way back to the mountains. And many of the constables were also less than enthusiastic.

So far, however, from what Marshall has heard, most of the soldiers had spent the days sitting around drinking and flirting with the settlers' daughters. There had been no sign of Sheedy at any of the properties.

'Someone mentioned that the woman with them was your servant at some time,' Blessington said as they crossed the field and neared the house.

'Yes. That's true.'

'Hmph. They really are degraded, some of them, aren't they?'

'Who are?'

Blessington looked at him. 'The female convicts.'

'Oh,' Marshall said. 'Yes. Yes, I suppose they are.'

He had been thinking: the last time the Sheedy gang had been sighted there had reportedly been no woman with them.

'Last time I was in Hobart Town I saw a couple of them fighting in the street. One was pulling the other's hair, and then the other one punched her. With her fist, mind you. Fair in the face. And the swearing and cursing that was coming from them—it was really quite something,' Blessington said, laughing.

'Hm,' Marshall said, forced a grin.

Giggling came from the lawn. Blessington's daughter, Louisa. Pullen had strung a rope between two trees, was trying to walk across it. He had just fallen off.

'Daddy,' she called, 'Lieutenant Pullen is going to leave the army and join the circus!'

Blessington turned to Marshall, raised his eyebrows.

All the talk was of China. They were going to the coast. Had a boat organised, Matt boasted, drunk. He picked up the bottle, swigged. His beard had grown back. He was ugly. Ugly and there was something wrong with him—worse than before. It was as though whatever faint stitching had held him together had finally come apart.

The next day when he hit her she walked off into the scrub but he came after her, scruffed her. 'Where do you think you're going?' He said she should be more grateful, said again that he'd saved her; that she owed him, that she'd be dead without him. Then he said that in China he'd get her whatever she wanted, that he'd get her whatever she wanted in China.

...

'You should come. Come to China, Bridge. It'll be better when we're there,' Sam said. He looked at Matt, who was sitting on a rock sharpening his knife. 'He'll be better. He'll be alright once we're there.'

...

Henry spoke over his shoulder. 'This is part of Cantwell's property. Owns just about half the flaming colony. His shepherd's a bloke called Peter Murray. Met him a couple of times.'

They were coming up to the hut when Henry stopped. Matt stopped behind him. On the ground ahead of them a man lay face down, a spear sticking out of the middle of his back and one out of the side of his thigh.

'Aw,' Henry said. 'He don't look too well.'

Matt bent over the man. 'Hasn't been well for a while.'

His clothes were ripped at the bottom of his ribcage and the flesh there ruined where something had been feeding on him.

Henry looked around, drew his gun and went up to the hut door. He pushed it open then came back out. 'Nothing left here.'

Matt walked up to the hut, looked inside. 'We keep going.'

...

They camped that night by a slow-moving creek, the water tea-coloured, doilies of foam floating on its surface.

Henry was quieter than usual. There was another man with them—Pascoe. They had picked him up; he was taking them to the coast, Matt said. Pascoe was on edge, wanted to camp somewhere else. 'They'll get us. Come get us in the night while we're sleeping. I tell ya, they will, they'll get us.'

'If they're gunna get us, they'll get us anywhere. Here, there . . .' Henry stretched out his arm, indicating the land all around. 'Anywhere.'

'Reckon we should take it in turns to watch out.'

Matt chucked wood on the fire, a splash of sparks. 'You so worried about them, you watch.'

Bridget lay awake, could hear Pascoe moving around. There was a crack in the branches on the other side of the river.

Pascoe hissed at Matt, 'Wake up.'

'I'm fucking awake.'

'You hear that?'

'What?'

'That were too loud for an animal.'

'Go fucking shoot it then.' Matt rolled over, his back to Pascoe.

Pascoe walked down to the creek, stood near the bank looking. She heard him come back again.

Matt sat up. 'For fuck's sake, fucking lie down.'

'They'll kill us.'

'Don't shut up, I'll kill you myself,' Matt said.

...

They slogged their way through mud up to their knees. It had been showering most of the morning. Matt yelled ahead to Pascoe, 'Are you sure you know where the bloody hell you're going?'

His voice flew back on the wind. 'This's the shortest way.'

They had been walking for days. On the way to China, Matt said in the dark, his breath stinking like something dead.

At the end of the plain they stood on a hummock. The plain before them looked like the one they had just crossed: long yellow grass shiny with moisture extending out towards a treed ridge in the distance. Plumes of dark cloud massed above them and soon spat their wet peril. They stood like cattle under a tree that was hardly any shelter at all. Bridget felt the water make it through her clothes, tiny rills of it run down her front. Her hair was soaked through, water dripping off the ends of it. Next to her Sam was standing looking up into the thin canopy, rain falling into his face.

...

The hut was behind a marshland of reeds and the sound of frogs peppered the night. The men—Slambow, Havercock and Canning—as dank and dark as the hut they lived in. Their clothes dark blue and brown, their skin tan with dirt, their faces shadowy and set in harshness, they seemed to have been taken over by the black corners of the hut, to have become of the dirt and shadow, no longer at all separate from it, so that when one of them rose and moved, the fire flicking over his form, he was like a spectre stepping out of darkness. And behind them, even more within the dark than the men, four women, bent over their work, quiet as mounds of dirt. The brown children played mostly outside the hut, thrashed like angry snakes, until one of the men came out, at which they moved further away from the hut, or grew quiet, looked down at the ground, all thrash and buzz gone from their lithe little bodies. Slambow wore a sealskin hat, arms covered with tattoos, hair thick with grease around a scarred face. Havercock also tattooed, dry and brittle-looking, like beached seaweed. Canning, quiet, a faraway look in his eyes and a smile like a waving flag—the only one of the three whose facial muscles bore the memory of mirth.

...

At first glance she thought it was sky, took a moment to realise what she was looking at: water. A lot of water. Water stretching all the way to a hazy horizon. Soon the smell of salt was strong. From up on a rise they could see down over the river that snaked out to the coast, wide at its mouth. Then, there ahead of them was a long stretch of white beach, dunes behind it all the way along except where the river came in.

The river water was still and dark brown, tea tree growing close to its banks. Closer to the beach the river opened out and black swans with red beaks bobbed around, the wind ruffling their feathers. The five of them trekked along the side of the estuary, walked into the wind, their heads down, the sand whipping up into their faces. Huge waves rolled in, the sea a mass of white breakers. 'They won't be getting in here in this,' Henry yelled.

Slambow led them down the beach a long way from the river mouth to a place where the shore became rocky and another river entered. They sat up in the dunes behind the shore out of the howling wind, looked out onto the grey coughing sea. Bridget wanted to get up and run, keep running back towards the plains. Matt would come after her, cart her back here. He was focused on the sea now though, concentrating. She might be able to sneak away. Pascoe had stayed up at the hut, was going back to the road. She could follow him back to the road. Where then though? Where from the road?

She wouldn't be able to get away anyway. At night, if she so much as moved, he woke up. He'd come after her. She wouldn't get more than a few yards through the dunes before he'd have hold of her.

The boat was going to New South Wales. She'd find a way to get away from him then, stay in New South Wales. The panic that was in her wanted her moving. But she sat. She sat and the fear turned to heat that spread through her, had her feeling sick.

They sat in the dunes for a long time but the ocean kept on being black and lumpy, and only black and lumpy; there was no boat.

As they waited the wind dropped and the moon came up. It was quiet without the roar of the waves, the night clear and still, moon shining gold on black water.

...

For the next four days and nights they camped in the dunes, Henry and Sam going back and forth to the hut, bringing food and water. Sam shot a black swan that they roasted. It was on the fifth day, later in the afternoon, that Sam saw it. A boat, sails full, a good way out from the shore. 'You beauty,' Matt said. 'We're going, boys! We're going!' He was loud now, was jumping around in the sand like a puppy. Sam started hooting and crying. Only Bridget and Henry stood still looking at the boat.

Matt and Sam ran down to the water, Henry walking behind them. Bridget followed them down, stood back near the dunes. It wasn't coming in. The boat was going past. Matt ran up and down the beach yelling, waving his arms. When it was well gone he sat down in the shallow river that ran across the sand towards the waves. She was a long way behind him but she could see his shoulders shaking, could just hear the low sound of his keening. Sam walked over and stood next to him. Henry sat down where he was, picked up clods of sand and threw them at the water. Bridget watched the boat getting small. She imagined being on it, going back to England; a great roar of longing reached out after it.

...

'Arseholes. Bastards. Curs and sons of bitches.' Matt was walking and swearing, ranting about someone in Hobart Town. It had been clear, arranged. He'd paid him. He would kill him. He would fucking kill the mongrel. Why was every bloody person he ever met such an untrustworthy goddamn bugger of a filthy fucking cur?

No one else spoke. Everyone walked.

...

Again the plains rolled out like dough below them, wet and shining. Matt had been quiet for a few hours, his brow knotted in its well-worn frown. He dropped a sack of flour in front of her feet. 'Make damper.'

She left the sack there, didn't immediately pick it up. She was sick of him and his orders. Sick of everything about him.

He grabbed the back of her neck, held it hard, his thumb and forefinger biting into her muscles.

He picked up the sack of flour and before she knew what was happening her face was in it. He was pushing the back of her head. She needed to breathe, her nose filled with flour. She needed to cough but couldn't; there was no room, no air. Flour clogged her throat and a loud rasp came from her.

Suddenly she was released.

She gulped and coughed, held her head.

Henry had the sack, pushed Matt. 'Easy. Settle down.'

Matt stood there, eyes like a frightened horse.

Her legs were shaking. She needed to sit. Needed to sit.

Matt walked off.

Her legs folded under her and she half sat, half fell where she was.

Henry put a water bladder in front of her face. She took it off him, sat it on the ground. She sat there trying to breathe, looked up to see Sam standing staring at her, mute. She looked away from him.

They took two horses from a big house on a brisk, sunny afternoon, camped just before dark on a rocky hill among trees. It was windy enough for the boughs to crack and for the falling of bark to have Matt on his feet peering through the trees. The horses were restless, stomping and snorting, pulling on their tethers. Matt paced for a while and then sat on a fallen log close to where the fire smoked. A moment later one of the dogs barked and Matt was up. He kicked Henry. Henry groaned. 'Bit of bloody wind.'

'Shut up. Listen.'

Bridget sat up. There was a noise, faint but audible, from down the slope. Someone had shouted.

Matt was listening intently. She could go. Go now. The men had been discussing crossing the road—it mustn't be too far away.

She was about to move when Henry got to his feet, gun out. 'Get the horses!'

There was a flurry of activity. Sam had hold of one of the horse's bridles and, spooked, it pulled back, wrenching his shoulder. Henry grabbed the reins and a second later was up in the saddle. Matt had one foot in the stirrup of the other horse;

as he lifted himself up a shot passed behind the horse. Henry returned fire and now Matt's horse bolted forward, almost unseating him. He circled back. 'Get up! Get up!'

There were more voices now, more shouting. 'We've got them, sir. We've got them!'

Matt's hand was out, the palm facing up. She didn't move.

There was a shot. Caesar whimpered, his hindquarters collapsed into the ground.

Another shot. Sam was up on the horse behind Henry but now he fell to the side. Henry swore. The horse spun around and Sam fell. He groaned, held his hand out to Henry above him. Matt looked down at Sam. He was lying on the ground, his back bleeding. Matt yelled at her again. 'Get up!'

'You can't leave him!'

Another shot came. She stepped forward and the next thing she knew she was pressed against Matt's back and the dying light was full of the sound of the horse's hooves striking rock, of the flick of branches.

...

A crack of light showed near the horizon, a great shimmering yolk growing from it. The horses were walking now, their heads low. She took her stiff hand away from Matt's waist, where it had been clamped for hours, let it drop near her thigh.

They would stop soon and she would be able to get down. She let her head drop. Blood. There was blood all over her hand. Up ahead Henry stopped, turned around and the look on his face confirmed it. 'Jesus Christ.'

She almost fell as she reached the ground, her legs so unused to taking her weight. Henry took most of Matt's weight, lowered him down.

'Need a rest,' Matt said. His eyes were glassy.

'Why the bloody hell didn't you say something?' Henry looked around. 'Fuck.'

'Just need a rest. Get back on. I'll get back on.'

'You're shot in the guts, man.'

'I'll be right.' Matt's eyes half closed.

'Stay here with him. I'm going to get someone. You hear me? Stay here with him. Find some water. Can you do that?' Henry grabbed the horse's reins.

'Where are you going? You can't just leave me here with him.'

'Don't go anywhere. Stay here. You better bloody do this, you hear me? You fucking look after him. Look after him.' He turned the horse, was gone in a shower of soil.

'Don't know where he thinks he's going.' Talking hurt him, his hand going to his waist.

Matt sat up a bit, lifted his shirt and looked. The wound was dark red in the middle, where there was a hole, brighter towards the edges. The hair of his stomach sticky with blood.

He swore and lay back down.

Bridget walked down the slope and listened, stood seeking the sound of water as golden light spilled over the hills.

He was sitting up, one arm on the ground supporting him, the other one holding the bottom of the horse's leg. There was a knife on the ground next to him. When he heard her, he stopped, turned around. His mouth was red. The animal flicked its leg. Matt tightened his grip, put his mouth back over the wound he'd made.

He slept. She watched the horse, a trickle of dry blood now underneath the wound on its leg. He had cut the reins of the bridle and used the leather to hobble it. Her mouth was dry; she was dizzy from lack of sleep and food. She patted the horse's neck, squatted beside it. It looked down at her, curious.

Its flesh was warm against her mouth. She sucked and it lifted its leg in protest, put it down. She tried again. Nothing. Sucked harder this time.

The blood came in a gush, warm and salty in her mouth. After she'd drunk from it she lay on the ground and slept.

When she woke, there was a fly on his left cheek. Matt didn't flinch. The fly stayed there. It flew off and another one landed on the blood on his shirt and then hovered before landing closer to the middle of the wound.

Bridget stood up. The blue sky had gone, clouds bunched around the middle, more of them coming in now to join the council. She looked up at the rock mass behind them, along the plain towards a stand of trees. His eyes were closed. She stood there staring at him, at the body drained of tension, at the fly above his right eyebrow.

The horse was lying down. It wouldn't get up. She pulled on its head and it made an attempt. Then its head sunk to the ground again, its eyes closed.

'Come on. Get up.'

The horse's belly rose and fell. Its eyes slowly opened and closed again.

Bridget sat looking at the horse. A crow stood on a rock a few yards away watching her, tilting its head this way and that as though trying to solve the puzzle that she was.

She picked up the gun from where it lay next to Matt, put her hands under his shoulder and pushed him up to get the powder horn off him, a small handful left in it.

In the night the horse died. Not long after the devils arrived. She lay against the horse's cold side battling sleep, ready with a stick to beat the animals off. Sleep claimed her and she woke to find one of them right next to her, pulling at the flesh of the horse's leg. She hit the animal hard and it squealed and ran off. She could hear them over near Matt. The wet sound of flesh. In the morning light Matt's side was bright red where they had torn it. There were scrape marks on the ground where the pulling had moved his body.

No sign of Henry. No sign of anyone. The valley was filled with death. She picked up the gun from the ground. Then she stood there looking around, trying to see which way to go.

Dogs' cries echoed around the valley and the sound of men shouting reached up the slope. For a while they seemed to have been coming up the valley somewhere to her left, but now it sounded like they were almost directly behind her. She could see the mountain's peak above her, the slope was scrubby and steep and soon she was climbing more than running, rock under her feet giving way and crashing down the slope behind her. She slipped, grabbed a sharp bush that cut her hand. She hoisted herself up again and scrambled over a flat rock then squeezed up through a crevice to an area of loose, smaller rock. She climbed up the side of it and then, when her breath was coming too fast and hard, she stopped, dared to look down. She heard the dogs again but now they seemed to have moved to the right side of the valley and were coming up there towards the foot of the mountain. The cloud was low and it had already started to drizzle.

It was harder to climb now with the rock slippery and she'd come to the steepest part. The peak that was now beginning to be shrouded by cloud was not far above her. Here a spring came out from under one of the rocks. She stopped to drink. She could hear nothing now, but thought she caught a glimpse of the men moving through the trees way below. The cloud was creeping down lower, making its way steadily towards her. She came to a split in the rock shaped like an upside-down V, deep enough for her to fit in.

The weather continued to come in from the other side of the mountain, the clouds darkening. She sat trying to hear through the rain, wondering if they would come up here in this weather. There was no sound now except the howl of the wind across the side of the mountain and the thrashing of the stubby gnarled trees that grew on the slope around her.

She shivered. Darkness came quickly and the storm took hold. If they were coming now, let them come. There was nothing to do but wait.

The storm seemed to possess the strength to pick the mountain up and toss it aside. But the mountain held and Bridget held, although she shivered and her mind grew hazy and hunger gnawed at her. There would be no sleep, only this strange drifting as the world of dreams seeped out of the rock with the cold. In the blackness she saw Rose Hadley.

Bridget had been young, there with her family, most of the district out to see it. When the man slipped the noose over Rose's head Kate had squeezed Bridget's hand. Barbara's voice in her ear later: 'That's what happens to girls who don't behave themselves.'

The memory of Rose Hadley taunted her, poked its bony finger at her face. You, it said. *You.*

Hunger grew sharper, the cold more intense; it curled up in Bridget's bones and purred with sinister content. She rested her head against rock and waited while the demons came and clawed at her face, her ears, her throat, summoned the dark shapes that rode on the back of hunger, of tiredness, that wheezed and unfurled their long, thin black tongues, whispering their words of possession into her ear. She forced herself to look at them, which they hated, and they retreated, their squeals on the wind. They would be back though. They would be back.

By dawn the rain was light and the wind had settled but the mountain was still cloaked in mist so that Bridget could see only a few feet in front of her. She waited until it lifted then found her way back to the spring she had drunk from before and now instead of being a trickle it spread out over the rocks below it.

She climbed slowly to the top of the mountain that was now clear of cloud. The cold wind blew her wet hair and bit through her coat. The ground dropped off sharply, too sharp to climb down. The wind ripped the clouds across the sky, the hills in the distance in shadow and then light and then shadow again as the clouds passed over them.

She could see nothing moving in the landscape, no sign of the men. But that didn't mean they weren't down there somewhere in the trees, waiting.

...

There were four men standing watching her. She was lying at the bottom of a steep drop among leaves. She tried to get up but it hurt. They started talking then. One of them came forward and pointed at her. He pointed again and she looked down to see the powder horn around her neck. She understood he wanted it. She took it off and held it out to him. He grabbed it, thrust another container at her. Water. She drank all of it and he took the container back. He spoke to the man standing behind him then, looked back at her and motioned up the slope. She remembered the fall now, her foot off the side of rock, falling and rolling for a long time.

They made their way easily through the scrub, stopped and waited as she limped her way up the slope. At first it was a sound, a sound without a name, and then as she followed them towards it and the sound became louder there was a word: *river*. River.

At the top of the slope they stood talking. They were talking about her, she thought. One of them looked at her and pointed to the river. Then they turned around and headed back along the slope.

...

She pushed through the scrub with a surge of energy that brought her out onto a column of rock. At the bottom of it flowed an almost-black river laced with trails of white, a rapid further down where it slipped through a gorge. She went back into the scrub and beat down through it to the rapid and then below it to where she could lean down from a rock and touch the water. She lay with her stomach on the rock and drank.

The land on the other side moved in a gentle wave, the trees seeming to slowly rise and fall, and there, near them, was a white building. A cottage. Smoke was coming out of its chimney, rising, rising into the sky. She could smell it in the air. The smell of smoke.

...

She stood behind the tree, dripping wet, her breath a rasp from the cold river crossing. The back of the house was only yards away. Between her and the house there was a pigpen, a pig standing close to the fence. She stood there watching it. The door to the cottage opened and someone came out with a bucket, emptied it into the pen and went back inside. She waited for more movement from the house and when there was none, she walked straight to the pen, stepped in between the railings and put her hand in the slop, pushed the handful into her mouth. The pig tried to push in and she shoved it out of the way. It squealed. Bridget swallowed, took another handful of the food.

The cottage door opened again. A girl stood in the doorway, hands on her hips. 'What are you doing? Mary, Mother of God, get out of there! What are you doing?'

She swallowed, scooped up another handful of the slop.

A woman came out and stood next to the girl, put her hand to her mouth. 'Goodness gracious me. What . . . ?'

'It's a woman,' the girl said. 'It's a woman.'

Bridget felt her stomach turn, reached out for the fence.

It had been the woman who walked forward and opened the gate. The pig had run out, nearly knocking the girl over. The little woman had tried to take Bridget's weight. 'Come on,' she said, 'let's get you inside,' and then the girl had been on the other side of Bridget.

They sat at the table and watched as Bridget ate and then the woman stood next to her while she was sick onto the ground outside. The girl had come in and out of a room with buckets of water and then the woman held Bridget's naked arm to support her while she stepped into the tub.

Later she lay on a wide bed in a clean, tidy room. On the wall was a painting of what looked like an English lane and house. She fell asleep, was aware sometime, maybe more than once, of someone coming into the room, going again. She woke, sat up, drank from a cup the woman held and then slept again.

The next time she woke there were voices outside the door. A man's voice. 'I will go in tomorrow.'

'She needs a doctor, that gash on her head is nasty. It needs seeing to.' The woman now. Bridget remembered her: short and grey-haired with the voice of a little girl.

Bridget put her hand up to her head, found the cut above her right eyebrow. She tried to remember. She didn't know how she had done it. She must have fallen. Had she fallen? Now she did remember. The gun had gone in the fall. She had been trying to shoot something—an animal. They were too fast, thumped away into the bushes. She remembered the men, the river, she had taken her coat off before the river crossing, left it on a rock. She looked around for her clothes, remembered taking them off by the tub. She was wearing a gown now, crisp and clean-smelling, white.

'Who is going to pay for this?'

'We don't know yet, do we? Surely we have to give her the benefit of the doubt. Anything could've happened.'

'What happened is that she's a runaway convict.'

'You don't know that.'

'Look at her hair,' he said. 'And why was she dressed like that?'

And the woman: 'We don't *know*. You don't know what's happened, Peter. She's ill, for goodness' sake. Look how thin she is.'

'Yes, she's ill. And what I know is that there is a woman in my house—in my bed, for that matter—who looks like she's just crawled out of the fires of hell and who smells worse than a fox.'

'I'm just saying, you don't know what's—'

'Yes. I don't know what's happened.'

Bridget sat up. Her mouth was dry. Very dry. There was a table next to the bed, a glass and a jug of water. She picked the jug up and drank from it.

There was silence outside and then the door opened.

'Hello. You're awake. We wondered when you would wake up.'

Bridget put the jug down, sat up further.

The woman smiled. 'How are you feeling? I have some hot soup ready for you. I will bring it in.'

The woman left the room again, shut the door behind her.

Outside the door there was whispering. She sat on the bed looking around the room; a pile of folded clothes on top of the dresser, a brush next to them. The room was bright with the white of the curtains and bedding.

The woman came back into the room carrying a tray with a bowl on it and a hunk of bread. She moved the jug and put the tray on the table. 'I imagine you are quite hungry.'

Bridget nodded.

The woman sat on the edge of the bed and watched Bridget as she ate.

'It's been a while since you've eaten,' she tried.

'Where is this place?'

'So you are lost then?' the woman said, her voice full of both hope and relief. 'I knew you must have been lost.'

Bridget nodded.

'This is Meadowvale, on the North Esk River. Where are you from, dear?'

'Norfolk Plains,' she said, the first place she thought of.

She could see the woman thinking.

The door opened then and a tall man came in, his face serious. He took in the scene before him. 'My wife was worried you were dead,' he said.

'We'll talk later,' the woman said, gave the man a look of warning. 'You rest for now. Rest.' She ushered the man out of the room.

...

In the night Bridget woke up. The letter. It was in the pocket of the shirt she'd been wearing. She got up and went out into the hall. She stopped when she heard the man's raised voice. 'Take her in to the constable.'

'No reason to suspect her, Peter.'

'You think far too well of people, Alice. Did you see her boots?'

'What about them?'

'The state of them.'

'She's probably very poor. How do you know what Mary looked like when she went looking for a stable?'

'I'm not even going to answer that.'

'I'm just saying—'

'I know what you're saying.' A silence, and then: 'You amaze me, Alice, you really do. What about that necklace? If she's so poor, what's she doing with that?'

The woman said something Bridget couldn't hear then and Bridget put her hand up to her neck, felt the pendant.

'We're not keeping her here.'

'Keep your voice down.'

...

'There we go then,' the missus said, opening the curtains. 'Rest and some good food, we'll keep on bathing that wound and you should be as good as new.' She asked Bridget did they need to get word to anyone; her husband would surely be concerned, and what about children?

'No,' Bridget said.

The missus turned and looked at her then, disappointment and sadness showing in her eyes before she turned away.

'I need my shirt,' Bridget said.

'Oh,' the woman said.

She came back in holding it out in front of her like it was a dead thing. 'This?'

Bridget nodded.

After the woman was gone she fished in the pocket, sat holding the note.

...

She dressed in the dress and underwear the woman had given her, all of it too big. She sat at the table with them. The man said Grace and then they ate in silence. She felt the man watching her. 'There were bushrangers shot not far from here just recently,' he said. Bridget looked up, met his gaze.

'Apparently there was a woman with them.'

She speared a chunk of potato.

'Do we need to talk about this now, Peter?' the woman said, but she didn't look at Bridget and her voice was quiet.

He didn't say anything else but she felt him watching her.

...

Bridget lay awake until well after the house was quiet. She'd asked the convict girl, their servant, what the nearest town was. Launceston, the girl said, about ten miles away.

Against the wall in the sitting room was a cabinet. Bridget

got up, slowly slid the top drawer open. A knife. A small silver tin. She looked back at the door to the bedroom, picked up the knife. In the kitchen she took bread and a sack, a lump of ham.

Outside a triangle of silver spread over the river.

She went quickly along the road. Two men on horseback passed by and then a shiny carriage with four people inside, a young woman with flaxen braids, her pale face pressed to the window. For a long time after that there was nothing. Then there was the sound of rattling wheels and a bullock cart came into view, a man and a woman sitting up front, two animals pulling a cart loaded with goods.

She stepped out into the road and they slowed. She said her name was Mathilda and she had been in Norfolk Plains visiting her sister and was headed south to Hobart Town. They were going to Ross, the man said, she could get on the back with the children, concern and doubt filling the woman's face.

She sat on the back on top of a crate, the littlest of the three girls staring at her the whole time.

'I want to go home,' the girl said. 'Susie doesn't like it here one little bit,' she said. She was looking down at the dolly that she held with both hands.

The girl looked up at Bridget. 'She doesn't like it,' she repeated.

'Susan, be quiet,' the man said.

The girl lowered her head.

Bridget looked behind her. The road was clear.

...

They dropped her off at twilight just before the small town of Ross. She walked along the quiet street and then along a track that followed alongside the wide river the town was built on. There was a stone house close to the river, at the end of it a timber barn, its door open. Inside was a pen with a horse in it. The animal watched her. She tripped over something then walked into straw, lay down near the snorting horse. At dawn she opened the stable door, saw a bonnet on the line, snatched it before she ran towards the road.

...

A grey day, drizzling on and off, the road quiet. She stayed close to it, sometimes walking along the actual track. When she heard the cart coming she stood for a while watching it and then started to walk. She walked ahead of it and then stopped to look again. A man drove the cart alone, a brown horse pulling it. She stood and watched as it came closer. The man had a moustache but no beard, he wore a shirt and waistcoat, a long coat over it spread out either side of him on the seat. He stopped the horse, was looking at her as though he expected to recognise her. 'Hello,' he said, more loudly than necessary. 'Looks like rain.'

She nodded.

'Where are you headed?'

'Hobart Town.'

He looked at the sack she held. 'Well. Hop up if you would like to.'

She looked back up the road. Then she stepped up onto the cart.

He drove in silence and then he turned to her. 'My name's Patterson, George Patterson; some dim-witted buggers, like the much-esteemed magistrate who has a property adjacent to mine, call me Georgie Porgie. When he's had a drop, that is. Sober, you couldn't fault him. Charming man. The colony is swarming with them, don't you think?' He laughed. 'Don't mind me . . . What's your name?'

'Mathilda.'

'Don't mind me, Mathilda, I'm a cynical bastard—life'll do that to you, won't it? Don't you envy children? I do. I envy them. I don't like them much, they whine too much for me, but I envy them all the same. Where are your children, Mathilda?'

Bridget looked down at her feet.

'Sorry,' he said, 'none of my business. It's annoying, isn't it? The questions people ask. Why are people so nosy? Do you ever wonder that, Mathilda?'

Bridget thought about jumping off, stared at the worn toe of her boot.

A man passed them walking the other way along the road. Bridget pulled the bonnet in close around her face. George noticed her do it, looked at her.

'So what are you going to tell me, Mathilda? Tell me something.'

'What?'

'I don't know. Anything.'

She shrugged. 'Nothing to tell.' Her voice sounded strange to her own ears, as though she hadn't heard it for a very long time, maybe never.

'Ah, you see, that just means you have more to tell than most.' The man winked and tapped the side of his nose.

She wanted to get off again, put her hands on the seat either side of her thighs to hold herself there.

...

They came to a hill on the right-hand side of the track, a lesser track leading up to a small cottage sitting halfway up it. 'This is Mrs Laughton's place,' he said. 'I buy flowers from her every time I come past.'

He turned the horse off the main track and they passed behind an outcrop of rock and then along in front of a paling fence that surrounded the cottage. Between the fence and the house was a garden full of flowers, a shock of colour against the grey of the cottage. As George got down off the cart the door opened and a woman came out, her hands held protectively over her stomach. Behind her in the doorway stood a girl, her hair long and dark, her skin pale. George bowed low. 'Mrs Laughton, how do you do today?'

'Alright, Mr Patterson. Will you take some flowers?' The woman glanced at Bridget.

'Well, why not?'

She turned and said something to the girl, who went back inside and then came out with a knife. The girl stayed near the door while the woman walked down to the garden and started cutting.

'Nice day, isn't it, Miss Emma?' George called.

'It's nice enough, I suppose,' the girl said.

'Emma.' The woman stood up from her flower-cutting. 'Be polite, please.'

George was not put off. 'Yes, Miss Emma, it is that. It is nice enough.'

They all stood there and then the woman stood up from the flowerbed and gave the bunch of flowers to him.

'Beautiful, Mrs Laughton. Beautiful!' He pulled a coin out of his pocket and gave it to her and she flushed red.

'Thank you, Mr Patterson. I . . . we . . .'

'That's quite alright; your flowers are worth every penny of it.' He looked up at the girl who hovered in the doorway, her arms crossed.

'Well, see you next time.'

'Will you be by again soon?'

'I hope so.'

He flicked the reins and headed the horse back down the hill.

'She's lovely, isn't she? The girl, I mean. Beautiful.'

'I don't know.'

'You don't know?' He looked over at her. 'Piffle. Of course she is. You don't have to be a man to see that. In fact, in my experience women are a hundred times more observant than men. My daughter is always trying to bring women home for me to meet—widows for the most part. "She's very handsome, Father," she says. Ah, but they never are! So, I take that back, whatever I said. My wife died you see, quite some time ago now. No one likes to talk about it, but it's going to happen to all of us sometime.' He glanced at her, drove in silence until they reached the road again. 'You're not a very happy person, are you, Mathilda?'

The question shocked her.

He threw his arms up in the air and nearly knocked her.

'Happy? What is happy? What am I saying? Who is happy, Mathilda? Eh? Who?'

He was singing now. A song she'd never heard before. '*Old Happy Mac. Old Happy Mac was a happy chap. Dear old Happy Mac.*' Then he stopped singing and went along frowning again, and the next time he spoke he was serious.

'Her husband died a year or so ago. I suppose they'll go soon. Where and do what, I don't know. Anyway, it makes me gloomy, thinking about what her life will probably be. Emma's, I mean. You can see it, can't you? All laid out before her. Still, you never know. The wind might change, pick her up and blow her off somewhere else—somewhere better, perhaps. I can't help thinking she deserves better, not that she did anything to be so beautiful, that was just luck. Old doctor luck. Good old doctor luck, eh?'

He was quiet for a while and then he hit his hand on his thigh so that she jumped in her seat. 'Oh, it's a fine day, isn't it? The sun is out, the birds are singing, you and I are having a nice chat, what more could you want? Hmm? Isn't it perfect? Perrrfection, that's what it is.'

He slowed the cart to cross a wet ditch. Bridget jumped, fell, but quickly got to her feet. She heard him calling out, 'Mathilda!' as she ran.

Seven other people stood waiting for the ferry to take them across the river to the Hobart Town side. When the ferryman came to Bridget she gave him a silver thimble that had been inside the tin she'd taken. He looked at her, studied her face. She thought he was going to give it back but then he nodded towards the ferry. All the way across she felt him watching her.

She had only walked a few yards on the other side when he called out. 'Eh, what's ya name?'

She looked back at him, but then turned around and walked quickly.

...

By the time she came to a cluster of huts at the top of the hill that led down into Hobart Town it was close to dark. She passed a semi-cleared area where a bullock was tied to a tree stump, the animal turning its head slowly as she passed.

Outside one of the huts, a small girl squatted down and spread her hands on the ground. She closed her fist and squeezed mud through her small fingers. A woman appeared and picked her up, wiped the girl's nose with her hand. The girl pulled her head back away from the intrusion, put her hand on her mother's face. She started to cry then and the woman took her inside.

Somewhere nearby someone was chopping wood. The air smelled of smoke. Between the huts she caught a glimpse of a girl carrying a bucket that banged against her leg, water slopping over the sides.

Bridget went down the road and, at the turn-off to the right that led along to Marshall's, she stopped, the shape of the house and of cattle grazing in the fields on either side of the lane leading up to it visible in the growing darkness. She stood looking at the house and then continued down the hill.

She turned a corner and walked along a narrow road. A boy stood in the middle of the road with a plank of wood. Another one threw a ball to him and the boy hit it with the wood. It rolled past her and one of the boys sprinted after it. A door opened and a woman called the boys inside. The smells of cooking wafted from the huts and filled the street.

She followed the creek up the hill, where the street became a rutted muddy track. The first few drops of rain fell. Right at the end of the track, at the base of the hill, she stopped. She had seen Beth, who had been on the ship with her, a few times at the Bird in Hand. Then one day she had been doing an errand in town for Mrs Marshall and had run into her in the street. Beth had brought her up this hill, showed her the hut she was living in. She had married a man with a Ticket of Leave and been assigned to him.

There was a fenced yard at the side of the hut that hadn't been there before. Close by a bullock bellowed. Something moved in the tree next to where she stood—a possum. There was no sound from inside the hut. The timber shutters were closed over the windows. Bridget walked up to the door and knocked.

The door opened.

Beth.

3

HEADWATER

From the outside it looked the same: same sign, same lamp, same curtains—one of them ripped near the edge just as it had been before. The curtains over the window were half open so that inside she could see a few people sitting around a table playing cards, none of them familiar. A man she didn't know came out, looked her over before going up the lane, and the heavy timber door came to rest again in the frame. A skinny-looking dog appeared at the end of the lane, stopped there and looked down towards where she stood and then kept going on its way. The next person who came out was a woman, a shawl around her shoulders. Bridget stepped out of the shadows. The woman put her hand up to her chest. 'You scared the life out of me.'

'Daniel Rooke in there? You know him?'

The woman eyed her, appraising. 'Maybe . . . why?'

'Need to talk to him.'

'He's in there.'

'Can you get him?'

The woman screwed her nose up, her look suspicious now. 'Who will I say wants him?'

'Just ask him to come out.'

She stood there waiting. The door opened but it wasn't him. It was a woman who hurried off up the lane. She thought maybe the woman hadn't got him at all, or that she was lying and he wasn't in there. But then the door opened again and he was standing there, the woman Bridget had spoken to standing behind him peering over his shoulder. 'It's alright, Molly,' he said, and reluctantly the woman shut the door.

'Didn't expect to see you here,' he said.

Beth said there'd been talk around town—Bridget Crack had taken up with Matthew Sheedy and his lot.

'Where's Eliza?'

Beth had told her Eliza wasn't in Hobart Town anymore, had been reassigned to the Interior.

'Ain't seen her,' he said. 'Reassigned months ago, Norfolk Plains.'

She put her hand into the dress pocket then, pulled out the necklace.

He looked behind him and then nodded towards the end of the lane.

There were three buildings built close to this side of the creek, a field with a few cattle grazing on the other side, one of them with brown and white markings, the patches of white glowing under the moon. Bridget and Daniel stood down the bank, close to the water. Daniel turned the necklace over in his hand. She wanted a ticket, she said, for a ship to England.

He looked at her, seeing if she was serious. 'Not that easy,' he said. 'Need a different name, papers. Travelling alone'd look suspicious. Need someone to go with you, a husband.' Said he could find out when there was a ship, if someone was going to England and would do it, and do it for what he could get for the necklace, minus his commission—a third, and the cost of a fare. He'd ask around; she should come back to the public house in a week.

...

Beth's husband had died only months after she married him. 'God rest his soul, he wasn't a bad man,' she said, busy at the fireplace, her broad back to Bridget. The hut and bit of land that had been his were hers now. She had been reassigned to a master in town whom she worked for during the day and she was allowed to return to her own place in the evenings. 'Not such a bad situation.'

Bridget had bristled when she'd said it. Why couldn't she say that? *Not such a bad situation.*

Because of Mary. This was all Mary's fault.

But it wasn't—she deserved it. *What happens to bad girls.*

At the hut during the days she slept. In between sleeping, in the long crawl of hours that she lay awake, she was aware of Marshall's house a mile up the road. Remembered Mary standing in the kitchen, all puffed up like a bird who'd just shaken itself after a bath. 'They're causing a terrible lot of trouble.' She'd been talking about bushrangers. Said as though it was bad, but a thrill there in her voice. She might even have said his name. *Matthew Sheedy*: a sound like a sneeze back then and not much more. Again this feeling of 'back then' . . . not that long ago, but another time entirely. She rolled over to try to get away from it, eyed the feeling darkly.

...

Bridget was asleep when the hut door flew open and Beth shut it hard behind her. She stood inside breathing hard, had been running. 'They got him. He's caught. Henry Evans. They got him. He were caught the day before yesterday, they've got him in gaol at Launceston. I just seen Tott Clancy, who knows whenever someone farts in the colony before they even know it themself and he said they got Henry Evans, that someone had come down from Launceston, said the news were everywhere.'

'Alive?'

'S'pose so. He's in gaol. They wouldn't bother putting him in gaol if he were dead, would they?'

She had to go, she said, had just come to tell her.

...

It was nearly a week later when Beth turned up in the afternoon with the news that Henry Evans was being brought into town. She was going down the hill to have a look on the way back to her master's place, Bridget was to stay there.

Bridget stood at the door and listened. Sounds of cheering and whistling came up from the town. She sat down in the chair by the table, got up again and walked back over to the door. She opened it and looked out. The bloke from the hut nearby had come to the door the other night, peered into the dark hut behind Beth. 'Got a visitor?'

'No, I haven't, and if I did, what business would it be of yours?'

'Numbskull there said he seen someone.'

'Did he, now? And what do I care about what he says?'

Beth had shut the door. 'Dunno who the good Lord

thought he was kidding: "love your neighbour as yourself"—he obviously never lived next to Jimmy bloody Ferguson.'

Bridget went back to the table for the bonnet, tied it close around her face.

...

The main street was packed with people. A shot was fired into the air and a soldier yelled for everyone to get back, get back. Bridget pushed through the crowd in time to see the cart coming along. It was pulled by one horse, soldiers walking beside it. People flocked towards the cart and Bridget was pushed forward with the surge of the crowd. The soldiers pushed people back. Another shot was fired into the air. He was sitting on the back of the cart, looking into the distance behind him. There was dried blood on the side of his face. His hands were tied behind his back and his big body was rocking with the movement of the cart. Behind Bridget someone yelled out, 'God be with you, Henry!'

Through the crowd she saw him, walking close to the cart. Marshall. Captain Marshall. She pushed back through the crowd, hurried back up to Beth's hut, shut the door behind her. She stood with her back against the door, trying to catch her breath.

...

'I can organise it, but it'll take time,' Daniel said. He knew someone, lived out of the way, she could go and stay there until it was organised. Amy Jenkins, her name.

Beth had been telling her to hand herself in. 'They're not gunna hang you, if that's what you're thinking. They'll put you in the gaol for a while, reassign you. That's it.' But she didn't sound sure, Bridget thought.

...

'Jimmy came over again asking,' Beth said, the pitch of her voice heightened a little, a miniscule waver in it. 'Dunno who the Lord thought he was kidding with that "love your neighbour as yourself" business—he obviously never lived next to Jimmy Ferguson.' The sound of it altogether different from the last time she'd said it—forced frivolity in it now where before there was disdain, and now a short laugh came after it, nervous and thin.

...

Daniel led Bridget to a hut, where he introduced her to a man called Tranter who had a bullock already harnessed to a cart, ready to go.

It was hours later, the afternoon sloping towards evening, when they stopped at a hut near the river. Tranter got down off the cart and a man came out of the hut and Tranter got down and spoke to him, gave him money.

The man walked ahead of her, held a lantern up in front of them. The night was cloudy and the river was as dark the sky. The boat sat tied up to a narrow jetty, the water plink-plinking quietly against it. He held the side of the boat while she stepped in and then untied the rope and stepped in after her. Beth had given her a jacket that she now pulled tight around herself.

It was a quick row across, but there was no jetty on the other side. He held on to a handful of reeds while she stepped out into the water and then climbed up the bank. He pointed down the river. 'The road's that way. Walk down there and you'll come to the place where the ferry pulls in; that's where the road starts.' He nodded, picked up the oars again and she stood there until he'd melted into the blackness.

The day had started out sunny but there were only a few patches of blue left now, and by the time the track opened up into treeless flat land the sky was all grey. Muddy tracks crossed a rough field where logs had been dragged along the ground. Further on, a cottage built from rocks sat alone on scrubby land. She stopped and watched the cottage for a while, walked up close to it and stopped again. A dog barked and then the door of the cottage opened and an old woman shuffled out. Bridget bought bread and lamb from her with money Daniel had given her and the woman stood on the doorstep looking at her and kept watching as Bridget walked along the track.

After another mile or so the track met with the creek it had been following and she sat down to rest. The sky was growing darker grey now.

At Green Ponds, Daniel said, go to the first place past the public house, tell the bloke there I sent you, he'll tell you where to find Amy. At Green Ponds she found the hut and a man with a tattoo on the side of his neck who sent her along this track: about two mile along look for a hill on the right, rocky with two humps. A creek flows along at the bottom of it. Look for the two-hump hill.

Bridget looked back along the way she had come. Maybe she'd missed it? She scanned the landscape for a hill with two humps. There was a hill beyond the stumpy field but no two humps. Mist was easing its way over it now, obscuring it. A fine net of drizzle settled over her hair. She walked on.

...

Rain veiled the two-humped hill and Bridget peered at the hut through the blur.

'Who is it?'

Bridget spoke to the door. 'Mathilda. Mathilda Maloney.'

A lock was slid across and the door opened to reveal a thin fair woman with nervous eyes, the hut behind her a tumble of children, dogs and animal skins.

...

Amy Jenkins had pale blue eyes that might have been darker had life not drained the colour out of them. She had the face of a person who moved, who worked, who spoke without knowing why they were doing it anymore. Tiredness was living in her bones, but her eyes betrayed guilt, an apology that she could not do more. Amy Jenkins was a husk waiting for a wind. Her children were wild. They were mean to their mother and mean to the animals.

The hut was full of kangaroo skins she used to make caps that she sold to the government. They were for the parties of soldiers and constables who went out after bushrangers, to keep their heads warm, she said.

At the fire with a child on her hip Amy apologised, her voice small. 'Sorry we ain't got much. How's it ya ain't got nowhere to go? Husband run off s'pose.'

Bridget nodded.

'You was in Hobart Town then?' she asked later.

'Yes,' Bridget said.

'Don't say much, do ya?'

...

She sat close to the fire near Amy, a roo skin draped over her knees. Squinting to see in the half-light, she shoved the needle into the fur, pushed until she felt it pop through the skin on the other side, then pushed again until it went through the second skin. She pulled the sinew tight and started again. Amy had been talking but now she had gone quiet and they sewed to the sound of the popping fire and the sleeping children's breathing.

Here they were, preserved in detail. The detail without the whole. Deep lines at the sides of the eyes, becoming lighter towards the hairline. Bright blue eyes lit with mischief. Fine light freckles sprinkled across a beautifully shaped nose turned up very slightly at the end. The green of fields, the light of stars twinkling over England.

Pull the needle out, push the needle in. Out. In. While they fade and fade and fade, and come and go and fade. While they are sewn into this cap—a tapestry of fur and faces and memories.

Bridget got up, chucked the skin and needle down on the floor, wrenched the door open and went out. She wasn't sitting there sewing caps for those bastards to wear while they came looking for her. She wasn't doing it.

A slight wind had come up and it raked over the plain. She took a few deep breaths. The wind mucked with her hair, its chilly fingers toying with the fine hairs on her cheeks and stinging her eyes.

She waited for it to blow the images away.

...

Amy sat on the constable's knee, one arm around his neck. The man that had turned up with him sat near the fire, drinking and looking furtively at Bridget. 'Come on,' Amy said, held a bottle up to Bridget, 'have a bloody drink. She's not very friendly,' she said to the constable. 'Know what she needs.' She giggled.

'Might not be needing these no more,' the constable said, after Amy shoved a cap on his head, pulled it down low. He pushed the fur away from his eyes. 'Henry Evans is to be hung next week. That's it for bushrangers.'

'For now, anyway,' the other one said.

Bridget waited a moment then picked up the whiskey bottle and swigged hard. They all watched her, Amy's face showing her surprise.

She lay on a straw mattress on the floor with the children, Amy noisy with the contstable on the other side of the room, the other constable curled by the fire.

She couldn't sleep; saw the scaffold, a mob gathered around it.

...

Out on the track she walked back and forth, the rasp of her breath loud in the dark.

...

In the morning, after the constables were gone, Amy didn't speak to her. Finally she said: 'You could of gived something to Risby, ya know. I don't get their business, I ain't got nothing.'

'Why didn't you say there were constables coming?'

'What's it to you?'

Bridget didn't answer.

...

That afternoon, while Amy was sleeping, Bridget took the little money she could find—most of it had been hers anyway—and what food she could carry and, cursing Daniel for sending her to a woman who made caps for constables, she headed back to the main road.

Between tree trunks, sky and water melded in a blur of greyness. Drizzle swirled and branches hissed and Marshall stared at the reverend's black shoes in the wet grass. It was summer, almost Christmas, but a cold day. 'Thou, who for the sins of others didst thyself hang on the cursed tree, rescue his departing soul from eternal misery, and forgive him in the abundant riches of thy mercy.' On the other side of the grave, the reverend continued to compete with the wind. There was no one there to hear him, however, but Marshall and the trees and the convict servant resting with a spade against a tree trunk yards away. The body in the ground was that of a sheep thief, Albert Little; it had been taken down from the scaffold that morning.

Two eagles battled the harsh currents above the cliff as Marshall, present at the burial as the governor's representative, stood with cold feet, acutely aware of the rise of dirt behind him that was Sheedy's grave. The morning of Sheedy and Merriweather's burial had been as windy as this one, the sound of waves breaking on rocks reaching up from the cove below. Marshall recalled how, as he had stood here in the cold wind, whitecaps lettering the water, he had not felt the sense of pride and accomplishment he had heard in the voices of Colonel Gower and Bartholomew White, and the voices of the others who had brought the bodies into town. He had not even felt the sense of something finished, of relief—no feeling of the correctness of the situation. What he had felt was a slight sense of wonder: one of those shapes in the ground was what had led Bridget Crack into the bush. That shape was a thing she had been with, known, possibly even loved. He had reminded himself that the dead man was a thief and a murderer; that he was a general malefactor; that his association with Bridget Crack was the least of what he was. But the whole thing had seemed altogether strange. Despite all the evidence, he still did not know how to put her with them. In his mind she did not fit there.

In a few weeks' time Henry Evans would join Sheedy, Merriweather, Little and all the other condemned men and women who now lay here. That burial would be a good deal more public. The bodies of Sheedy and Merriweather, wrapped in hessian, had been loaded onto a cart and transported to the remote graveyard early in the morning in relative secrecy. Following the hanging as it would, Evans's burial would be far more difficult to conceal. Hordes would follow the soldiers here, jostling for a view of the grave.

One of the eagles was swept out over the water while the other hovered in place. 'God is mighty,' the reverend said, his black robes blowing in the wind. They turned their backs on Little and as he passed by Sheedy's grave, Marshall thought of her again. A report had come down from Launceston in November saying that a Mr Gleeson had found an escaped female convict in his yard. His property, Meadowvale, was not all that far from the location where Sheedy's body had been found. Gleeson's wife had nursed her and she had stolen from them and run off. The woman was now thought to have been Bridget Crack.

That was over a month ago, and since then nothing had been heard of her.

As they walked down the damp slope Marshall heard the scrape of the convict servant's shovel.

'Look at that,' the reverend said, pointing at the headland, where one of the eagles was hovering low over the ground. 'It must have found something.'

Bridget stepped out in front of the cart.

The bullock pulled up. The driver sat and stared mutely at her.

'Going north,' she said.

He looked for a little longer. 'Going a few mile,' he stated.

She shrugged.

He picked up the reins. 'Get up then.'

...

She sat on the back of the cart and they followed a track past a herd of cattle, some lifting their heads to look as the cart rolled by. Two figures came into view up the road, both of them wearing red. As they came closer she saw the guns slung over their shoulders. Her heart started to race and she looked behind them and then, as the soldiers came closer, she kept her eyes on her feet. They acknowledged the man as they passed.

A while later they passed a man on horseback who waved to the man driving the cart and noted her presence, the question clear on his face.

They crossed a creek where two pieces of split timber had been placed across it and then went up a wooded hill and down into an open valley. They had been going for some time when the ground got marshy and one of the wheels became stuck. He hadn't said anything since picking her up. Now he got down, looked at the wheel. 'Get off,' he said. She got down and he pulled at the bullock's head. The animal pulled but the cart remained stuck. He walked away from the cart towards the creek. She watched him picking up branches, breaking them under his foot. He came back with an armful of sticks that he put down in front of the wheel. This time when the bullock pulled the cart rolled forward. 'Stay off,' he said. 'You'll have to walk a while.' He grabbed the gun from the seat and walked next to the animal's head.

After a while he stopped, turned and walked to the back of the cart, where she had also stopped. He stood in front of her. 'What's your name?'

'Mathilda.'

He nodded. 'Mathilda.'

He went to grab her shoulder and she stepped back.

He stood staring at her, then walked back to the bullock's head, picked up the reins and moved it on. When the ground became drier he stopped the bullock and got up into the seat. He didn't look at her. She got on the back. When they came down the hill to a cluster of cottages she got off. He turned and looked at her then turned back, cracked the whip next to the bullock's rump.

...

The road to Norfolk Plains followed a flat slow river, the town itself consisting of a few big buildings on a plain. A black horse was tied to a post outside a two-storey building, a pile of fresh shit steaming on the ground behind it. It stepped back into the pile and then lowered its head to doze. Two young girls, well dressed, came out of the building and crossed the road, giggling as they went, one whispering to the other behind her hand.

Bridget pulled the bonnet around her face and went further up the road.

A man walked past with a pick over his shoulder and then two boys ran by, one chasing the other. The boy behind picked up a rock and pelted it at the other one. It hit him in the shoulder and he turned around and swore at the other boy, laughed and kept running.

Daniel had said Eliza was here. That Eliza had been reassigned to Norfolk Plains. Bridget asked a girl in convict clothes where there was a public house, followed her directions to a hut near the river.

Inside, Bridget scanned the room while unfamiliar faces turned to look then went back to their drinks, their cards and conversations.

'Want a drink, do ya, sweetheart?'

'You know Eliza Maloney?'

'Liza Maloney.' The man swayed. 'Nah. Anyone here know Liza Maloney?'

A pudgy woman with a handful of cards looked over. 'Gone. Launceston. Went to the gaol then reassigned there. Why?'

Over in the corner of the room now Bridget saw a man looking at her. She recognised him, had seen him somewhere before. She could see he was thinking, trying to place her too. The memory came to her, with it a cold sweat. At the lake. She remembered rum running down his chin, the hard cold glare in his eyes. One of the surveyor's men.

Bridget turned around, went out the door.

Along the road she thought she heard someone following her. She turned around. There was a man yards back. Not the surveyor's man, and didn't look to be in a hurry, but she ran for a while anyway.

A mile or so along the river she saw a convict man alone in a field, ploughing. She watched him and then went over to him.

The main road went to Launceston, he told her. Walk out to the main road then follow it. Or, it was about twelve mile down the river. 'You'd have to cross the river first and there's not much track or nothing. I wouldn't be going that way.' Was she on her own? he wanted to know then. Need somewhere to stay?

No, she said. She didn't.

...

The cottage sat on flat cleared land, a fenced paddock behind it, a donkey dozing there. Beyond that was an area of burnt stumps dotting a plain where a flock of sheep grazed and water sat in the lowest part of the land like a shallow lake, the wind scouring its shining surface. Next to the paddock was a haystack and a bullock cart, the shafts resting on the ground. A cow tied to the outside of the paddock fence was watching a brown dog that had just squeezed underneath the fence and was now cocking its leg against a post.

The hut's chimney was smoking but there was no sign of anyone. In the paddock the dog had noticed the donkey, wandered towards it and then stopped. It watched the donkey and then gave one short bark at the resting animal, who looked at the dog and then went back to its dozing. The dog barked again and then kept up its barking until the donkey tossed its head impatiently. The dog responded by getting down low, its rear stuck up in the air. It continued to bark, trying to engage the donkey in some kind of play that the donkey took exception to and, seeming in no mood for the dog's games, it ran at the dog, head down and teeth bared. The dog quickly took off back under the fence, the cow watching it go, and ran to the back of the cottage, where it stood looking back at the paddock before it lay down in the dirt. The donkey stood near the fence for a while, twitching its ears, and then resumed its dozing in the new spot.

Behind her among the wattles where she stood watching there was a grave—a pile of grey stones with a wooden cross at the head of the pile. She went on up the rocky hill around the cottage and came down on the far side of it. Further on was another cottage, a woman working in the garden that was between it and the cart track. While Bridget watched the cottage door opened and a little boy ran out, went through the fence into the garden and stood next to the woman digging. Another woman came out, stood at the fence and then went through and picked up the child, who screamed and kicked his legs as she carried him back to the cottage. A few minutes later the woman in the garden stopped digging, wiped her hands on her apron, left the garden and went inside.

All day yesterday Bridget had pushed through bush above the river, had spent a cold night under a rock overhang. The night before she had slept in a smoke house, eaten curing meat.

This morning she'd come to a house and circled around it, found a cart track and walked along it until the furrows in the soil became deeper and she felt herself to be on a well-used track, up and down slopes, through mud to this group of cottages.

...

The sun crept towards the horizon and the track led through forest. Bridget ate the three eggs she had taken from a chicken coop at the back of the last cottage. On dark she stood on a rise; lights twinkled below and tendrils of smoke rose to join a blanket of fog that hovered above the lights. The track widened as it led down the hill, the dark shapes of houses either side of it.

There was a bang and she fled from her place in the middle of the road to the trees on the other side. The bang had come from a cottage on the other side of the track and now its door opened and a woman yelled: 'I don't care, do I? I don't give a damn. Why don't you bugger off?' A person came out the door towards the road. A man. He stood out on the road looking back at the cottage and then he turned and went down the hill, disappearing into the dark. The hut door shut and behind it the woman yelled again. 'I told you, get down off there. Now!'

...

The town's dirt streets were quiet in the early evening, the odd lantern glowing over a doorway here and there. Bridget stuck close to the buildings, turned up a lane where there was a place with a group of men milling out the front on the street, a lantern casting light over them. The windows of the building were lit with candles, and laughter, music and singing came from inside. Someone pulled the door open and there was a burst of noise and light; they went in and it was gone again. Bridget crept up the lane and stood in a narrow gap between two buildings, the ground here stinking of piss.

She watched the men in the street for a while then went back down, asked if any of them knew Eliza Maloney. One of them nodded, said she was a servant at a big place out of town. He pointed. 'Guildford's place,' he said.

Behind him there was a pole, a sign nailed to it. WANTED. Under it was her name. The man saw her staring at it, glanced at the sign and then back at her.

She turned and walked quickly away, felt him watching her. She continued up the hill, stopped at a stable. It was empty. No one around. Inside she slumped down in the darkest corner, pulled straw around herself.

...

The stately house sat at the top of a slope, casting its importance out over the land below it. The land between the house and the river had been cleared and planted out with English grasses which grew greener than the native grass. Some new trees had been planted and, close to the riverbank at the bottom of the lawn, there was an ornate bench overlooking the river and a small jetty with a boat tied up to it.

Bridget went around to the back of the house, stood there a long time looking at it. She tried to imagine Eliza in there, what she might be doing. The sun had sunk behind the hills and shadow lay down softly over the fields around the house.

She found what she thought might be the door to the servants' quarters and knocked.

'Eliza Maloney here?'

The girl who'd opened the door shook her head. 'Liza ain't here no more.'

'Where's she's gone?'

'They sent her to the Factory.'

'When?

'Month ago now woulda been.'

Bridget looked at the empty yard behind her and back to the girl. 'Can you get me bread?'

The girl shook her head. 'Can't. Isa wouldn't like it.'

'Come on—just a bit.'

'Can't.'

Bridget turned as if to walk away from the door, then spun around suddenly just as the girl was shutting it, barged past her into the kitchen, grabbed a whole loaf of bread from the table.

'Hey! Hey, come back here! Hey!'

But Bridget was running now, across the grass and down towards the river where two black swans took off squawking into the sky.

...

Cowpats littered the grass, the wet ground full of holes from the animals' hooves. Below her the fog was lifting to reveal the town, damp with dew and strange and new under the glare of daylight. Last night she'd gone back to the stable—a horse in it and voices nearby. She'd kept going up the hill then beyond the flicker of lights until there were no more huts, no more cleared or half-cleared plots, until she could sense the town below her but could see or hear nothing of it. She found a leaf-filled hollow in the ground and lay down in it.

Across the field the land sloped away and she walked to a creek that flowed down out of the hills. A cottage sat on a cleared rise above the creek. Behind it was an open-fronted shed where a young girl was milking a cow. From inside the cottage someone called the girl, who got up from her stool and went inside, leaving the pail. Bridget ran across the creek, picked up the bucket and guzzled, some of the milk escaping down the front of her dress.

'Well, hurry up.' The voice came from inside the cottage. Bridget put the bucket down as the girl came out the door. As she ran she heard the girl call out, 'Mama, Mama, someone's stealing our milk!' Bridget didn't look back, ran up the creek.

She followed the creek upstream to a small pool, ferns growing all around it. She sat on a log listening for a long time then started back down the creek.

She was careful to stay out of sight passing the cottage. There was no sign now of anyone near the shed and the cow was gone.

Below the cottage the trees around the creek thinned and she could see the other cottages that dotted its banks, and the rest of the town down in the valley's basin. She crossed the creek and followed it down on the other side to a place where some of the understorey on the bank had been taken out, the biggest of the trees felled. She saw a small slab hut, a rock chimney at one end. There was no smoke coming from the chimney. The ground was covered in sheep shit, a lot of it fairly fresh, and there were axe marks in the tree next to her. She took a few more steps towards the back of the hut and stopped. The wind was a quiet hiss. Nearby there was the splutter of the creek and a little way off the maw of a crow.

Bridget walked around to the front of the hut where the door was open a few inches. There was a hole for a window, a sack hanging over the opening. On the ground near the door there was a sheep skull. A magpie turned its beady eye towards her, hopped across the short coarse grass. It stopped and turned its head to the side as though questioning her and then flew up onto a branch. She pushed the door and it opened with a creak to reveal darkness, a dirt floor.

In the fireplace there was a half-burnt log. Near it was a small table and behind her on the floor a mattress, some of the hessian covering ripped and the straw coming out. She stood in the darkness of the hut, then went back outside and continued down the hill.

Soon the trees thinned more, there were more stumps, and she could see down to the ploughed field below where only a few lone trees remained. Between the ploughed field and the creek, close to where the trees ended, there was a cottage. She walked near the creek now and got to within fifty yards of it. There was a squeal and then two children appeared from around the side of the cottage, one running after the other. The little one who was being chased ran into the cottage and slammed the door behind him. The girl who'd been chasing him turned and walked to a sprawling tree near the side of the house where a swing had been hung from a low bough. She sat on the seat and pushed off, swung slowly, her head down. A few minutes later a woman came out the door. 'Elizabeth, you come here now.'

The girl looked up then, ignored the woman, went back to her swinging.

'If I have to come over there you will get it. I'm warning you.'

The woman was staring at the girl on the swing, her hands on her hips. The girl slowly got off the swing and walked over to the woman, who clipped her on the side of the head as she went inside, pulled the door shut behind them.

Bridget came down towards the swing and over to a timber shelter between the swing and the creek. Inside there was a plough, a bullock harness, a cart, sheepskins slung over the side of it, and tied across the shelter, a line with kangaroo skins hanging from it. She stood just inside against the back wall, the open front of the shelter being visible from the cottage door. Inside the cottage a child was crying.

A moment later Bridget was about to step out of the shelter when the cottage door opened again and the woman came out, a bucket in her hand. Bridget stepped back against the wall and as she did she knocked a spade next to her that fell down onto a pot. There was a clatter and the woman stopped where she was only yards away, turned towards the shed and looked straight at Bridget.

For a moment both of them stood completely still, staring. Something familiar about the woman—the eyes close together, a scar across the cheek. The memory came to her from a long, long way off, landed like a bird on water. Anne. It was Anne. From the gaol.

The woman put the bucket down, looked behind her. 'Lizzy, go and get the gun. Now. Hurry.'

Bridget took a step. The shock was visible in the woman's

face. She craned her neck forward. 'Bridget? Bridget Crack? Is that you?'

The girl had come running out of the house with a gun, stood next to Anne holding it.

'Dear God, what has happened to you? My God, you're skin and bone, look at you. What . . . what are you doing here?'

Bridget's voice seemed to have escaped.

'What are you doing? Are you in trouble? I could've shot you.' Anne was staring at her, waiting for an answer. 'Where'd you come from?'

Bridget shook her head.

'What happened to you?' She was looking at Bridget's dress. 'Did you know I were here? How'd you find me?'

She didn't speak and Anne watched her, waiting.

Bridget couldn't look at her anymore, focused on the ground near Anne's feet.

Anne looked over her shoulder at the cottage. 'Come on. Come in then.'

...

The room was crowded and warm, a fire blazing in the fireplace at one end. When they entered, the little boy she had seen before was trying to wrestle a doll out of the girl's hand while an older girl sat in a chair near the fire sewing. Now all three of them were staring at her. 'Stop staring, all of you,' Anne said, then turned to Bridget. 'Sit down.'

The table she sat at was covered with things: a loaf of bread that Bridget had to stop herself from reaching out for, a bowl of salt, a tin pot, a half-sewn dress with pins along the bottom, dirty plates, a cup, a flask, and on top of the dress a dried snakeskin. Anne reached over her for the loaf of bread, cut a few pieces and put two in front of Bridget. 'Here. Eat.'

The older girl had resumed her sewing but was sneaking glances, while the younger two children still stood near the table staring.

Anne turned around. 'Outside.'

They didn't move.

'Now. Outside.'

They went out.

'Frances, take your sewing into the other room.'

The girl got up, collected her sewing things from the floor.

'They'll be the death of me, I swear. The trouble is, he lets them do whatever they like. Thinks because their mother died they should be able to do what they want. That's all very well, but he's not the one with them all day, is he?'

She went to the door, yelled out, 'Elizabeth, take that bucket and fill it up! Bring it in here!'

A few minutes later the girl came in, slopping water on the floor, went out again. Anne tipped some of it into a pot hanging over the fire. 'He was working at the same place as me, got his Ticket. I knew them both and then she died. She wasn't really a friend; I knew her is all. Anyway, a few months later he left and the next time I saw him he had this place and he asked me to marry him. I got assigned to him so now he's my master. And now I've got these bloody children to look after and no doubt soon I'll have more. At least they'll be mine though; maybe that way I won't think about killing them so often.' She laughed.

Anne sat in the chair at the end of the table. Bridget could feel her gaze on the side of her face. 'So. Are you going to tell me?'

Bridget shrugged. 'Nothing to tell.'

'I find you snooping around in my shed looking half starved, filthy as a dog rolled in shit and you say there's nothing to tell. Rubbish.'

'I need somewhere to go for a while.'

'What happened? Did you leave your master's? Did something happen? You've been in the bush.'

Bridget looked up at her. 'How do you know that?'

Anne laughed. 'Well you don't look like you've been sleeping in silk sheets, put it that way.'

'The place I got sent up-country—there was no missus there.'

'And you left?'

'I was going to Hobart Town.' Bridget stood up, walked over to the fire. 'I got lost. It wasn't my fault.'

'You just have to turn yourself in. They'll charge you with absconding, send you to the Factory for a while and then put you back out with a new master.'

Bridget was shaking her head. 'I can't.'

'Why not? I saw Mary-Ann Daly a while ago, she left her master's place for a week, went off with some fella she found at the public house and all they did when they found her was give her a telling-off and sent her back to her master. Then she left again and the same thing happened. I mean, you remember Mary-Ann, she—'

'A man got killed.'

'What man?'

'I was there. I got lost and they found me, some bushrangers; I was with them, and a man got shot.'

'You were with bushrangers?' Anne stared at her. 'You took up with bushrangers?' She started to laugh.

'I didn't *take up* with them.'

Anne stopped laughing. 'What, they nabbed you?'

'I don't know. I don't know what happened.'

'What do you mean, you don't know what happened?'

Bridget felt something fierce grip her and she swung around. 'I don't know. That's what I said. I don't know, alright.'

Anne leaned back in the chair. 'Alright. Alright.'

...

She must have fallen asleep because it was suddenly almost dark. Anne was at the table lighting a candle. She took Bridget around a partition to where there was a tub of water on the floor, held her hand out for the filthy dress, gave Bridget another one to put on. Bridget had just put the clean dress on and come back around the partition when outside a dog barked and then the door opened and a man walked in. He looked at Bridget while he took his hat off.

The boy rushed up to him. 'Guess what, Papa?'

'What?'

'I killed a snake.'

'Did you?'

'Yeah, and it was a vicious one too. Here's the skin. Look!'

'This's Bridget,' Anne said. 'We were in the gaol together.'

The boy had taken the skin off the table and was holding it up in front of his father, who ignored him, still looking at Bridget. 'Oh yeah. And what's she doing here?'

'She's staying a few nights.'

'What are we running, a boarding house or something?'

'What do you think, Papa?' the boy said.

Bridget stood up. 'I'll go.'

'Sit down,' Anne said. She turned to the older girl. 'Frances, take Bridget up to the hut. Get the lamp and the fur blanket.'

Frances stood where she was, looking at her father, while Anne stared him down.

'Go on then, take her,' he said. 'I don't bloody care.'

As Bridget and Frances walked out the door she heard the boy again: 'It's a good one, Papa, isn't it?'

She followed the girl across the creek and up the slope to the dark shape of the hut among the trees. The girl pushed the door open and the lamp lit up the inside of the empty hut that Bridget had come across earlier that morning. Frances put the lamp on the barrel. 'There was a man here a while ago, our servant, but he's gone now.'

Bridget nodded. Anne had lit the end of a thick stick in the fire and given it to Bridget to bring up here. It was smoking now and she bent over and put it on the ground near the fireplace.

'Are you really a bushranger?'

Bridget turned around and the girl looked down at the ground.

'I heard you talking to Anne—to Mother.'

'No. And don't you go saying that to no one.'

The girl nodded, picked up the lamp and, without looking up or saying anything else, she left, the light in her hand swaying as she went down through the trees.

...

In the morning Anne brought meat, milk and bread to the hut. 'You have to give yourself in.'

'Shouldn't of told him my name.'

Anne stood above her, watching her while she ate, hands on her hips. 'Worst they'll do is reassign you for life. And what does that matter? None of us are going back anyway.'

'Or they'll hang me.'

'They won't hang you, Bridget. What have you done? You didn't do anything.'

Bridget chewed the meat, washed it down with milk.

'Well, where are you going to go?'

'England.'

Anne didn't say anything but Bridget sensed her watching. Then she said she had to go, would be back later.

...

In the afternoon Bridget went down to the cottage, asked if there was a piece of paper. There wasn't but she gave some money to Frances, who went down to the town to get her a piece.

> im not at amy jenkins any more she makes caps for cunstables is there any news i need some news

She wrote Anne's name and that she was in Launceston.

...

Bridget stood near the fireplace in the hut. Someone had engraved the initials M.L. into one of the rocks above the fireplace. Who was M.L.? Why did they put that there? Michael Lockley. Michael Landgridge. Micky Long.

She stood looking at the greying wood of the door, walked over and pushed the bolt across. She stood with one hand still on the bolt, her head against the rough wood of the door. Then she sat down on the mattress, went back through it all again, everything that had happened to get her here, where she was now. Tried to think. She didn't know what, but something. She wrapped her arms around her body.

...

Anne came to the hut, stood inside the door, her arms crossed. 'There's a Wanted sign for you in the town.'

Bridget didn't look up at her. Didn't answer.

'What are you going to do?'

Bridget said nothing.

'I can't keep you here forever.'

When Bridget still didn't speak Anne turned around and went out, left the door open behind her.

...

She would get a letter soon, she told her, would get news about the ship to England. Anne was quiet. Bridget pressed money into Anne's hand. 'I'll hear soon. Soon.' During the days she'd been helping Anne at the cottage. At night she was restless in the hut. 'Stay up at the hut,' Anne said now, 'don't come down here.'

...

B.C. She engraved it into one of the rocks. There was nothing else to do.

...

Anne brought the note to the hut. 'Is this what you're waiting for?'

> i told you i will see what i can do
> D.R.

It was still early but the main street was alive with action. People walked and ran and rode, came in and out of buildings, some of them glancing at Bridget as they passed, others intent on their morning business. A lady in a salmon dress walked by, the morning sun shining on her hair.

Bridget stopped a woman who dragged a snotty child along behind her, asked where she would find the constable. The woman pointed to a brick building down the street on the other side.

The building was red brick, smaller than the buildings on either side of it, the door timber. There was nothing remarkable about the front of it except for the iron bars over the windows. When the door opened she turned to face the road, her back to the building and the two men who came out.

'Yeah, well, I don't know, he had his work cut out for him if you ask me,' one of the men said as he passed behind her.

The other one laughed. 'I s'pose so.' She watched them walk down the road then stop when a boy ran up to the shorter of the two. 'Constable Foster, sir, someone's took our pig. Ma says she knows who it were, it were that bastard Gilroy, and she says can you go and get him.'

The man said something to the boy that she couldn't hear and then the two men kept walking and the boy ran off down the road.

Bridget stood there while the sun warmed the bricks and warmed her back and people's voices floated behind her. She looked back at the building the two men had come out of, then she turned away, joined the river of life that was the road.

The two-storey stone house was built close to the road. Around the back there were outbuildings, a stable and a fenced garden, a small hut facing the garden. The door to the hut was half open, the yard between it and the house empty except for some chickens scratching around. She crossed the yard to the hut and stood behind it. A man came from down the side of the main house walking straight towards where she stood. She pushed herself against the back of the hut, heard his footsteps coming closer. The hut door scraped open. The timber wall was thin and she could hear him inside. Something dropped, a dull thud, and the man swore.

The door opened again and his footsteps retreated. She waited a few minutes and then moved along the side of the hut, peered around at the main house. Seeing no one, she slipped in the hut door.

There was a small table up one end close to the fire, a good half a loaf of bread sitting on it. She pulled a hunk off the loaf. There was a tinderbox on the table, a blanket thrown across a hammock in the corner of the hut. On the floor near the fire was a leather knapsack, a powder horn lying next to it. She picked up the knapsack and shoved the bread and the tinderbox into it, grabbed the powder horn and the blanket from the hammock and was about to leave when she saw the man coming back. She froze where she was and then moved quickly into the corner behind the door. There was another sound, the crack of a whip. It sounded like a bullock cart and it must have pulled up close to the back of the hut because she could hear the voices clearly.

'I left Healy out there. He'll walk back in later on. Let the bullock rest for a while. Tomorrow morning you can take it into Hobart Town. Pick up Rowley's order while you're there, drop it in on the way back.'

'Yes, sir. Mr Dwyer said he should have that harness ready for you by the twelfth; should I stay on and get that while I'm there, sir?'

'Alright, I suppose so, yes. Before you go in the morning, come to the house.'

'Yes, sir.'

'Oh, and Carson . . .'

'Yes, sir?'

'Oh, never mind. I'll talk to you later.'

The whip cracked again and she heard the wheels of the bullock cart.

She pushed herself hard against the wall now.

The man walked to the hut door. She could see him through the crack, only inches away. He stopped, looked towards the house. Then he turned and walked back that way.

She breathed now, waited another minute, came out from behind the door. Outside there was no sign of him. She ran into the trees beyond the garden.

...

In the hills behind the house she sat down and emptied out the knapsack. In the bottom of it there was a small canister of gunpowder and an empty water bladder. The tinderbox was wood, smaller than the one Matt had carried, but inside was the flint, steel and a bit of straw. She hit the flint against the steel. Nothing. She tried again and again and eventually produced a spark. She collected dry leaves, twigs and branches and this time let the spark fall into the dry straw that lit a leaf, the leaf lighting a stick. Soon there was smoke and she squatted by her fire adding stick after stick. She went to slept that night by the fire with the blanket over her, woke to its ashes and ate some bread.

She had just tied the blanket to the top of the knapsack when she looked up to see someone coming through the trees about fifty yards from where she sat. She snatched the tinderbox and the knapsack, got to her feet.

'Hey, stop! Stop there.'

Halfway down the slope she slipped and turned to see two figures coming down the hill behind her.

She was up again, branches whipping her face as she ran down into a gully and then uphill. She climbed, grabbed branches and pulled herself up, going deeper into the hill's scrub. They were further behind her now, but still coming. Up ahead there was a rock like a huge tooth jutting out of the ground. She stood behind it, pushed herself against it.

Bridget stood completely still, no movement in her body at all except the rise and fall of her chest. She heard the crunch of a boot and then the voice, close.

'She can't be far away.'

The sound of someone crashing through scrub and then another voice. 'Fancy getting robbed by a woman.'

'I don't care who it was. I want my stuff.'

For a moment they were silent. Then: 'We'll go back down. You can take the cart to Rawlings', get word to Oatlands.'

She stood there until long after they were gone.

...

There were four of them. Sawyers. They were working in a clearing about a hundred yards from the river. Two of them were sawing in a pit and another two were carrying planks between the pit and a timber stack underneath a tree. A couple of bullocks dozed near the pit and a black dog lay to one side of them. Barely visible, hidden as it was among the trees between the clearing and the river, was a bark hut.

The sound of a plank being dropped onto the pile rang out through the clearing and was loud even where she stood. It hit the pile and bounced off and one of the men grabbed his foot. 'For God's sake.' He straightened. 'Told you not to throw the fucking thing. Nearly broke my bloody foot.' He swore again and the other one said something and then they both lifted the plank up off the ground. 'Put it this time, don't chuck it.'

One of the men appeared out of the pit. 'Carter being too rough with ya, Dolly?'

There was the sound of wood hitting wood again, not as loud this time. The man who'd hurt his foot turned. 'End up like bloody Peterson, laid up, and you blokes'll be another man short. Then see how bloody funny it'd be.'

'I didn't even chuck it, it just fell.'

'Bullshit ya didn't.'

They walked back to the pit.

As she watched another man appeared from out of the trees in front of the hut. He walked with a limp, a stick to support himself. He came up the middle of the clearing and when he arrived at the pit two of them stopped work and talked to him and the dog got up and went over to him and stood there wagging its tail. One of the men pointed towards the river and the crippled man looked in that direction and then they talked a while longer. When the two men went back to work he limped back to the hut where he sat on a log smoking.

Bridget stood watching and, as she did, the sun that had been out for most of the day sank down behind the hills. The bush drained of colour and cold rose from the damp ground. She made her way back to the river, the men's voices fading into the darkening afternoon.

...

She spent the night by the river without a fire and in the morning returned to the clearing. There was a rise at the top end of the clearing from where she had a decent view and it was far enough away that the dog wouldn't hear or smell her—although there was no sign of the dog yet today. The bullocks stood yoked to a cart that was loaded with timber. Their heads were down and they were dozing as though they might have been standing there for some time. Down in the forest, smoke bled out of the hut's chimney up into the canopy. She shifted her weight, looked into the bush behind her.

She had been standing there for a long time before three of the men came out of the hut and walked up to the bullocks. They were talking, but it was too far away to make out what they were saying. One of them fiddled with the bullocks' harness and then another man came from the hut and walked up to join the others at the bullocks. He and another man got up on the seat and the other two sat on the timber on the back of the cart. They drove the bullocks out of the clearing and into the forest.

She stayed there on the rise a while and then came down and crossed the track where they had gone. It led through the forest to the river. Close to the hut she stood by a gum. There was a lock hanging from the hut door but it was not done up. There was still smoke coming from the chimney.

There was a noise from the hut—the door being unbolted from the inside—and then the limping man she had seen yesterday came out, the dog next to him. The hut door was left open. When the man got to the woodpile, Bridget went to the hut door, peered into the darkness. There was no one else inside.

In the night she curled up by a creek among ferns. At dawn there was a rustle behind her. She rolled over to see a wombat disappearing into the thick scrub. Bridget grabbed the gun, got to her feet and fired. The thing uttered an awful sound but kept going. She went after it, got a glimpse of its wide grey back, reloaded the gun and fired again.

She pulled it out from under the bush by its back leg. It was heavy and still alive, spitting and growling, bleeding from its hindquarters that were a mess from the shot. She found a rock, pounded it between the eyes. She hit it again but it wouldn't die. The damn thing wouldn't die.

She stood over its bloody carcass, the rock in her hand by her side. It was done. It was dead. She dropped the rock.

She sat by the creek, carved a chunk of flesh off the back end of the animal and sat it on the coals next to her. She waved her hand over the wound where flies were settling, carved off another piece of meat. She carried the thing for a while but it was heavy and flies were following her, settling all over it. She cut another few bits off it and left it.

...

West, Sully had said, out beyond the settlement on the Clyde River. There is a river. *One place a person might still be left in peace.* Bridget had been travelling south, following the road but staying in the hills to the west of it. She held the gun she had taken from the sawyers close to her side.

...

The sky was all blue and a warm breeze licked the day. The edges of the mammoth craggy mountains behind the hills were clear and certain under the hard sun and birds chattered excitedly, spreading news of a golden morning. She passed a cottage where part of the thatching had come off the roof and a spade with no handle leaned up against the door. She stopped in front of it. A crop of potatoes and cabbages was growing in a patch at one end of the cottage and at the other end a fruit tree. Near where she stood there was a small pine tree and even closer, only a yard ahead of her on the track, was a kangaroo's foot, the fur damp and muddy, a host of flies sitting on it.

Bridget walked on along the track and into the gum trees and around to the back of the cottage. There was a dog near the back of the building tied to a post and lying on the ground. It heard her and stood up, barked in her direction, pulled against the rope that held it. Bridget stayed near the line of trees waiting. No one came from the cottage. Behind the potato patch there was a rope between two trees, two shirts and a pair of trousers hanging from it. Beyond that a field planted out with corn. The dog was tall and skinny—a hunting dog. She took a few steps towards the potato patch and the dog barked again and she stopped where she was, looked back over the field. The dog had sat down and was now wagging its tail ferociously so that its whole backside wagged. It got up again, jumped, straining on its rope and then it sat down again and wagged and whimpered. A young dog maybe, rusty in colour, a long snout, a mangy ragged-looking thing.

She pulled up three potatoes, ripped the shirts and trousers off the line and cut the line at both ends, quickly coiled it. Then she ran back into the trees. The dog barked again. She stopped. There was still no sign of anyone around the cottage. She dumped the clothes and rope by a tree, walked back to the dog, who started jumping again so high and energetically now that it almost flipped. She stood a yard in front of it. It sat on the ground wagging its tail, its head down as though expecting to be told off. She slowly put her hand out and it sniffed and then licked her hand. She looked around again, cut the rope near the post and the dog ran next to her to the trees.

...

There were five of them, all of them a decent size, grazing on flat grassy land, the trees sparse here, the understorey light. They stood watching the roos and the dog looked up at her as though to ask permission. 'Not yet.' She held the hair at the back of his neck. The animals had heard them and were on edge—she wanted to wait for them to settle. One of them, one of the biggest, hopped a couple of yards and a few of the others looked up then returned to their grazing.

'Alright, go.' She let him go and he sped out of the bushes and instantly the roos took off, their huge hind legs propelling them up and forward, all of their attention on fleeing. The dog had chosen his target already: the smallest one at the back of the group. The dog's hind legs gathered up under his body and then made contact with the ground ever so briefly until they were drawn up again. The muscles of his body rippled, his line did not falter, he was gaining on the animal. He almost flew for seconds at a time, nothing of his agile body in contact with the ground. Then he came up next to it, grabbed it around its throat and took it down. The rest of the group continued in their flight as the dog stilled the struggling animal then turned towards the place where Bridget stood, ready to deliver up his work. He was a good hunter. She strode over, patted and praised him, lifted the heavy, bleeding animal off the ground.

...

The creek glinted in the afternoon sun, the water curving smoothly over a submerged log and then spitting and splashing like a party of demons before collecting itself and progressing on downstream in a more mellow fashion. A small bird, its head marked with the same blue as the sky and a tail like a fan, hopped from branch to branch. Flames rose up from the fire's coals like genies, dancing in the daylight.

Bridget pulled the cooked piece of meat off the stick and ate it, threw another piece to the dog. Bury—his name. He'd needed a name. Bury St Edmunds. The village her sister had moved to when she married. Bridget chucked another piece of meat to the dog and he gulped it down, then sat a yard away watching her eat hers. He was distracted by a fly on his coat that he snapped at and then his brown shiny gaze was back, intent, watching the meat on her stick, monitoring her every move until she threw him another piece.

In the night she lay curled around him, his warmth seeping into her body. His coat was short and rough, burnt orange. In the middle of his chest the hairs met in a swirl and sat up in a tiny crest. He was the shape of most of the island's hunting dogs, his stomach pulling up into the high hindquarters, the tail long and thin, although even more lean than most. The skin on his head was tight over the bone, the eyes sitting in the skull, brown and perfectly round, the soft lids graced with short eyelashes darker than the colour of his coat. The black snout was wet with moisture and there was crust in the corners of his glassy eyes. She lay against him, the dark close around them. He let out a whimper—he was dreaming, his legs moving, running. He was running in his sleep. She put her hand on his coat, on the warmth of him.

The cave was part of an outcrop of rock, dry as a scab halfway up the steep slope, trees and scrub growing close all around it, the river fast below it, shallow, the bottom measled with pebbles. Along from the cave was a rock column and balanced on top of it, as though it had been placed there gently for some later use, was an almost-square rock. The cave was deep with a low roof that had a hole in it about twice the size of Bridget's head. Inside the floor was fine silt that had been undisturbed when she arrived and now was messy with foot and paw prints and tracks from dragging branches.

The fire jumped and sprang and then became nothing but a quiet glow, the occasional flick of flame across the coals. She hacked meat off the carcass that lay on the floor next to her, pushed the meat onto the stick and squatted close to the little fire. Juice dripped onto the singing embers. She sat up in the back of the cave and ate, the gun on the ground next to her. Bury was sitting obediently a yard away from the carcass, staring at it and licking his chops. She sawed more flesh off the animal, chucked him some.

...

The dog sat on the ground next to her wagging his tail and looking up at her from time to time as if to ask was something going to happen now. What are we waiting for? He was torn between wanting to sit there like she had told him to and the desire to get up and run—not for any particular reason, as far as she could tell, but for the sake of running. She dropped her hand onto his head.

She'd been here in the daylight once before, had seen a man come up from the river to the cottage and go inside. Today a line of smoke trailed from the stone cottage's chimney, but they hadn't seen anyone. The bullock was there like before, standing in a yard at the back of the house. Beyond the bullock yard was a flock of sheep, and not far from where they grazed a field of corn. On the other side of the cottage from the bullock yard was a garden thick and alive with vegetables.

It was upstream from the cave, not far. She had been here twice now in the night, taken corn and potatoes. Last time it had been a bright moon, but on the way back to the cave her foot had gone down in a hole and her ankle had rolled badly. It had been hot and swollen and she had not been able to put much weight on it for days.

They had been standing there a long time when a servant girl came out with a basket and went down to the river. The cottage door opened again and three children ran out and joined the girl. She had taken a dress out of the basket and was washing it. As she washed, the three children played near her. The girl picked up a rock and threw it into the river.

'That's hardly very far at all.'

The servant girl turned to the boy. 'You mind your manners. That was a fine throw, Lucy, don't listen to him.'

'I'm throwing now. Watch me! I'm throwing now.' The other girl threw a rock. A moment later one of them hit the other and then they all screamed and bawled and the servant girl yelled at them that if they didn't stop it they could all go to bed. They were quiet for a few minutes then, but soon they were fighting again and the servant girl ordered them inside. Not long after, she took her washing up to the line near the cottage, hung it, and then she too disappeared inside.

Bridget tied Bury to a tree. He wagged his tail, strained against the rope and then sat down, resigned.

The girl had come back out into the yard and was spreading grain for the chickens when Bridget stepped out from behind the cottage.

She put her hand to her chest. 'Lord above, you scared the Devil out of me.' She looked beyond the house. 'Where did you come from? What do you want?'

'Flour, bread. Can you get some bread?'

'Who are you, where did you come from?'

The girl was young, clearly scared. Bridget looked behind her. The cottage door was open. 'There anyone there?'

'Yes,' the girl said, lying badly, her eyes gauzy with it. 'If you're in some kind of trouble—'

Bridget pushed past her.

'You can't go in there.' The girl was coming along close behind her. A dog that was chained up on the other side of the cottage started to bark.

In the kitchen Bridget grabbed bread, flour and pork, stuffed it into the knapsack.

'Those are not yours. Put them back. You can't take them.' She was crying now. 'Please, the missus is awful kind.' She grabbed at Bridget. Bridget pushed her hard back against a bench.

When she came back up the hill Bury barked.

'Shut up.' She walked up to him and grabbed his snout in her hand. 'Be quiet.'

...

At the cave Bridget sat eating bread with the gun next to her. It was a dark afternoon, the sky grey and lumpy.

It had been raining for most of three days. They were out of meat. Without salt there was no way to preserve the meat they got. Bury was hungry. She had given him part of the hunk of pork she had taken from the place. It was too wet to hunt, no kangaroos around in the rain. She sat and looked out at the wall of rain, the river gushing below. 'Daniel's drunk our money.' She knew it; she told the dog. 'He's drunk our money.'

...

The wet land was shiny under bright sunlight. They got a good-sized animal quickly and easily. The clearing where they hunted was not far from the cave, downstream a little way, on the other side of the river. The river had been easy to cross but was flowing faster now after the rain and twice on the way back she nearly lost her footing. Bury was swept a way down the river before he found his way out of the current and swam to the bank, emerged on the other side with his coat stuck flat to his skin. He wagged his soaking tail, shook until all his fur stuck up. Bridget carried the roo around her shoulders, blood dripping from its neck onto the ground and onto the back of her trousers.

Back in the cave they ate and later she cleaned the skin as much as she could. It was her second kangaroo skin. The other one was up the end of the cave where she had put it to dry out. A mat of flies sat on it and buzzed around it, attracted to the bits of flesh that were still stuck to the skin. She put the new one with it.

She took everything out of the knapsack. A shirt. A tinderbox. The rope. The water bladder. A knife and pipe from the sawyers. A skerrick of gunpowder she'd taken from another hut. She laid them out on the floor, sat there looking at all of it. Her blanket was at the back of the cave where she had left it. She got that now, put it down on the floor near everything else, brought the two skins over from the end of the cave, put them close to the blanket. Then she sat down again, sat staring at the tinderbox, the knife, the row of things. Then she packed things back into the knapsack, shoved it into a hole at the back of the cave. She sat back on the floor with the skins and the blanket, the gun on the ground next to her. Dull green hills, brutally silent, acres of tea-coloured sky infused with pink. She picked up the gun, put it on her knee.

...

They had been down to the clearing again, had stayed there a long time, but there were no animals that morning. Around midday they crossed back over the river and scrambled up the slope towards the cave. As she came near it she stopped. There were footprints in the silt, fresh; not hers, larger. Her blanket was still there. The kangaroo skins were still there. Her knapsack with everything in it she had taken with her.

She turned around and looked over to the valley where the cottage was.

Governor Arthur straightened a book on his desk, wiped away imaginary dust. 'Captain Marshall, let me say this: in the end, I am little concerned with the offender's sex. I don't really care if the thief is an hermaphrodite. What I am concerned with is the maintenance of order in this colony. That is my role, to maintain order, and whether it be a man, a woman, a monkey or any other creature threatening that order, I do not care. What I care about is that they are brought to order, and imminently. Do I make myself clear?'

'Yes, sir.'

'Need I remind you, Captain, that she was present in the houses of both Mr Scanlon, when he was robbed, and Mr Goodwin, who was robbed and killed?'

'No, sir. I am aware of that.'

'Thank you, Captain. You may go. And take your *six* men with you.'

...

Outside Marshall closed the gate and started along the road, Sergeant Barker coming along next to him.

'Captain?'

'Yes, Sergeant?'

'What's a . . . a herm . . . herm . . . agrovide?'

The captain cleared his throat. 'Do you mean an hermaphrodite, Sergeant?'

The sergeant nodded. 'Yeah. What is it, sir?'

'Ah, it's someone, or something, that can mate with itself. It's male and female at the same time.'

'Really, sir?'

'Yes.'

'What, it can fuck itself, sir?'

'In a way, I suppose, yes, Sergeant. If you want to put it like that.'

'Bloody hell. That sounds alright. You sure about that, sir?'

'Yes, I am. Fairly sure.'

'Well, fuck me. Thank you, Captain.'

Marshall watched the sergeant turn the corner and go off up the road whistling, his walk jaunty, everything about his going suggesting he were mightily pleased with himself.

...

The party headed by Captain Marshall left Hobart Town at first light the next morning, stopped for lunch at the McCarthy residence, where Mrs McCarthy welcomed the captain graciously into her home. The rest of the soldiers were led around the back to the servants' quarters, where they would dine on bread and beef.

The meal was an ample one of lamb, potato and beans. Marshall, however, found he had little appetite and was rather distracted. When Mrs McCarthy enquired as to the health of Mrs Marshall her question was met with silence, only the repeat of it eliciting a response.

'Ah, yes, well. She's well . . . thank you.'

During the meal the rain that had been threatening all morning began to drum steadily on the roof. Drops raced down the muslin-framed window and the landscape outside disappeared behind a veil of water.

'Well, it would be absurd to go out there in this weather. You must wait here until it eases. I will have Emily bring tea.' Mrs McCarthy left no room for a response, immediately summoning the servant girl.

'Yes, better rest up, it's a big job you've got to do.' Mr McCarthy winked at Marshall. The captain felt himself failing in his battle to reserve judgement on this smug, self-assured man who in conversing adopted a position of leaning back in his chair, one leg crossed over the other, an all-knowing grin tormenting his rather large V-shaped face. Marshall, ever an advocate for diplomacy and mutual respect, firmly discouraged intolerance, both in himself and others, and went to great pains to reflect these values in his manner. However, when he spoke his tone was curt.

'Thank you for that advice, Mr McCarthy.'

'I only meant that—'

'I am quite aware of what you meant. Thank you.'

The servant girl entered the room and Marshall, shaken by his loss of control, was quite relieved when Mrs McCarthy seized the opportunity to jump up and clap her hands together. 'Ah, here we are. Who'll have tea then?'

Tea continued to be poured amid somewhat awkward conversation. Finally, around two-thirty, the captain offered his sincere thanks to Mrs McCarthy, gathered his soldiers and set out on the puddled road for Lovely Banks.

...

In the late afternoon the grey cloud mass split to reveal canyons of deep blue. White clouds with edges as sharp as cut-outs sat high in the sky like snow-covered mountains. The pungent smell of wet vegetation spiced the air and as the sun grew closer to the horizon, a queer yellow glow settled over the land. Marshall rode through this uneasy splendour, his thoughts dipping and surging with the rhythm of the horse's walk. It was a beautiful part of the country, an area of grassy woodland, well suited to grazing. Little surprise it was so popular among the settlers. There was, however, always the feeling of danger—not just physical, although he knew it existed; what bothered him more was the sense of spiritual danger. He had tried to explain it to Eleanor once, early on. 'Oh, Richard,' she laughed, 'I wonder these large thoughts of yours don't drive you to the grave. Must you be such a sombre bore?' She held up one of two beaded doilies on the table next to her. 'Which one of these should I give to Mrs Arthur, do you think?'

Eleanor may have been right about him—for too long he had chewed the same raw material, constantly failing to produce anything resembling a clear thought or direction. A smarter man might have admitted defeat by now, but his mulish mind, indifferent to its owner's welfare, persisted.

...

Notification had arrived from a settler in Ross that there was someone living in a cave who he believed to be stealing from him. The settler's convict servant had described a woman who had come to the house and stolen food. The constable at Ross had done nothing but send the report on to Hobart Town.

Marshall had wished to come out here alone, but the governor had insisted that he be accompanied by Lieutenant Pullen—and by these other buffoons, no less.

There was a mole near her lip. It had been written in the report. The convict servant had stated that the woman who barged in and took the bread and pork had a mole near her lip.

It was in her convict record too, listed under 'Remarks'.

He remembered it well. He should not have, but he did. And it bothered him.

Behind him now laughter cut a swathe through his thoughts. He turned around to see John Macintosh off his horse with his trousers down around his ankles, the look on his face one of shock rapidly turning to anger. Above him Hawkins sat in his saddle holding a whip in his hand, grinning from ear to ear, as the men around him fell forward onto their horse's necks, laughing.

'Fuck you, Hawkins. You think you are so fucking funny. Ha fucking ha. Wait till I hack your balls off in your fucking sleep and see how funny you are.'

The men laughed harder as Hawkins put his hand down onto his crotch and crossed his eyes.

Macintosh had obviously got down off his horse to relieve himself and Hawkins had hit him across his bare buttocks with a whip. He was always the butt of their jokes, although not usually so literally. And Hawkins was a troublemaker, a bully who needed to be the centre of attention. He had the men's admiration, although Marshall thought it a thin kind of admiration and wondered if they feared him more than they liked him. Feared his ridicule and, for some reason, desired his tinny approval.

It was his duty to intervene but it seemed the damage had been done and really he didn't care. Pullen could do it. It was fast becoming his expedition, Marshall trailing like a ghost. Let them carry on, let them do as they would. They might kill each other one by one behind him and he would keep riding. Even when there was no one left, still he would keep riding. Such was his mood.

...

On reaching Lovely Banks, Stratton, Mr Hooper's servant, took their horses and the men set about creating a fire outside the wheat shed where they were to sleep. Lieutenant Pullen and Sergeant Barker borrowed Hooper's dogs and set off in search of kangaroo, returning soon after with two. By the fire Barker cut off the animals' heads and threw them to the dogs. Taking a swig from the cup beside him, he ran his knife down the belly of the first one and began peeling back the grey fur to expose the meat. Marshall, not hungry, wandered towards a stand of gums a little way off.

It was just on dark and the last smears of indignant daylight lent blue to night's black. One by one the stars appeared and hung in the sky like tiny spiders on the end of infinitesimal threads. Marshall walked on through the trees and picked his way carefully up a rocky rise, where he watched as the day finally withdrew, taking with it the certainty of shape. In the distance he could just pick out the dark outline of the Sweet Water Hills. To the west, behind the Lovely Banks homestead, a hill rose up, now settled under the shadow that earlier it had thrown out over the paddock below. In the morning they would proceed north to Salt Pan Plains, where they would leave the horses and head west towards the tiers along Blackman's River—where, if the informant was correct, they would find her.

He wondered what he was doing out here. Some people were dealt a bad hand in life. He did believe that. He strove to see all people as equal, as they were in the eyes of the Lord—something that he knew Eleanor hated. 'Those who are good will be rewarded and the Evil will be punished,' she said, 'which is precisely what they deserve, and exactly as it ought to be.' He wished he thought it were so simple. And anyway, the real truth of it, perhaps, was that he sought to ease his own guilt. He still felt somehow to blame. Of course it wasn't his fault. The girl—or woman, he supposed she was—could and would do as she wished. But he still couldn't help feeling that something had gone wrong. If he'd have been better . . . Perhaps he *had* caused it—whatever chain of events had come about. Eleanor had taken a dislike to the girl. He worried that she had sensed his interest in her. After Mary had gone to Eleanor crying that Bridget had tried to kill her, Eleanor had insisted she go. When he said he didn't believe everything that Mary said was gospel Eleanor had yelled at him that she wasn't having Bridget there a second longer and that she was going to go down into town herself to get the constable. He had told her they would speak about it later as he had to go. When he had come back that afternoon Bridget was gone. Eleanor had done just as she said she would.

Some time ago Marshall had been walking along the road and had met Mr Price, the surveyor. He asked him had he seen

Bridget Crack at the lake, with the men, with the bushrangers. Price had said yes, he had seen her. When Marshall asked did he think . . . had she appeared . . . *coerced*, Price had stood in the road and looked at him a moment. 'Coerced?'

'Yes, I just wondered if, well, if she gave the impression of being there of her own free will, or if indeed—'

The captain was stopped by the look on Price's face. He appeared overly interested, intrigued. There was the flicker of a grin, then he said: 'No, Captain. No, I don't think she was coerced.' And he excused himself and walked on.

The next time Marshall had seen him was at a social gathering that Eleanor had insisted they attend. Price had come up next to him, a drink in his hand. His face was flushed. 'So,' he said, making himself comfortable against the wall, 'you know Mr Ainsley, don't you, Captain?'

'I know of him. Why is that?'

'I heard he married his convict servant.' He grinned into his glass, turned it in his hand, then looked up for the captain's response.

'Is that right? I had not heard.' (He had, in fact—it had been spoken about all over the town.)

Price was now looking across the room at a fair girl who had just smiled at him. He pulled himself away from the wall, passed uncomfortably close to Marshall, whispered with whiskey breath as he went: 'They're all whores, Captain.'

...

In the middle of the night Marshall woke. He had been dreaming: he was sitting up in a bed and there on the end of the bed was a fox. Behind it an open window, moonlight streaming in through the window onto the fox. It was standing there watching him, its fur rich orange, the colour of fire. Then it turned around and in one leap was gone. The dream changed then and he was no longer in a bedroom but standing at the base of a mountain. He looked up at the top of it and just then realised what was about to happen. He turned and ran, but behind him the whole mountain started to crumble. Rock tumbled down and covered him. He tried to dig himself out, to find air, to find light, to get out from underneath the rubble. He was just about to suffocate when he woke himself up.

He sat up, looked around at the sleeping men. The air in the shed was full of the musty smell of grain. The only sounds were of the men breathing and the hiss of a possum. He was awake now and he remained sitting, staring into the dark.

...

It was several hours since the men had left the cottage of the settler who had made the report. They had been following the northern bank of the Blackman's River. About half a mile back the scrub by the river had got too thick and they had been forced to make their way further north. Now they were pushing through a net of thick scrub, trying to find their way back to it. Marshall had just noticed that the air was getting damper when up ahead of him Pullen raised his arm. They had indeed made it back to the river. Above its bank, almost indistinguishable among the trees, was a cave. A number of trees grew very close to either end. As they stood looking a dog started barking, the sound coming from the cave.

Next to Marshall, Pullen was making wild signals with his arms, directing some of the men along the river. The men hesitated, looked to Marshall, seeking his command.

'Wait,' Marshall whispered.

'For what?'

'Just wait a minute.'

Marshall looked up at the cave, put his hands around his mouth. 'Is there anyone there? Bridget Crack? This is Captain Marshall. Please come out.'

Seconds later a shot came from the cave and narrowly missed Pullen's head. He raised his gun, fired at the side of the cave. Automatically the soldiers behind him followed suit and a volley of shots ricocheted off the rock.

'Hold your fire!'

Pullen's eyes widened. 'What? Do you want us all dead?'

'I said hold your fire.'

'I'm sorry, sir, but surely you don't expect—'

Stones scattered. A figure appeared running across the slope of loose rock, a dog behind it. Pullen, the self-proclaimed finest shot in the regiment, aimed at the running figure. The sound rang in Marshall's ears. 'Damn you!' Fear gripped him as he waited for her to fall. And then for a moment he was confused. There was a flash of grey as the figure disappeared into the trees, a dog going after it.

Pullen turned, 'Alright, men, let's go.'

'No! Stay here. I order you. Stay where you are.'

...

Marshall ran hard, followed the sounds of her retreat. He caught glimpses of her ahead of him. He saw her trip, fall forward. Then she was up again, but it was enough for him to gain ground. When he came up close behind her he called out for her to stop, please stop. To his surprise she did stop, a gun hanging from her hand at her side. She turned to face him.

Marshall stood looking at the figure in front of him, barely recognisable as the striking girl who had got up into his carriage that day. She looked for all the world more like an animal than a human being, let alone a woman. Her eyes were the same, although harder perhaps, the crystalline green having more of a shattered look than he remembered; like rare rocks that had sustained an impact not quite enough to break them, only to create shock lines, tiny cracks, through the weaker points. Her face was filthy and her hair hung matted around her face. Cheeks drawn, skin stuck to bone, eyes big in the head. On her feet she wore shoes of some kind that appeared, like the vest she wore, to have been sewn together in the most extraordinary way. In her body she possessed the alertness of the hunted, every sense wired, the muscles taut and active in their stillness, as though they too listened. He could see nothing in her eyes to show whether she recognised him. Surely she must; he was little changed. His own musket was in his right hand by his side and her eyes flicked down to it. If he moved it, she would run, he was sure of it. She was summing him up, he knew, trying to decide what options were open to her. 'Please come with me. I don't know what happened, but you cannot . . . There is nowhere to go here.'

Her eyes, which had been wide open, narrowed slightly. Emotion—of what kind he could not quite tell—pricked their cool surface.

'Please . . . look at you. Honestly, I . . .'

She said nothing, only continued scrutinising him, probing more deeply now, her sharp eyes, finely tuned tools of extraction, boring and flicking. Then, without warning, she turned and ran.

'Bridget!' Instinctively Marshall raised his gun but immediately let it fall to his side again.

...

Marshall stood still listening to the crack of branches. He listened until there was no more trace of her going, until all he could hear was the slight whisper of wind through the gums. High up in the trees leaves twirled, flashing silver in the light. On the ground in the place where her feet had been the flattened grass began to move, to rise slowly, like a concussed man from a road. Marshall felt suddenly tired, very tired. He let the gun drop to the ground. Behind him was a clearing and he turned and walked to the middle of it.

The cold moist wind that ran down off the mountain grazed his cheek. Such a quiet place. And that same timeless quality he always felt in these places. What was time in the face of all this space, all this stillness? Nothing. A laughable concept. Yet another crutch pulled out from under a man, leaving him naked and howling. How we build these ideas to lean on. Hoping they'll hold our panic at bay, we push them ahead of us into the darkness. In the end, he thought, they crumble easily, turning out to be nothing but towers of sand.

He stood perfectly still, allowing the cool air to snake around his back. For as far as he could see tree trunks charged straight and true towards the sky. It was such an effortless kind of trying they managed. Striving graciously and succeeding—a sweet, enviable condition. Higher up, wisps of cloud raced east towards freedom, away from the imposing black rock where birds of prey soared on their luck, waiting for pickings.

Bridget stood on top of the rock, the river below her, the dawn light a powder pink dust over the hills. As she stood there the sun showed itself behind the hill and rose like a god, huge and quaking in the sky, preaching its bright gold word over the land.

She stepped down off the rock and hit her thigh, signalling for the dog to follow.

He stood where he was, looking at her.

'Come on.'

He picked his way down off the rock, followed along behind her and then walked next to her along the top of the hill.

The ground was dry and craggy, the hill messy with outcrops of rock. The grasses that grew around the rocks and between the grey-barked trees had turned brown under the sun.

Up the slope the dog stopped, turned back to look at her and then stood there waiting. She came up next to him, dropped her hand onto the back of his neck and he fell in next to her.

Captain Marshall put the newspaper down on Arthur's desk, walked over to the window. Three ships sat at anchor in the bay, their masts swaying, the river busy with white-caps. Beyond them, on the hill overlooking the bay, the work of clearing the land was progressing. When he had arrived, only three years ago, most of that hill had been covered in timber and now it had been cleared almost to the top. The town was growing. And in the last three months Arthur had signed off on hundreds of new land grants in the Interior.

Arthur had only days ago issued an order stating that the military and settlers could use force to drive natives away from properties. The settlers already had been using force, Marshall had thought. But the military—that was something new. And the paper Arthur had just shown him, the *Colonial Times*, contained a letter from a settler lamenting that he had to build a wall around his house to protect himself and his family. *In the name of Heaven, is it not high time to resort to strong and decisive measures?*

'They will have to be removed from the settled areas,' Arthur said now. 'That is the fact of the matter.'

Marshall's thought was: How? How would they be removed? But he didn't ask. He had a feeling he already knew.

...

That night, having heard about the governor's order, Jane came to the house. She had been staying with Mrs Potter.

'You have to do something about it.'

'What am I to do? There *is* nothing I can do.' He was tired, not in the mood for Jane, once again, telling him—lecturing him—about how things *ought* to be.

'Speak to Arthur,' she said.

He told her that Arthur was not going to listen to him, and neither indeed was the Colonial Office.

The natives needed, she said—as she had before—to be educated, brought to God, not hunted down and killed.

For God's sake, she knew he agreed with her. Why was she huffing and puffing at him like this? Perhaps what she hadn't considered was that the natives themselves had shown few signs of being interested in her proffered education. There had been a group of them camped down at the bay near the town. Jane had visited them weekly, had arranged for them to have clothes and blankets. He'd been in the store one day, had overheard a woman say to another: 'I just saw Jane Marshall down at the bay feeding the orang-outangs.' He had been ashamed to observe the feeling of embarrassment it stirred in him. He ought to have felt pride in her philanthropy. After the hanging of the two native men the group by the bay had left. They had not returned and he had been rather grateful.

'You can't make pets of them, Jane,' he said now.

'They were not my *pets*.' She spat it at him: *pets*.

He repeated Arthur's assurance—that force would only be applied to drive them away from homes and property where necessary.

'And who will decide, Richard, what is *necessary*?'

Yes. He should have known she would ask that.

Damn it. He'd hoped for a quiet evening, for a convivial visit from her. Was it so much to ask for? He did not have these *answers*—none for Jane and few for himself. He wished someone had more for him.

...

Marshall stood in the middle of the road. The sky was hard blue, clouds dragged and smeared across it. Still, like the day had inhaled and was holding its breath. He had been following the governor and Mr Ridgeway, a surveyor from New South Wales, around the town most of the morning. Ridgeway had come to create a new plan for the town; its shape and its streets were currently dictated to a large degree by the creek that flowed through it. Ridgeway was proposing a grid system, he and Arthur discussing the ins and outs of bridges and roads and where they would go. Marshall made his excuses then went up the hill towards his house.

...

At home he took the letter from his brother out of the drawer where it had been sitting for the past month. A good friend of his had taken over a senior position at Dublin Castle, it said. He felt certain of Richard being able to secure a good position there, should he wish to return to Britain.

Eleanor had been expressing again how much she missed her family, firmly reiterating her dislike of Van Diemen's Land. Some days she hardly spoke to him.

Early in their marriage Eleanor had attempted to get to know him, to create warmth between them, and he had not reciprocated as he should have. He ought to have at least tried. They were both unhappy. And he must accept some responsibility for it. She wanted to return to England and he wondered if perhaps he owed her that. There was, she'd told him, a ship leaving in three weeks.

He put the letter away, got up and went over to the curtain, looked down into the empty yard.

He had told both Pullen and Arthur that Bridget Crack had run, and that he'd not been able to get a shot at her through the trees. There had been no questions asked, but they had been there in the silences.

...

Marshall crossed the creek, was coming back from the hut where he'd been speaking to Kelly. Near the dairy he stopped, faced back to the creek, watched it flow down through the gully. Behind him the cow flicked its tail. Steam rose from the animal's fresh shit, the smell of it strong on the cool air. Further behind him, he heard a sound, turned around to see the convict servant girl Martha come out of the house with a bucket. She went to the pump and put the bucket on the ground. Marshall watched while she filled it. She leaned over to pick it up, lifted. He saw her arm take the weight of it, her spine curve as she rose, then her body moving, supple, feet one in front of the other across the yard.

She came across the soldier near a bridge riding the road alone, talking to himself.

'You wouldn't know, because you're only a horse. That's what you are, a horse. And ya have to be what you are. There's no escaping it, see, horse. If you're a horse, you're a horse, and that's the truth of the matter. That—is the truth of the matter. And who says what the truth is? God does. God—says the truth. Not you, horse. Not you.' He pointed at the animal's head. 'And that is my point. That you, are only a horse.'

It was close to sunset. Bridget watched him. He had let go of the reins. The horse stopped and stood there in the middle of the road. The man did nothing. His chin dropped onto his chest. He was asleep. Drunk.

The horse wandered to the side of the road where Bridget was, started to graze. Bury had been standing next to her watching but now he suddenly ran out, snapping at the horse's legs.

The horse took off fast. The man was unseated and fell, but a foot caught in the stirrup. The horse cantered away, the man dragging along the road behind it.

The man was lying still, the leg in the stirrup, the horse blowing breath from flared nostrils, lifting one hoof then another nervously. Bridget came up behind them on the dark road and the horse took a few steps forward, the man dragged with it. She stood over him. His eyes opened, his hand came up and he pointed to the leg. Bridget put her hand on the horse's rump, shushed it. Pulled the foot out of the stirrup. The man groaned and the leg fell to the ground. He was breathing hard, his eyes flickering open and closed. 'Catherine,' he said. Bridget put her hand down and felt in his coat pocket. Three coins. The horse was standing in the bush near the road, its head turned to them. Bridget looked back at the man. 'Are we home, Catherine?'

'Yeah,' Bridget muttered, 'we're home.'

...

The town was a spread of buildings around the east bank of the Clyde River, a couple made of brick, most of them makeshift and timber. She found the bakery and the store, bought bread and flour with the money from the soldier, the baker watching her as she left, his gaze ripe with suspicion.

On the edge of the settlement she followed a cart track that led up the west side of the wide river to a fork in the track, one track following the river she had come up, the other, a less-used track following a creek. As she stood there a boy appeared up ahead pulling a small cart behind him. As he came closer she saw that in the cart he had traps and a dead possum.

She looked along the lesser track, asked him was there a river out there. 'A river? Plenty a rivers out there, miss.' The track went nowhere, he said, to a few huts and then to the mountains. 'Just stops.'

Bridget waited until he was gone and then turned onto the faint track.

...

The log was damp and slippery and she crossed it on her stomach, inching her way across, her knees gripping the sides of the log, pushing the knapsack along in front of her. It stopped a yard or so short of the other bank, its branches splaying out into the water. She stood up, measuring the distance, and then jumped—did not quite make it from where the log ended to the bank, her back foot dragging in the water, her boot now soaking wet. She looked back at Bury, who was standing on the end of the log wagging his tail. He made the leap easily.

The cold drained down off the hills now to sit heavily over the river, the dark and the cold curling around the ferns, around the rocks and trunks of trees, curling and more of it coming, the dark water getting darker, the hollows inside the trees filling with cold.

...

The hut sat among gums, had a lean to it, one end of the roof pressing into the trunk of the tree that grew next to it. At the other end of the roof was a stone chimney. She was only about twenty yards from it, having come that close before she noticed it. The dog was a bit ahead of her and she called him back now. He stood beside her and eventually, when nothing seemed to be happening, he sat down, looking up at her now and then as though questioning the delay.

There was no smoke coming from the chimney and nothing out the front of the hut. The two windows were rectangular holes in the slab wall—they were framed but nothing filled or covered them. She crept forward and finally kicked the door open. It was empty, only a log of wood sitting end-up close to the fireplace. The dog sniffed around the gaps between the wall and the floor. On the window frame Bridget found a rusted knife and in the corner by the fireplace, an empty bottle.

She pulled the door wide open. Outside the stones of the chimney were damp and moss grew in the gaps between them. On the ground around the back there was a small clean skull and a few other bones. There was a hollowed-out log, the faint red of blood colouring the grain of the wood where someone had used it to salt meat. She stood back at the front of the hut looking around and listening—birds, the sound of branches brushing the air, and the flow of the river, almost indistinguishable from the wind.

Downstream on the other side of the river Bury had caught a roo. She came up the slope, the animal heavy over her shoulder. She dropped it, stopped to rest. Bury started to bark then stood next to her, his hackles raised, snarling. He was looking into the bush to Bridget's right. She drew the gun but couldn't see anything. There was no powder in the gun. The dog was focused on something, his growl low. And now she saw it. Among the trees not fifteen yards away a man stood watching her. There was another one, further back into the trees. The front one stepped forward, pointed the spear that he held at the kangaroo, beckoned for her to give it to him.

The dog's growl lowered.

'My dog got it.'

He stepped forward and reached for the roo and Bury flew at his hand. The man jumped back and pushed the dog's chest with the spear and now the dog wrapped its jaw around the wooden base of the weapon. The man shook the spear but the dog held tight. The one behind him raised his spear.

Bridget stood in front of the dog. 'No.' She spoke firmly to Bury. 'Let it go. Let go.'

Bury let go of the spear and she kicked the roo. 'Take it. Here, take it.'

The man turned around and said something to the one behind him, picked up the roo and dragged it off into the scrub.

...

Night and day she slept fitfully on the hut floor. She was out of flour. She had been eating fern fronds from near the river.

She went down to the river and came back up with the bottle full. There was a cold wind up and she closed the hut door against it, although it still rushed boldly in through the gaps that were the windows, moved through the fibres of the timber walls. It knew this material, knew it as tree, as its own kin.

She laid red berries out on the hut floor and counted them. Eleven. Eleven berries. The dog got up to look. 'Stay!' she yelled at him, and he slunk back to the corner.

She paced the hut. The cough she'd had for a while had turned into a hack and she doubled over in the corner, spat out the door.

...

Flames picked fussily at the few sticks in the fireplace. The paper was soft and dirty, had worn through at the folds so that the letter was now in pieces, the writing faint. She held the pieces in her hand, tipped them absently onto the sticks.

She put her hands in the fireplace, into the soft grey ash gone cold now. The letter. The letter was in here. Had she put it in here? It was in here. She needed it. Had to have it. She got down on her knees, both hands in the ash, stopped there like that. She stood up, put her face in her sooty hands.

...

She lay in the corner of the hut. The dog was watching her. He got up and came over, stood there wagging his tail. He watched her for a while then went back over to the door and lay near it.

...

Light was coming through the window, washing over her where she sat slumped against the hut wall. Her arm rested on her leg, the inside of it facing up to expose the charcoal shape there. She stared at the tattoo, at the new moon on her arm.

There was a voice coming from somewhere. Someone was singing. Was it Eliza? '*Will you come with me over the mountain?*' Eliza had sung that song.

Another noise now. A gunshot. Reverberating around the hills. Was it? No! A cough. It was her father coughing. Sitting up in bed. The doctor there, going out through the doorway, ducking his head. He is dead now. Father is dead. It seemed—unreal, just a thought, just—nothing. Nothing at all. But she knew it was true.

...

'*She opened the door saying, Maybe I'll choose, to come with you over the mountain.*'

...

She was aware of Bury close by. She reached out. A damp sensation. Bury licking her hand.

...

It was windy, tree branches creaking and moaning around the hut. Bury stood up and barked.

Bridget scrabbled for the gun.

She crawled to the wall and dragged herself up, peered out the window.

There was someone there. There was someone behind the tree.

She leaned against the wall, listening.

Bury barked at her then he stopped watching, whined as he flopped to the floor.

They might have some food. Whoever they were; they might have food.

Bury had got a small animal, close to the hut. But they needed more food.

...

Bridget pushed the hut door open, light came yelling and screaming at her.

No one.

Nothing.

She put her hands up to her face, dug her fingernails into her cheeks.

...

He was scratching at the door, whimpering. No, he couldn't go out there. They had to stay in here.

...

She sat on the floor, her back against the wall. She was neither awake nor asleep, but in this new drifting place between. Darkness flowed into the hut and in it she saw someone. They were standing on a lane above a field looking at a leafless tree. Behind them was a cottage. It was the cottage she had lived in as a child. It was her; she was the person standing on the lane. A flock of birds rose out of the tree now. All of them flew off but one and this one hovered above her, a small brown bird that was the only thing in a vast and all-blue sky. She was in the sky, weightless, air all around her. And then something . . . What was it? A gunshot. Falling now, falling into black. And then running. She was running. Running fast down the lane and across a field, feet pounding the ground, chest straining. She stopped on the unfamiliar field then, looked up into the sky. Above her a white cloud broke apart, bits of it drifting away from each other. Killing itself into pieces. Killing itself into pieces to be free.

Bridget woke up breathing fast, wondered where she was, gazed into the darkness of the hut.

...

Dog? Come over here.

Dog? Are you there?

Dog?

The wind blew against Marshall's back, sails the colour of bone above him, bulging with air. The ship had not long ago turned her bow from Hobart Town. In approximately six months they would reach England.

Jane was staying. The last few times he had seen her she had been polite. *Polite.* He understood that this had happened. He did not entirely understand why.

He stood facing back towards the cove now, his imagination taking him west, sweeping him out beyond New Town, across the Derwent River, over to the place where the mountains scratched at the sky, and beyond them past lakes and high wet plains where wind raked its cool hand through long tough grass. Small brown heads balanced on long blades, nodding. The grass agreeing. Yes, it said. Yes, I know. But what it was agreeing with, nobody knew. Then further, deeper west, where mountain hugged mountain, where trees strived for the sky, where soil took everything that was dead and made it its own. West, where a river rushed past an island, past a cross that was only a shape in rain. Where fishes' gills opened and closed, opened and closed regardless of a woman, of her footsteps through forest, regardless of anyone's stories about anything, of names, or dates, or language.

The water of this broad river that the ship now floated on all came from there, came raging and panting and merely, relentlessly, flowing from out there. Behind him now it widened into the bay called Storm.

He walked to the side of the ship and looked down at the surface of the water where the boards met a shimmering, moving pattern of black. Nothing there for him.

Bridget tucked soil around a little tree. Apple. An apple tree. She stood up to survey her work. Yes, yes, the garden was coming along, although the battle with the possums raged on of course, Primmy swearing and cursing, shooting into the night. Below her the field was full of cattle and their shit, holes from their feet, gums at the bottom of the slope below it.

Yes—how it would go. That was how it would go. The wedding at St David's Church, on the corner there, with the bells ringing out over the bay the way they did. She would wear a new dress. Outside the church she'd climb up onto the cart. It'd be laden with supplies. The donkey—he would be tied to the back of it. Primmy would climb up next to her, his grey eyes smiling, Sy on the back. They would go up through Hobart Town and people they didn't even know would wave and cheer. Sy would stand up in the back of the cart. 'And we'll have a pig too, won't we, Primmy, a pig?' he'd say. They'd follow the river along to the ferry and a swan, big and sleek, black feathers shining, would land, would slide across the water. Sy would point, full of excitement. 'Whoa, did you see that?'

When they got there, to the land that was theirs, to the

land by the river under the mountain where the sun was out and shining on green grass Sully would be there. He would be there and he would have finished the cottage already. He would have planted a vegetable garden and flowers too—daffodils and pansies, some rose bushes. Bridget would come out of the cottage with a basket of bread and ham, her belly round and firm in front of her. Primmy would walk over then and put his arm around her and they would all stand under the mountain and look over the field. Yes, that is how it would go.

She put her hand out to the dog. She was too tired to talk, but she told him in her mind so that he would know: that is how it will go. It will all be alright.

...

She used Bury to help herself get up. Going back to Hobart Town, she thought, was talking in her head to the dog again. Going back now. Give ourselves in. He whimpered and she laughed. You're not going to get *hung*. Don't be silly, she thought. He was a silly dog sometimes. Such a silly dog.

The river had risen up over the rope that was slung across it and was roaring, stampeding, rushing away from the mountains. The dog sat next to her, barked at the charging water. When she took a step he stayed where he was, wagged his tail and barked again.

Cold gripped her legs. Her foot looked for a steady rock against the drag of the water.

...

Everything turned to hissing white.

...

The dog stood above a pool of deep, shushed water shaded by the riverbank. He took a few steps and stood close to the edge of the bank, where he looked down and cried.

The dog sat. The dog sat down to wait and sat there as the sun lowered behind the hill opposite him. He blinked and slanting late-afternoon light shone on his round brown eye.

Author's note and acknowledgements

Bridget Crack is a fictional character; however, in creating her and the story I have been influenced by, and drawn on, a wide range of historical material. My reading about Tasmanian bushrangers, particularly Matthew Brady and his gang (1824–6), inspired some of the events that take place during Bridget's time with Sheedy. The Proclamation on page 117 is taken directly from one issued by Governor Arthur and printed in the *Hobart Town Gazette* (4 March 1826) in regard to the Brady gang; I have changed the names and added text of my own.

The reverend's reading on page 239 is adapted from an excerpt from Reverend Knopwood's diary. The texts he quotes on pages 96–7 are from Proverbs 12:3, Proverbs 12:4 and Genesis 2:10, from the *Holy Bible according to the authorized version*, Cambridge, 1817. 'In the name of Heaven, is it not high time to resort to strong and decisive measures?' (on page 294) comes from the *Colonial Advocate,* May 1828 (cited in Nicholas Clements' *The Black War: Fear, sex and resistance in Tasmania*, University of Queensland Press, Brisbane, 2014).

I'd like to acknowledge the creative works used within the novel: William Wordsworth's 'I Wandered Lonely as a

Cloud' (pages 88–9); an extract from Mary Shelley's *Mathilda* (page 34); and lines from an old Irish folk song, 'Come with Me Over the Mountain' (page 305). 'By the Living Harry', quoted on page v, is from Pete Hay's *Physick,* Shoestring Press, Nottingham, UK, 2016, reproduced with the author's permission.

I am indebted to the Australian Society of Authors Mentorship Program, which was integral in the development of the manuscript, and to the Copyright Agency for its support of the ASA Mentorship Program through its Cultural Fund.

Thanks to everyone who assisted me in the development of this novel: Olga Lorenzo, Sue Saliba and students of RMIT's Professional Writing and Editing program for early encouragement; Adam Ford, Peggy Frew and Marg Boyce for feedback on an early draft; Jode Satya, Miriam Ceh and Nicky Adams for their reading of later drafts. Huge thanks to my ASA mentor Judith Lukin Amundsen for her thoughtful and provocative questions and for her belief in the manuscript. Similarly, to my agent Grace Heifetz for her support and her passion for *Bridget Crack.* Thanks to Professor Peter Stanley at the UNSW, Canberra, for generously sharing his knowledge of the British Army, and to Rebecca Starford and Ali Lavau, who both contributed editorial guidance. I'm grateful to Sarah Baker and the team at Allen & Unwin, and to Christa Moffitt for her cover design.

To Ralf Rehak, I am grateful for so much, including insightful queries and many, many cups of tea. And finally, my heartfelt thanks to my publisher Jane Palfreyman.